Gathering Evidence

Martin MacInnes's first novel, *Infinite Ground*, was shortlisted for the Saltire Awards and won the 2017 Somerset Maugham award. He has previously won the Manchester Fiction Prize and the Scottish Book Trust New Writers Award. He lives in Fife.

Also by Martin MacInnes

Infinite Ground

Gathering Evidence

MARTIN MACINNES

Atlantic Books
London

Published in hardback in Great Britain in 2020 by Atlantic Books,
an imprint of Atlantic Books Ltd.

10 9 8 7 6 5 4 3 2 1

A CIP catalogue record for this book is available
from the British Library.

Hardback ISBN: 978 1 78649 345 3
E-book ISBN: 978 1 78649 346 0

Printed in Great Britain by TJ International Ltd, Padstow, Cornwall

Atlantic Books
An imprint of Atlantic Books Ltd
Ormond House
26–27 Boswell Street
London
WC1N 3JZ

www.atlantic-books.co.uk

Gathering Evidence

PART ONE

Nest

The concept was simple: the user donated data and the app displayed the pattern. The data came from users' phones, tracking movement. The pattern – a looping line, branching off, folding back on itself – updated in real time, rotating in bright colour against the dark phone screen.

Users checked on their aesthetics day-to-day. They saw a correspondence between mood and pattern. Initial comments were ironic, generating memes, but after a tiring or frustrating day, coming home to the pattern was a consolation. People reported seeing the pattern – its growing complexity, its turning knots of activity – and feeling that someone was listening to them, paying attention to them, responding to them.

The app's signal innovation was its sensitivity to motion. Rather than mapping a user's broad direction, drawing a diagonal line as they walked or drove across the city, the app took its measurement closer to the ground. It recorded the way a vehicle behaved, the lurches and minor vibrations shaking the carriage. It noted the firmness with which pedestrians pressed on the ground and the distance they sprang on the next step. It read pauses as people anticipated and moved aside for others, as they stopped to take a call or as they looked at an advertisement or another person or a feature of the landscape. It inferred whether the user was proactive in avoiding collisions. It tracked changes in pedestrian speed and rhythm and correlated these with the music the user listened to; it then identified when the user was thinking about the piece of music and when they were thinking in a way that resembled the mood of the music.

Users became adept at reading the pattern. There was something in the shape, a meaning you picked up in a glance, a significance in the difference between the two most recent iterations. Inside this discrepancy was the story of what happened to you.

The app was especially useful after fraught or anxious encounters, events with uncertain outcomes such as a first date or job interview. Not knowing how to feel afterwards, one solution was to look at the pattern. There, you saw an indication of the other's attitude, implied in your small responsive movements. Providing you kept it close, the tracker was sufficiently alert to absorb many hundreds of gestures. A glance at the image showed how many times you crossed your arms, craned your neck, looked distractedly over your shoulder, leaned in at the meeting-room desk, sat back in the comfortable chair at the bar.

The benefits of the app extended further. Users measured their state, deciding to walk out in order to come back and see how they came through in the pattern. Tests could be open, performed without set purpose, or directed. Unsure how to act in a given situation, you could walk, think about the issue, the various factors that made it hard to decide, and track your thinking. The app grew more sensitive, learning the particular rhythms of its user, and received a regular stream of automatic software updates increasing the power and range of its sensors.

There were relatively minor social effects in the beginning. Meetings changed, users wishing to accelerate past the provisional experience to find out what it meant. Public transport was affected, users refusing to board certain vehicles. Communities tallied segments from multiple patterns to measure and evaluate services. Drivers, servers and assistants generated open profiles based on data derived from the app, and employment in public-facing work became contingent on the app's measurement of quality of experience.

Though mobile devices typically remained slender and light, users felt an extra weight from the pattern inside. People were uncomfortable and anxious if dispossessed of their phones. Seats in public transport were fitted with a pair of narrow lateral cushions supporting the head in a fixed position, looking downwards, and blocking peripheral visual information. Chairs in office environments were designed to offer increased support to the strained neck, and mattresses were built with hollow grooves ready to tip back and lay your head inside, in relief.

With the development of new hardware, fittings on the phone that would pick up movement on the inside and periphery of the body, and with new, extensive changes to the terms and conditions, the app, which remained free to use, was branded with a name – Nest. Shortly after, to make readings even more authentic, more powerful and accurate, and to make the experience more comfortable, remote body-sensors were distributed. These sensors, placed initially behind the ear and on the hip, were neither conspicuous nor intrusive, appearing as tiny moles on the skin's surface. Previous motion capture, which included heart rate and body temperature, had been tentative, limited to the distant reception picked up by the phone device itself. The new updated hardware, combined with significantly more sophisticated and powerful software, made earlier nest forms comically inept.

Data was captured from a variety of time scales, microseconds to months, and from every available spatial perspective – the trunk and limbs of the moving body, the changing oxygen concentration in each microlitre of blood. Movement was rendered in patterns of far greater detail, in vast, coiling depth, and from many different and complementary perspectives, each of which was available to view on the original phone screen and on user-endorsed, encryption-secured external devices; this allowed for a much greater and more speculative pattern analysis.

Sensors tracked sleep, making recommendations on diet and exercise and suggesting changes leading to better rest and health. The app adjusted morning alarms as close as possible to optimal points in the sleep cycle. It informed users how long they had dreamed and split up dream activity into distinct narratives. It exposed dream content through users' expressive physiology – pulse and breath, temperature, eyelid-motion tracking phantom objects. It monitored limb movements, the number of times the body turned and any words spoken from inside the dream world.

Data was incorporated into many areas. Open access to nest patterns during work hours was made a condition of employment. Performance reviews and salaries were tied to nest readings. Employment could be revoked because of non-conscious evidence.

The app detected illness before substantial development. The best chance of catching and excising a tumour was to follow the pattern. The evidence existed in the total record of behaviour, bearing something alien and new inside it. It found signs of depression and mental illness through associated patterns in body movement. It made confident assertions as to when someone was in the process of changing their mind.

Nests began and ended as a single line. Flatlines recalled birth, a record of arrival, a beginning in a strange and unimaginable place. Subsequent versions replaced flatlines – in birth and death – with rougher fibres, neither resolving into nor beginning ultimately from a single line. For a spell, activity extended into embryonic development and disposal of the corpse. Fetal nests provided valuable insight, allowing family to posit character and resemblance before the person was born. Several institutions and corporations offered incentives to share this data, awarding scholarships and positions to promising candidates. Insurance firms provided attractive rates to clients, conditional on nest activity being supplied. The decay of the deceased body also fed the nest: patterns formed while the corpse dispersed. This data too was interpreted. After intense religious lobbying, the app was modified and an artificial clear line reinserted to mark the definitive beginning and end of the person.

Beyond data voluntarily shared with employers, insurance firms, medics and security forces, users guarded their nests. Each pattern's repetitions and escalations generated unique security criteria, nest-prints being akin to behavioural fingerprints. If a device was intercepted by another user, it wouldn't function; the corresponding identity must be physically proximate for the device to open. The advantages of nest-print security over standard biometrics was in the near impossibility of mimicry. Nest-print – a unique unconscious pattern generated repeatedly by each user in the course of their flowing behaviour – wasn't something that could be lifted out by a third party, as a body part might be. Nest-prints were created by tens of thousands of active movements ongoing inside and on the edge of the body; attempted hacks – users surveilled over long periods, their habits and mannerisms aped

– were bound to fail by virtue of the sheer range and depth of the data fields fed into the nest.

Users spoke of having a relationship with their nest, describing the product as an entity itself, with agency. A common comparison was to domestic animals. Advantages emerged independently, organically, as users, eager to support the well-being of their nest, took better care of themselves. In periods of sickness, the pattern became dimmer, pulsed slower and sometimes appeared to barely move at all. Users made every effort to ensure the same lifelessness never again afflicted their nest.

A number of different settings were available to display nests. The default setting remained a black background, the nest a spinning 3D object, but alternative pattern displays were added regularly, each elaborating on and complementing the core design. Nest software converted data into landscape simulations. Animal simulation was popular, user data articulated by the movement of a chosen species, every aspect of which conformed to both the local detail and the general pattern of the individual's life. Users could watch the simulation from several perspectives and at a range of speeds, observing the failures and pains and satisfactions the animals met; they could then switch to a time-lapse showing the origin and development of the species, its migratory patterns and changing rates of mortality and reproduction, all the while knowing every detail was an illustration of their own life, formed only by their movements, their decisions, conscious or not, knowing everything ultimately came from them.

Simulations were developed of fully inhabited cities, planets, galaxies and universes, again exactly corresponding to the individual's data; a simple scaling process, the activity regulating the growth of the pale crescent at the base of a fingernail was expressed, in one example, through the drama across twelve months of a family of three.

Finally, users were able to hold their nest in their hands. The heart-sized hologram was fitted with tactile boosters, giving the impression of smoothness and roughness, weight and temperature. Users made formal nest displays, presenting their pattern to another person, handing over the hologram in a highly charged symbolic act, securing strong, long-lasting bonds. Couples cared for each other's nest, feeling the heat and weight of the other in their hands. Using a partner's nest as a light and heat source was popular among young users, who sometimes renounced all other sources of artificial energy, living, for as long as was possible, exclusively on the power generated by the other person.

Couples observed the effects of nests projected onto walls. They replayed segments of pattern and altered the display speed. The nest made a storm of light, turning in a spiral that entranced them. The darkness of the room was ruptured by a strobe effect that distorted their perception of time.

Hallucination and observation were difficult to separate. Couples saw significance everywhere. They read language in the patterns and they reached out, trying to hold the meaning that had already gone. They saw people and places, memories the source user had buried long ago, reanimated through transcribed physiological rhythm. Unspeakable stories, frightening exhibitions of creation. Pattern inside pattern, each layer opening to a further one beneath. Among the images forming and dissolving were large urban vistas, rows of superstructures, smooth black monoliths reaching into space.

Images broke, turning into tubular forms and gently waving fibres – the user's genetic structure, the electrochemical composition coincident with the memories and the neural cascade taking place while the individual watched. Couples, underneath and inside the images, reached to them, tried to grasp or wrestle them away, to treasure or destroy them, punish them for what they signified, what they were unable to accommodate inside. This ritual behaviour supported, encouraged and prolonged lovemaking, and people often claimed children were conceived in these nest ceremonies.

An update to the immersive holographic feature – popular among couples and its potential beginning to be exploited in other areas, including psychotherapy, the criminal justice system and medicine – enabled a user to appoint, at any time, a single other person as their nest custodian. The custodian would receive, from the moment the appointment was formalised, a live replica of the other's nest, their own heart-sized copy of the spinning 3D object, developing and updating in parallel to the source life. This was a significant stage in the development of nest technology, marking a shift, after the identity euphoria of nest exhibitions, back towards the separation of user and nest. It was now possible to display a nest at great, even unlimited, distance from the user's physical instantiation.

Holographic identity displays continued with both partners present. But custodians' exclusive use of the nest copy began to dominate, then to obstruct, physical meetings between people. Custodians became addicted to the copy, spending long blocks of time visualising the development of their partner's life.

Users reserved areas of their house to keep the copy in, going out of their way to ensure it was well heated and insulated, that it got plenty of light. They put it in a protective box. They watched it, monitored it, came back to it, thought about it continually. They heard and felt it through the night, the heart-sized image of the person that they loved. People slept beside the representation, turning towards it, holding themselves against it, enjoying its pulse. They put blankets around the box to further protect it. A house containing a representation, a custodian's house, was always locked. Additional security systems were set up to protect the representation. There were frequent nightmares about water spilling over and extinguishing the form, ruining and breaking it, dousing a fire.

Dreams of power outages, faulty generators and reserves, of a whole city full of melted, expired nests.

Custodians were careful not to make too much noise or say anything unkind when the nest was present. They maintained they knew the nest worked unidirectionally, that it couldn't be influenced by factors remote from the source user. But the dissonance remained. There were reports of custodians attempting to feed the image.

After a limited trial, and with clear indications of where the application would lead, Nest Inc. approved a software update temporarily suspending the remote access feature, reinstating the original user as a necessary fixture beside his or her nest.

Nest-based artworks began quietly, with users designing tattoos matching recurrent motifs and stamping them on the source body part: walking patterns on feet, breathing rhythms on chest and throat. Brief fads included tattooing brain activity onto the scalp, carrying coded messages under the growing hair and inking the whole body in fragments that would only become visible under certain sound frequencies.

There was commercial potential in enabling users to incorporate nest patterns into food. Ready-made stencils, based on lines and curves invariably found in each nest, were sold in inexpensive packets. Elaborate personalised versions depicted whole stretches of an individual's behaviour. People baked and fried nest fragments, celebrating occasions and special moments. Users marked particular experiences they wanted to live again, identifying the associated nest activity and using it to shape edible matter.

Trauma sufferers were drawn to shaping, producing and eating material based on what had happened to them. One of the pleasures in eating your trauma was the strangeness of seeing and feeling the thing disappear – of holding the event in your hand, opening your mouth, incorporating it and making it nothing.

The adaptability, the versatility of a nest pattern was impressive. Nests offered direct, unmediated translation into music. Concerts were performed dramatising particular moments in a user's life. The nest of a user living to average age would be rendered in a musical piece with an estimated duration of twelve to thirteen billion years. Scaler technicians, working on software that would truncate musical life-pieces to weeks and hours, stated that the perspective admitted to humans was approximately equally near to the smallest known thing and the largest – that, according to best estimates, people occupied a position midway between nothing and everything.

First efforts to manipulate extra-terrestrial objects focused on asteroids. Semi-autonomous mechanical structures observed and adapted to the asteroid's trajectory, intercepted the rock body and began an extensive mining operation. The extracted ore was collected and shuttled back to Earth at regular intervals, a private enterprise launched by an anonymous individual. A press release revealed that the ore was of secondary importance to the mission, and its principal objective was to carve long stretches of a particular pattern, believed to belong to the deceased partner of the benefactor, onto the asteroid. The operation, still with no known end date, had achieved its first success. The press release stated that the carving, carried out simultaneously by thousands of smaller machines, reached far into the rock, significantly altering its mass and orbit. Video streams broadcast footage of the asteroid's movement, cutting from clips of the drilling to a higher vantage showing aspects of the carved design, to a distant shot, taken by one of the returning ore capsules, of the asteroid spinning in space.

The tribute to the deceased individual comprised three distinct stages: the hollows put into the object; the new course of its voyage through the solar system; and the more conventional reverential structures built, on Earth, by ore extracted from the asteroid.

Beyond this first experiment, plans were made to impart the whole of a nest onto an extra-terrestrial structure. The world's wealthiest individuals competed to fund these missions and project their nest in space. Previously, full-pattern renderings had taken place only virtually, in holograms or in other simulated representations. The reasons were strictly practical, nests comprising too much information to be rendered in terrestrial areas.

The process required use of a large, previously untouched object: a planet. Planets were to become representative entities, maintaining a one-to-one correspondence with the life of the source user. Teams of astronomers, astrophysicists and astroengineers consulted on potential effects, not only on the mass of the carved planet, and hence its orbit, but also on that of any of the chain of neighbouring moons, planets, satellites and asteroids, and of course on Earth itself. A project spokeswoman used the phrase 'altered heavens', and there was discussion at various levels of possible effects on the daily life of people on Earth. This, again, would be part of a larger exhibition, the continuous tribute to the user carved across the planet.

Environmentalists, biologists and animal rights activists submitted grave fears about the effects the changed night sky might have on any number of migrating species, from the former-Arctic tern to the mid-Atlantic giant green turtle, who were believed, in a process still not fully understood, to gather information from the magnetism of the Earth's core, from genetically instantiated ancestral memories and from the patterns and revolutions of the astral bodies seen in the seas under them and the sky above them. Should the night sky be even minutely altered from its predictable course, there were sure to be waves of catastrophic animal behaviour, not only in those larger vertebrate species that appealed to sympathy, but also in ecologically crucial species such as green locusts and melanaphis aphids, whose sudden astral miscalculations could set in chain disastrous effects on their plant symbionts, creating almost unimaginable ruin of the Earth's total food system. All of this, the full reach of each line of effects, derived directly from even the most idle moments in the source user's life.

Sociologists, economists and state administrators expressed fears about the unpredictable effects an alien sky might have on swathes of the human population. There was anxiety about sudden political turmoil and market ruptures after the ground and sky became unidentifiable, genuinely unpredictable human behaviour emerging from this abrupt sense of unmooring, of a global deracination – melatonin fluctuating, diurnal body settings running askew – as people's fundamental sense of instantiation, of duration, of being alive in time and space, was put into jeopardy. It would be all but impossible, experts said, to factor in the full range of possible effects. The smallest adaptation may ripple out into vast and overwhelming health and behavioural changes. Previously undisclosed reports noted correlations between the installation of larger satellites in low Earth orbit and spikes of resistance to previously reliable courses of medication. Artificial manipulation of the night sky, in such instances, appeared to produce infinitesimal changes in the rhythms of sunlight and passing time, changes still too subtle to measure instrumentally but picked up, nevertheless, unconsciously by animal and plant bodies. Fears grew over productivity and fertility; hysterical protests warned of threats to the continued existence of the species. Fractional, apparently negligible alterations to the course of the Earth's orbit – noted already in the most devastating earthquakes, which seemed to rip and gouge out slabs of time as well as space – may well upset the range of delicate, precariously balanced homeostatic controls keeping people alive. As declining fertility threatened future life, so too did suboptimal or erratic functioning of various autonomic processes, from the ability to breathe and walk, to the capacity of the inner ear to measure balance, to the immune system's success or failure in recognising a distinct and individual human body. Any and all of these autonomous controls may, at any time and under the slightest and most innocuous provocation, give up; the risk, then, so various experts argued, in so significantly adapting the sky was entirely unmerited.

Among the most powerful and vocal dissenters to planet manipulation were religious leaders, with representatives from various faiths united in agreeing it was an affront to the creator. Astroengineering, whether conceived for practical or aesthetic reasons, was an act of gargantuan egotism, idol worship on a hitherto unimagined scale. The project drew particularly vehement scorn from factions occupied with the question of the physical location of God, concerned at possible retribution on man for the folly of disturbing His position in the seat of the heavens. The transgression should not be risked and must be sabotaged by any means necessary. Long communal meditation and prayer sessions were devoted to obstructing this impending obscenity; leaders spoke of an instantaneous shattering of the fundaments of space and time, a sudden voiding of matter, of everything coming not into darkness but into absence of darkness and light.

Related protests gathered around other Nest Inc. transgressions, including the digital planets programmed to express a user's life. Religious sects requested full acknowledgement not only of these simulated planets, but of the countries, cities, flora, fauna and especially the sim-human populations inside them too. They demanded guarantees for the continued protection of these habitats and civilisations, the granting, to these vast populations, of full legal recognition, of confirmation of their status as autonomous, sentient beings. Sim-people generated their own nests, patterns which could be rendered in a further simulated world, itself containing a large population, leading to further nests and yet further, a process of apparently infinite regress. The priests submitted lengthy formal proposals to the administrators of Nest Inc., laying out a programme that would include translation efforts, teachings of the word of God and finally vast baptisms, sanctifying and realising simulated people by water. Engineers built comprehensive patches that would incorporate rudimentary religious instruction within digital planets; extensive missionary efforts would follow in due course. In addition to saving the populations' souls, they proposed amending all aspects of culture, from architectural standards to prohibitions on food, in order that these simulated planets would conform no longer to a single human individual but to God Himself, who has created all.

At the same time, religious factions discovered certain opportunities inside nests. Nests were a form of revelation, and it followed that careful attention paid to these patterns would bring believers closer to God. Again, affiliated coders and software engineers were instrumental. Tightly air-controlled networks of servers and terminals were built into desert cave channels, optimally conducting and preserving the information, as powerful deep-learning software parsed collections of donated nests, seeking out intimations of pattern and structure. Priest coders uploaded and copied nest after nest, enunciating long sequences of numbers. The software grew more sophisticated and powerful as greater data sets were fed to it, leading to exponential increases in productivity. The priests found they could train the software, that if they withheld data, it then attacked it more powerfully when fed. The effects after each starvation were more radical than the last. With every new batch, the priests spilled libations onto the earth floor, complementing the sacrament of the body that was eaten.

Significance and structure began appearing in the output. The priests were in no doubt, now, that what was unfurling around them was a message contained inside a code, a vast total code arrayed across the movement of every individual who had lived. Their fear was that the limited amount of data harvested – being only in the hundreds of millions of people at this stage – may not be sufficient to render the whole message comprehensible. They worked on and on in the caves, singing the scrolls of numbers quietly.

The priests knew it was vulgar to speculate on what was written in the code; it would be revealed in time, however long that may be. But they saw it was His voice. On several occasions they were struck and marked by emissions of electricity, the voice emitting loose pieces of the emerging message. They bowed, grateful for the pain and the marks bestowed on them.

The message accumulated, years and decades passing, the line of priests sustained by the select group of priestesses occupying a single narrow chamber in the caves. Both groups were affected by the voice, marked by its revelations, their bodies distorted into the shape best equipped to serve their purpose.

As the message was slowly revealed to them they finally saw what it was. Spoken through the rendered lives of all humankind, every person who had lived, was the true name of God. His name, resplendent but concealed, fragmented throughout creation, composed a series of instructions. The priests sang out and went prostrate before the name, which gathered and thickened in great dense blocks of information, and they began to build.

They gave thanks with every step, overflowing with gratitude. They saw, as the building went on, the divine perfection finally revealed in the name, and they saw that it could never have been other than this. With every addition they made, building it, they saw that the name was moving them backwards, that as they built they eroded time. At the end, when the weapon was complete, as the last deformed priest went to press the release signal, they saw what had happened and wept. They were transported, taken to the moment of creation. Pressing to signal the release of the warhead, time unfolded and they existed infinitely, in the boundless glory and wisdom of the name, and it was as if all of this, all of the Earth and all of the heavens, had never been.

PART TWO

Westenra Park

1

He noticed it for the first time driving Shel to the airport in the evening. As a precaution they'd given themselves an hour for the journey but the roads were oddly quiet. Passing through the marshes, it appeared suddenly ahead of them – a shift, a low cloud, a distortion. He slowed. They felt it again a minute later, a thick sheet of fog drifting in from the coast.

Flights were grounded and the terminal filled up, then surged over capacity. The air was terrible; it was difficult to move. People yelling, sudden spasms of movement, odd rippling effects from one end of the concourse to the other. Shel tried to get hold of her colleagues, who were connecting from separate cities. The signal came in and out; she couldn't get a good line. People butted against her, knocking her arm as she tried to create space to focus on the call. This was critical. She risked disrupting the whole project if she was late. John trailed her from desk to desk, pushing past the banks of static passengers. Shel ran through a list of contingency plans: the first flight was a short transfer; the crucial flight was the second one. There must be another way of getting there. Could they transfer her overland? She repeated – to herself, to him, to the official oppressed under a dozen shrieks – that she had no option, it was imperative, she simply had to make that second flight.

An announcement, a reprieve, barely credible – the flight was boarding. A sudden wave through the crowds, murmurs of confusion, excitement stirring. They had no time for goodbyes – a quick hug, a perfunctory kiss on the edge of security. He stood by the glass watching the runway, tracking the rows of studded red lights. He could only just make out the aircraft. Surely there was a mistake? Surely she wasn't flying in this?

He couldn't bear to watch the aircraft rise, fearing that something would emerge out of the fog, colliding with her plane, bringing it down. He turned away and found a café, sipping coffee and waiting in the terminal until the flight disappeared from the screen. Only three flights had departed in the previous two hours and everything still listed was cancelled or delayed.

Why, he thought, was she so determined to go, at any cost? She shouldn't put herself at risk. No-one would blame her for waiting, and the university would cover any fees. Of course he knew the answer was simple. He understood her work was a priority above all else. They had been through this many times over the past six years.

The uncertainty of Shel's flight; the lack of information on the project; the loud, hostile activity all around him – it was understandable he was anxious. Whenever she departed on fieldwork, he felt this low panic, a certainty something was about to go wrong. Things were more fraught this time because of the suddenness of the offer, the lack of preparation time, the minimal information made available to her group. And then the weather, the fog rising, the confusion at the airport.

He had been sitting at the café an hour when he grabbed at the phone vibrating in his jacket, almost dropped it. *Landed. Boarding again soon. Flight was fine. Love you, S.* He breathed out. He could leave – everything was okay. As he got up and exited the airport, calculating how much the extended stay in the car park was going to cost him, he remained mildly anxious, with a feeling of quiet, stubborn dread. He felt as if there was something he had either forgotten or had not yet realised, something floating on the edge of his vision.

He arrived home late and slept fitfully. The next morning he looked from the tall window onto the thick fog. He had no plans for the weekend so he stayed largely in the house, going out occasionally to the edge of the fields, distant headlamps glowing in the vapour. Shel wrote, confirming her second flight had landed and that she'd checked into the hotel. Everything was fine, she said, everything was okay. She had used the same expression twice in two days. It didn't sound like her. Was his anxiety so apparent? Generally they communicated little when she was out on research. She was to focus exclusively on the work; they'd get in touch only in an emergency. He started thumbing in a response, when a message came through, the network provider apologising for the recent loss of service – *circumstances beyond our control* – warning of further disruption in the days to come. He looked at the phone reception and saw the bars had disappeared.

He paced the house, unable to settle. He couldn't decide what to eat. He picked up one book then put it aside for another. The day passed and he retired to bed; he woke sober and alert in the early hours. He had never previously had any problems sleeping. It was one of the things in his life he was quietly grateful for – the inevitability of unconsciousness. As the disruption was so unusual he thought there might have been an outside cause – a siren, a distant car alarm, a change in temperature, a sudden flare of light at the window. He sat up, hearing only the faint, distant stirring of the trees beyond the fields. He was still adjusting to the sounds. The gulls' cries worst twice a day, the distant machinery in the fields, the cattle moaning in the night. The wind whistling inside the walls' hollows, the scurrying sounds beyond the plaster. The house was temporary. Construction was just beginning on their own place, in a new estate past the edge of a forest. The agent was supposed to update them this weekend, but his phone signal was still out, and the router in the living room had started blinking red.

It was the first time John had visited the estate since they'd signed the contract; the drive took a little longer as the fog had failed to clear completely. He pulled in to the makeshift car park, clipped the door closed and lifted up his hood. Deserted, the site looked enormous, much bigger than he remembered. The construction vehicles were parked at odd angles, as if the crew had left hurriedly, some sudden event causing them to scatter. There were stacks of slabs and slates, and barrows and carts had tipped over. Food wrappers stuck to the fence and a length of blue tarpaulin battered in the wind. A rope fence formed a second perimeter further into the site, and beyond this the dug ground was piled in a large spiralling cone shape. He ducked under the rope and walked towards the excavation, the long pit prepared for the first several houses, and peered inside.

His instinct was to immediately call Shel, though of course that wasn't possible. They were to go inside it? To build a home, a life, in the ground? A ladder was set into the pit. He glanced around and then he climbed down. Inside it was immediately darker and the surface was far away. He knelt and identified points where the roots had been grubbed out. You could still see the dips where they'd split and removed stones, the frowns the machinery left in the soil. He swept the looser dirt away, startled as something unpleasant brushed his hand – the chitinous casing of a black beetle, uncovered and dazzled on its back.

He climbed out. The fog was thickening again, the temperature dropping. He had to concentrate on his feet so he didn't disturb or trip on any of the materials. He glanced back to the excavation, then he heard something. He paused, focused. Someone was there. Someone was watching him. The tarp rattling in the breeze; the cameras he subconsciously registered hanging from the fence in nests. He stood listening, the vapour in the air leaving beads of moisture on his jacket. He heard nothing. Nothing was there.

He stopped before the tall fence at the outer limit, hearing it again. It wasn't the tarp. A high-pitched whistling sound, a turbulence. He looked up. He searched desperately for the source, but saw nothing. A bird? Tension in his chest, a shiver passing over him. Where was it? At the same time he felt sure someone was watching him, that he was no longer alone. He had to leave, now. Hurry over the fence, towards the car, quickly and safely home. But he didn't. Time seemed to slow. A faint, gaining arrowing sound, a darkness, a high-pitched trilling, a cool breeze almost on top of him, and blind impact.

II

Our access was revoked mid-flight and the news awaited us on the ground; despite all earlier assurances, we were no longer permitted to see the bodies. Alice began making calls before they'd opened the doors; medics checked our papers on the runway and had us cough into a mask with an attached tube that spooled out into a black box. There was a high-pitched whirring sound as the air travelled through the tubing. The task of managing even the mildest infectious disease in an airport seemed extraordinary. We were divided at Immigration, delayed further after our postponed flight. We met again, as agreed, in Arrivals, by the café we'd specified, three, not four – Alice, Jane and me – and now we waited for the doctor.

It was a remarkable opportunity. Almost nothing was known of the animals. Three times only in the past six years had a research team been invited in, though the offer came with certain restrictions. The team could spend a maximum of six weeks in the park. None of the findings could be published. Any and all information derived from the park remained the property of the affiliated group, and a non-disclosure agreement was essential.

There were rumours, but that researchers were occasionally invited in was at least proof the troop still existed. With little else to go on – especially now it seemed we weren't going to see the two bodies – we looked at our particular experience and specialities, hoping our composition might tell us something. I worked on hygiene and diet in higher primates. Alice's research was in group formation and flux. Jane, a mycologist – the youngest of us, though, I had to keep reminding myself, only a couple of years my junior – had limited field experience, with no prior research interest in primates at all. The final member was the doctor, a haematologist; he was to coordinate and lead the animals' blood analysis. I'd been forming tentative provisional theories from the outset. Something gone wrong in their food consumption? Specifically, relating to a fungus?

Two hours after clearing Immigration, and having left several messages, we were still waiting, no further towards understanding what had happened to the doctor. Had something come up in his own medical checks? There would be an odd inverted logic in the doctor, sent to take samples from the animals, being detained because of something found in his own blood.

Alice doubted he existed. Selecting and inviting an individual only to detain him at the border – it didn't make sense. We expected setbacks – our revoked access to the bodies confirmed this. The briefing stated we were to 'conduct an analysis of the bonobo troop' – this could mean almost anything. The one clear instruction was that we should bring out blood, and now our haematologist had disappeared.

Alice knew several people who had worked in service at the park headquarters. She said they wouldn't be able to tell us anything directly – their contracts had non-disclosures too – but she'd heard rumours about recent strange activity. These may have been deliberate leaks, managed by the group – it was difficult to believe anything would get out otherwise. The stories were inconsistent, with only one or two clearer details emerging, but what was in little doubt, and confirmed in our briefing, was that two adult bodies had been discovered. The rumours here spiralled: the animals had been found strung up high in the trees, their arms outstretched; they lay prone on the ground with identical bite marks from an unknown predator piercing their necks; they'd suffered a corrosive attack, the surface of their faces burned off. None of this was likely, exaggeration thriving in the information vacuum. Certainly, had the deaths indicated human attackers, we would never have been invited in. One consistent detail was the presence of a thick, black oil-like liquid emerging from the animals' mouths. And while this sounded a little melodramatic, and though there was no reference to it in the briefing, there remained the possibility of some truth in it.

  We continued to press the airport staff. The group's representatives were immediately visible by their khaki attire, their shorts, boots, their clipboards. Their accents were odd, a highly enunciated, unplaceable English. They weren't from here, but we couldn't put them in any particular country. They were unfailingly friendly and eager to help, at least until we showed them our papers and declared the issue.

'Above our grade, I'm afraid,' the young blonde woman said, smiling. 'I wish I could help, but you'll need to speak to someone else. Haven't you got a contact you should call?'

Already she'd turned away, accosted by a group trailing suitcases loudly along the marble floor. The airport, harvesting light through its open glass and steel structures, was enormous; had the doctor simply got lost?

Alice, calling round, finally managed to get hold of someone. The decision about the bodies was irrevocable; it was unfortunate, but there was nothing they could do. There would be further information once we arrived at the park headquarters, by the north gates. As regards the doctor, they weren't aware of any problems. As far as they knew, he had entered the country as scheduled. We should continue trying the number – surely it was a misunderstanding. I wondered if there was a problem with his passport, his visa. Perhaps he didn't have sufficient papers for the new equipment he was bringing.

Jane, reading through the thick file of reports we'd passed her, held a table at the café while Alice and I tried other lines for information. Had he a criminal record that brought up an alert on the Immigration database? Had he an unusual travel history? It was possible; a doctor working in innovative blood-transfer techniques was more likely than most to have experience of war zones. In that case, the fault lay with the group, who had failed to foresee the issues or take precautions against them. I dialled another department, held indefinitely on the line. I called home – the service was gone; it wasn't possible to leave a message.

Although tourists could no longer enter the park, the area still received considerable income and prestige merely from the fact the animals were there. Revenue was ascribed to 'proximate tourism' – people who wanted to be near, if not in contact with, the last of the bonobo chimpanzees. No reason was given for the park's public closure six years ago, and tourists were now kept to the lake resorts hundreds of miles away. For some time leading up to that, unsolicited researchers were stopped at the gates. Even as tourists we were barred on technicalities. Alice had been able to visit just once; a strange experience. The animals she saw were common chimpanzees, not bonobos, and not indigenous to the park.

The resorts clustered around the central lakes, large hotels and apartment compounds fringed by thin trees where tour operators led groups on tracking expeditions, with small numbers of captive chimpanzees released briefly to gasps and phone camera clicks. Although these weren't careful, discreet operations – the animals were sometimes seen being unloaded from vans – tour leaders insisted on editorial control of all video, signing off before it could be uploaded. They branded footage with inspirational quotes about conservation. Without directly saying so, they were able to present the idea the park remained open and thriving, home to a large, healthy, viable troop.

The park was owned and administered by a group of 'affiliates' working under the name Westenra Ecology and Bio-diversity Group. It was through this group that we received our invitation, and it was from their various offices we were trying to gather information. Although listed as independent, WEBG was funded by a large mining conglomerate. For the past eight years, formally – in reality much longer – this conglomerate had what amounted to a controlling interest in the country and was developing extensive land interests throughout three continents. It shipped in materials for a transient infrastructure, prefab blocks assembling into railways, housing, schools, prisons, retail estates. It built new massively expanded airports, then special transit zones linking them with the lake resorts, heavily policed and only accessible to citizens with expensive and difficult-to-acquire permits. The airports were in high demand as connection hubs and were becoming prestige destinations themselves. Increasingly, travellers spent up to a week in buildings just like this, never entering the country proper.

Heading back to the café, we passed kiosks selling merchandise and a theatre showing a loop of documentary films about the park. Interactive VR headsets were to be offered later in the year. Even virtual contact with the animals, it seemed, was more attractive if it took place nearer to them.

But the animals themselves weren't the attraction; it was the idea of them that brought people in. And the obvious thing to say is that if their attraction was virtual – if people were happy to meet them virtually – then their existence could be virtual too. There was little doubt tourists would continue coming after extinction was formally declared, an act the affiliates were still nervous about, reluctant to commit to and had managed to postpone, despite the definitive, irreversible point passing some time ago. In some ways, it would be much easier for the authorities to set up tours relating to the species if it was no longer present. They could at least get into the park then. There was the argument that one of the main obstacles to understanding the bonobo was the existence of the bonobo. With no more bodies to constitute the species, the whole space could be opened up, groups led in to survey the places they'd lived. National parks such as Westenra would be reset as extinction gardens, drawing in equally people who said they wanted to commemorate the loss and others who were simply curious about the place, as if the ground, and the trees, and the other animals, even the air, would appear wildly different because of the sudden loss of its apex species.

Of the two thousand bonobos still claimed to be alive, at least 90 per cent were captive in laboratories, zoos and private residences. The remaining two hundred or so 'wild' bonobos were allegedly based across three national parks, with Westenra holding the largest population. It was Alice's understanding that the real number was much lower, that, in spite of WEBG's statements, significantly fewer than fifty existed in the park in total. This, among many other things, we hoped to clarify immediately we met the gate staff. These animals had been forced to adapt all aspects of behaviour, from diet and territorialism to sexual practice. Such unnaturally small troops would inevitably accelerate malformation through inbreeding.

I imagined the confusion of extinction tourists watching the airport exhibitions, affected by altitude, by the slipped time zones and irregular sleep, by the scaling effect of looking down from the aircraft at the neat strips of land and river, seeing the bend of the coast, the waves as static, drawn on to the blue sea. Where had they gone? Had the animals simply starved, blending with smaller or slower species – plants, fungi, insects? Oil was interesting as a proximate extinction cause because it identified already extinct life, bringing fossilised matter out of the ground and reanimating it, fuelling aircraft through stacked small things, some of whom had had wings too. I moved past restricted areas, embassy points and tax-free zones, watching the air melt through the high glass walls, a weird contrast to the carefully conditioned atmosphere inside, listening to but unable to make out the urgent calls, the arrivals and departures, turnovers of hundreds of thousands of people, the almost religious incantation of the flight notices.

There was a lot to think about. Alice asked how much I knew about the doctor. I didn't know his nationality, history, where he was from. I didn't know where he had worked, didn't even know whether he had previous experience working with animals. This shouldn't have mattered; we were to assume responsibility for all direct interaction – the doctor was there specifically, and exclusively, to operate the device. The device was a new piece of medical equipment still undergoing trials, still in the experimental stage. The doctor would attend to the device, which – this was the extent we were told – attached to the blood vials and gave all but instant information on a range of properties contained inside. It was being branded as exciting new analytic software, and our best available means of finding out what was afflicting the animals.

Without the doctor, I thought, our whole project was in jeopardy. Not only would his expertise be missed – Alice noted he wasn't there only to measure the animals, but to monitor our own condition too, to judge how we were responding to the environment and the diet and to our prophylactics, and to treat us should anything go wrong – his device, with the blood-mapping software, would be absent too. In a best case scenario, our work would be delayed. We'd take the blood the way we were accustomed to, tranquillising the animals and inserting a syringe. We would store the vials in protective containers and we would have them tested in the lab as soon as we got out. Even this saw us potentially losing several critical weeks should something be present in the blood. With the doctor, and the new software, we could relay data back to the gates directly if anything appeared. Of course another possibility, one that was becoming increasingly likely the more it seemed WEBG was orchestrating all this, our blood samples would be taken from us the minute we left the park and we would remain ignorant of anything that was found in them.

Alice continued furiously tapping on her tablet, oblivious to the noise she was making. She looked up and warned Jane for the last time to cease using emojis in her communications: it wasn't appropriate. Especially animal emojis. 'There is an inverse relationship,' I said, 'between digital and biological populations in certain animals.' Jane, eyeing me askance, unsure if I was being serious, made herself even smaller, curling low down, deep inside the high-backed chair. She seemed a little overwhelmed by everything, pressing her screen up close to her face, shielding herself, becoming little more than a hoodie with a fringe.

I looked down and noticed my foot tapping independently. With an effort, I stilled it. Of course I was anxious, but I remained hopeful that nothing catastrophic had been found in the autopsies, that the authorities were simply making things difficult as a matter of course. And while it was almost expected of them that they would do this, I couldn't help worrying about some of the rumours. Had they meant to obstruct us all along? The important thing now, I told myself, was that we got into the park and checked over the rest of the troop. This remained our objective, and in this sense nothing substantive had changed at all.

I slept for a long time, waking initially unclear where I was, struggling for the light switch in a room that was completely dark and seemed to bar all sound, not only from the adjoining rooms and the corridor but also from the streets outside. I lifted my phone from the side table to check the time, but as soon as I removed the charge, the display cut. Reattaching it, it displayed again. I didn't understand: I'd set it to charge before I went to bed; I was sure I'd connected it properly.

I couldn't recall exactly where the hotel was. I'd had the beginnings of a headache and a loose, groggy sensation settling in my lower stomach on the drive in. I'd looked directly at the headrest on the seat in front then tilted my head back against the cushion with my eyes closed. I remembered few details: street vendors threading through traffic, iced-water passed to hands stretching out from windows; a thin palm tree, something fluttering inside, a large bat launching into flight.

We'd had two drivers – or, rather, one driver and a colleague whose role wasn't clear. They greeted us at the airport doors, showing their IDs with a weary smile, offering to carry some of our luggage but not protesting when we said there wasn't any need. We drove mostly in silence, and it was a relief to have left behind the scripted phrases and determined cheeriness of WEBG's airport staff. They were dressed casually, the accompanying driver in jeans and a red polo shirt, his colleague also in jeans and – unbelievably in this heat, though the car at least was cooler from the regulated air – a light sweater. They spoke to one another quietly and quickly, then, seeing me in the rearview mirror, reset and resumed in English. They asked us if we were comfortable and pointed to the small chilled bottles of water which we were free to drink from. They said the journey shouldn't take long, if we had any questions we should ask, otherwise, we should just relax.

'Actually,' I'd said, 'I can't get this charging socket to work.'

The co-driver found my eyes in the mirror and explained the sockets were being adapted and were temporarily inoperable. He apologised but said it wouldn't be long until we reached the hotel, where of course there would be ample charging sockets in reception, in the bar and in our rooms.

A knock on my door: Alice. She stood over me in apparent disappointment. Was I late? Had we agreed a time? 'They're sending staff to meet us here for lunch – 12.30. Okay?'

'Great, sure. Any more news?'

She'd already turned to go. 'They're meeting with us. That's the news. I'll see you in the foyer.'

They were already gathered by the time I arrived – Alice, Jane and presumably a WEBG rep – sitting on bulky leather sofas by a low table with a pot of coffee. Alice, looming over the others, glanced up at me from the wall side but neither she nor Jane spoke. The rep stood, smiling a little uncertainly. He was slim, of average height, dressed in a neat dark-blue suit with open collar. He smiled warmly as we shook hands, introducing himself – 'director of communications, but not at all as important as that makes me sound' – and immediately began apologising, first for the very limited time he had to meet with us and then, of course, for all this trouble. I sat on the sofa seat next to him – the only seat available – and poured myself a mug. As he continued speaking I looked away, trying to concentrate, still disoriented. I looked ahead, at the wall, then down onto the table, distracted by the synthetic flowers held in a small stone vase.

'Sorry,' I said, interrupting him. 'But can you tell us where he is?'

He paused, momentarily thrown. He visibly composed himself, smiled at me. 'As I was explaining, Miss—'

'Doctor.'

'Of course, my apologies. As I was saying, Dr Murray, this has all just,' he began waving his arm, almost knocking over the vase, 'been dealt with terribly, in the most unprofessional manner imaginable, and I can only begin to offer our sincerest apologies.'

'You don't need to keep apologising. You can just tell us what's happened.'

Alice looked at me again, as if trying to communicate something.

'There was an anomaly with your colleague's passport and identification.'

'What was the problem exactly?'

'We don't know. That's what we're trying to determine.'

'But you're speaking as if none of this is your fault.'

'We prepared all the relevant documentation and as far as we were aware everything was in order. We weren't to know that something like this would happen.'

'That's not what I mean.'

'I'm sorry?'

'You still haven't explained anything. Look, I'm sorry if I sound short, I'm tired from the journey and still a bit hazy. All I want to know is what's happening. A simple question. Where is he?'

'He's here.'

'Here? Can I see him?'

He smiled. 'Sorry, I mean to say he's in the country, here, although not officially. He's in one of the secure transit hotels at the airport; he doesn't need a visa to enter. The idea is that he waits until the anomaly is resolved, his passport's cleared and he joins your group. Although, he may well have decided, and you couldn't blame him really, to simply return home.'

'So you've seen him?'

'My colleagues have. I've spoken with him – he's perfectly well.'

'Can I see him? I want to talk to him. You understand I want to verify all this?'

'Of course I understand. But it's complicated. He's not permitted to leave the hotel.'

'Well, I'll go there.'

'You can't, not without voiding your own entry papers. Talk to him, by all means. Call him. You do have the details?'

'Yes, but—'

'Again, I am profoundly sorry about all this. Honestly, I wish it wasn't like this; we've done everything we can. I'm afraid parts of this are as much a mystery to me as they are to you.'

'But that doesn't make any sense.'

'What doesn't?'

'You invited him here – can't you clear it up? Can't you just approve him and push it through, whatever the problem is? You said it was a minor thing – can't you straighten it out?'

'I'm afraid you seem to be inflating our authority here. We're simply a collective concerned with protecting biodiversity. We have no say in matters concerning, for example, immigration.'

I breathed out, tried to compose myself.

Alice intervened. 'Okay. So, if he doesn't get out, if he can't join us, then what?'

'I don't follow.'

'He has all the equipment – not just the new device, but the extraction kit, everything for storing the blood. How do we continue without that?'

'Ah, some good news there. In the event he decides not to join you, for whatever reason, the clinic at HQ has offered to provide you with everything you'll need.'

Alice leaned in. 'You're sure of that?'

'I can absolutely guarantee it.'

'Well, that's something, I suppose,' Jane said.

'Wait, what do you mean "decides not to"?'

'Sorry? Look, I really don't have long at all – I have another appointment which I'm already running late for.'

'You're not serious? We haven't even mentioned the bodies – we were supposed to have an appointment to view the two bodies.'

He stood to go. Alice and Jane automatically rose with him.

'They'll get to that, as well, at the gates. They'll look after you there. Look, we're all on the same side here, you know. Try not to forget that. I'll continue to monitor the situation, but in any case, I should expect your colleague will be joining you here tonight.' He glanced over his shoulder, towards the exit, the dusty glare of the noon light streaming in with every push of the heavy revolving doors. He extended his hand again, made a broad smile, told us how wonderful it was to meet us and wished us every success on our trip. He was gone.

'That's all we're getting?'

'Look,' Alice said, keeping her voice down, 'does it matter? You don't want to push these people – it won't get us anywhere. The important thing is, he's here.'

'Really? You're happy to leave it like that?'

'I don't think we have any choice, Shel.'

'Jane, what do you think?'

'Well, he did at least say we'd get the equipment we need.'

'Exactly,' Alice said. 'I understand you're angry, but trust me, this won't achieve anything. We have to carry on. We have to do our best.'

I waited a moment, and as they walked towards the corridor I took a seat again in the foyer. There was a buzzing sound, circling, coming closer. I tried to swat at it, and it dipped away. It returned, and the same thing happened again. I stood up, waited for it to land on my jeans, my arm ready, outstretched, but again I missed. It hovered constantly, set the perfect distance from my reach. I snapped at it, uselessly, again and again. It read me perfectly and instantly, modelled me – my size, health, my reflexes, my capacity – appearing to know, in advance, exactly what I was going to do.

Though we left early, before 4 a.m., it took the best part of two hours to get out of the city. Construction was ramped up during the night, with many routes sectioned off. Before leaving, we re-confirmed our journey and estimated arrival time with the city authorities and with the north-gate staff. Even so, we were stopped four times by security forces, who used lights from their phones to study our identity papers and permits. On the third occasion, we had to get out of the car. Fear, confusion, oil-black air, legions of insects suddenly lit in blue-screen, but it was just another delay, and by dawn we'd outrun the suburbs into long stretches of patchwork farmland broken, intermittently, by tall retail developments and partly built hotels.

Alice hadn't spent significant time here in years, but as she was the only one at all familiar with the area we agreed that she should guide. As soon as we left the sprawling outskirts the roads became clear and straight, and with the mApp as well there wasn't any need for Alice's directions. I didn't mind driving, the roads quiet, looking onto long fields and palm forest; it gave me time to think. Alice and Jane spoke quietly from the back. Focused on the road, I couldn't understand them, heard only this odd, persistent drone.

We began to notice a difference in architecture further north, lower but more elaborate buildings, an absence of two-storey structures. There were isolated, sprawling private residences remote behind tall black gates, razor wire over the walls. Beyond these block buildings were unmarked ranges of field. Alice pointed to narrow tracks leading into the mines. Once or twice we glimpsed, in the distance, the plumes of chalk coming out of the cratered earth, the opened surfaces of vast quarries. To the west, the land began to rise, and we saw the first hints of the hills we were approaching. Though still on the edge of the primary rainy season, we passed through spells of lurid green, interrupting the starker ochre haze we'd become accustomed to. We started climbing more noticeably, bending slowly through cut mountain. I listened to the engine, rechecked the fuel. We hadn't seen another vehicle in some time. A ravine dropped beneath us, and I saw rows of perfectly lined terraces dug into a radically steep incline.

The conglomerate dug caves into the earth. As well as prospecting for oil they mined uranium, gold, copper, cobalt, coltan, diamond. Tantalum was extracted from coltan and poured into circuits to make phones and tablets and audio players. They put it in cameras, 3D printers, pacemakers and reflective lenses in glasses. They used tantalum to build platforms for virtual experiences whose primary purpose was distraction from, among other things, the conditions needed to create the devices and the social, ecological and climatic consequences of the mines. The increasingly disembodied nature of programs run on this hardware – VR holograms, whispered notifications of blood-pressure targets, automatic food replacements arriving silently at the door – was deliberate and ingenious, implying the technology was literally baseless, unlimited and independent, divorced from anachronistic categories such as fuel, labour, emissions, natural resources. It was as if product design exploited latent religiosity, a nostalgia for the belief that people too existed free from bodies.

It was impossible to convey how hopeless all this could seem. The more indirect and intercepted people's experience of the world became, the less significant it seemed that poorer quantities of the earth itself remained. As if vanished or damaged matter could simply be regenerated by simulacra.

Spokespersons announced the results of sponsored research claiming immersion in phone and tablet screens correlated with fewer air miles per person; at the same time, tantalum was fused in alloys in military jet engines that orchestrated the conflicts creating the conditions for the mines and quarries to thrive. One of the most absurd details was that the techniques supposed to alleviate, if only a little, catastrophic environmental damage – wind turbines, electric cars – themselves relied on quarried coltan.

According to formal notices, the country's decades-long conflict was presently somewhere between indefinitely prolonged ceasefire and resolution. The conglomerate received wide international acclaim for its efforts in brokering this. This was obviously bullshit. We were aware of the allegations that throughout the conflict the group remained not only immune and untouched, but it stoked and in some cases scripted its conflagrations, in line with the ebb and flow of prices and demand for the area's minerals. If the conflict was temporarily stilled, there were clear market reasons for it; as soon as conditions changed and these justifications vanished, the conflict could escalate again. At best, in agreeing to cooperate, albeit indirectly, we were foolish and naive. More realistically, we were passive and effectively complicit in what was happening. If we were invited to the park then there was a clear reason behind it, in the group's own interest. We were aiding them by ceding to their conditions and demands.

WEBG were effectively the conglomerate's PR division. They directly supported the mining. Their videos and reports consistently ignored the conflict around it and were so successful that tourist numbers stayed constant and unaffected through ceasefires and escalations. They just didn't talk about the war. The group even produced lines of electronics with a small green dot on top, indicating coltan sourced from the zone, a percentage of the profits of which went into supporting and looking after the animals in the park. Which was, of course, such a parody of the truth I didn't know where to begin.

There was no evidence anyone in the organisation had any kind of background in the natural sciences at all. They generated goodwill through sophisticated media management and curated tourism operations. They produced short video clips made from years-old footage and recycled material from outdated journals and disseminated them on social media. There was no research presence in the park, only guards making seasonal tours and drone cameras monitoring potential trespasses at the edges. It was a fluke they'd even picked up the two bodies.

The park itself was getting smaller and smaller, mining continuing to blast away the surrounding forests. In theory, you could never be quite sure when you were inside it, both because there was no physical barrier and because the edge kept changing, drawing in. The reason given for the authorities' refusal to build, as a last, desperate attempt to deter human interference, a steel wall around the entire perimeter, was that the construction would disrupt the animals, introducing new elements to the park and perhaps threatening plant, insect and bird species, with a knock-on effect on the primates. The reality was that the cost of building it was too high because it would never end. It wasn't a matter of building a single wall, but rather of erecting, dismantling and rebuilding the same wall continuously, endlessly, as the park drew itself in, ever smaller and tighter, until eventually there was nothing to encompass. Another advantage, from the authorities' perspective, in having no clear physical boundary – originally a principle enforced to allow natural species' migration – was that it was more difficult for outsiders to see just how small the park was becoming, how much land was sold and sheared off every year.

Maps were adapted to hide this, presenting outdated information. WEBG offered free downloads of mApps at the airport, a means of managing the information given to and produced by tourists. Alice said roads, villages, whole towns were named that hadn't existed for years. It didn't matter; all travel inside the zone was by permit only and under the guidance of tour leaders, carefully managed so the vanished areas would never be encountered. None of this was explicitly denied, spokespersons for WEBG and occasionally other affiliates preferring to avoid answers and instead make positive statements about the sophisticated technology they had created and how it was available to anyone who wanted it, free of charge. Interrogation was appropriated as PR opportunity, until people stopped asking questions.

The horizon was ridged in livid cloud, and it was about to fall dark. We had several hours still to drive. Jane cleared her throat. I thought with every passing hour she became more childlike. I thought I'd seen her pretending to sleep, as if she might discover something under false cover. I slowed, and we continued in silence. Settlements were arrangements of lights hung up in the darkness. They seemed bold. They seemed built against something. I was tired. Alice met my gaze in the mirror and asked me if I wanted to stop. I said no, I was fine. She continued to look at me.

'We'll pass one further town,' she said. 'There is a hotel – we can rest and leave early in the morning. It will make no difference.'

'No,' I said, 'I'm fine. There's not much further to go.'

I wasn't sure what it was at first because of the silence. The scene appeared to be missing something. The flashes were sudden, like mistakes in perception. Silver flashes on top of us every few seconds, lighting up, metallically, shards of the environment. The electricity seemed to affect us, inside, with additional tension, a heaviness put around our bodies. I kept both hands on the wheel and continued looking ahead, my back straight, as if the slightest movement might detonate a charge. The lightning continued without sound, without rain. We outran it, but I could hear the others shifting and turning in their seats, watching it, craning their necks at the odd strobe effect distorting the land and time behind us.

The park HQ – all that was really left of it – was three block buildings at the bottom of a dirt drive. I watched the thick moths turning in the beam of the headlights, fluttering and unfolding, and almost didn't notice the two figures emerging from the building furthest away. I turned off the lights and we stepped out of the car onto the soft, wet ground. The air was close and humid, a strong metallic smell carried from the rain, and beyond the HQ there were no buildings, no lights at all. The insects were loud, the cicadas' signalling twice as fast as my heart rate, and they seemed to clutter the hectic air. I noticed Jane wearing a strange expression, breathing through her nose, pursing her lips – she was afraid of inadvertently swallowing insects. The two figures broke into a light jog, though the distance was almost nothing and the rain had stopped and the lightning seemed to have abated, and they introduced themselves, extending their arms, insisting on helping us with our things.

Both Bryan and Selina spoke in that strongly enunciated English that was hard to pin down, clear but neutral, like the colourless accent of the internet itself, that we'd noted with several of the WEBG staff at the airport, though they had neither their ridiculous khaki uniforms nor their demanding cheeriness. 'How was your drive?' Selina asked, smiling warmly, and in the corridor light I saw several iron fillings. She looked around the same age as Alice, perhaps early forties; she was a little shorter than me, athletic, and held her red hair in a bun. 'We've had quite a storm,' she said, as Bryan, taking off his cap to reveal close-cropped hair, started hauling bags from the back of the pick-up. 'Thought you might be delayed. I am so grateful you've come here, we all are. We can't thank you enough, really. Anyway, we'll get to all that in the morning. You must be tired, hungry, I imagine. Why don't we eat first, then I can show you to your room?'

'I'd rather leave my things in the room first, if that's okay.'

'Of course.'

'I can never really relax until I've unpacked.'

'Ah,' she said. 'You might want to hold off unpacking until morning.'

'Why's that?'

'Well, the others are sleeping.'

'I don't understand.'

'You'd wake them, in the dorm. Everything shuts down fairly early here, I'm afraid.'

We left the bulk of our things inside the vehicle, Alice and Jane went to the kitchen and I said I would see them later. I entered our room, found the light switch and heard people stir

– a brief image of low movements in the stacked dormitory beds. I shut it off, whispered an apology, crept to my assigned bed and lay down exhausted. The insect noise was deafening, as if the walls, in the darkness, had collapsed. There was a thin perimeter curtain hanging from the bars of the bed above, and I pulled it to enclose me. We were higher than in the capital but the humidity seemed just as punishing. The ceiling fan spun limply, unable to end. I took out my phone one last time – nothing from John – and fell into sleep.

Bryan gave us a brief tour first thing in the morning. I suppose it was the names that had misled us. There were no gates – 'north gate' appeared to be a kind of euphemism – and the area certainly didn't function as any kind of recognisable headquarters. I found it hard to believe that this, several years ago, when the park still generated a large income, had been the main entrance. All that remained was a clinic, a limited domestic space and one small office, the 'administrative centre' where Selina and Bryan worked. We met one ranger, Frank, and the medic, Dr Andrews. Bryan told us a team had recently left for the city, while the cleaning staff would be arriving later in the day.

The other guests in the dorm were construction workers, here to work on the small fence just in sight of the clinic. The fence had stretched for only five kilometres. It was an artifice, installed for tourists when they were still permitted to enter the park. No-one explained why they were only taking it down now. Frank was helping cut the posts; the wire was heaped in loose coils behind the dorms. Without the fence, there was no clear entrance to the park, rather a narrow gravel road that dissolved into shrub and then, a little further on, an area of scattered trees, gradually becoming denser as the hills rose and a light mist obscured the rest.

I went to the kitchen, heard voices raised through the door and found Alice lecturing Jane. She held a small plastic bin, and I saw on her arm something that looked like stitching peeling itself open. I stepped back instinctively from the ants. Jane – ceasing her stiff, trance-like walk – muttered weak apologies. Alice paced to the sink, tried to blast the ants off. She showed me the object responsible – a single black banana peel.

'All food waste,' she said, 'goes in the freezer. *Here.* You can't leave it out,' she said. 'How long has it been there?'

'An hour,' Jane said.

We took our cereals, fruit and coffee through to the adjoining room and sat at the table. Jane's bowl was filled with milk, and she slouched forward on her chair, stirring the cereal round and round. Strands of her fringe fell over her face, almost dipping into the milk. Alice neatly cut up her fruit, appearing absorbed in the task. I was relieved, then, when Selina entered the room. She looked different from the previous evening, strained. There seemed a forced, almost manic element to her manner – I could all but hear her instructing herself to retain and hold focus.

'How did you all sleep?' she said, driving at a smile. 'The mattresses aren't the greatest, I know, but after a long drive you probably didn't notice?'

She sat down by Alice, holding a mug in both hands, centring herself through it. 'You must have a million questions. I almost don't know where to start.' The incident, she told us, had occurred two weeks ago; everything had been arranged in a great hurry. The rangers, on a routine tour of the upper west zone, discovered two adult bodies drying out in the heat, a cloud of flies around them. The bodies were laid on the ground with a black substance emerging from their mouths. No further superficial damage was discovered; the rumours were entirely fictitious. The bodies were brought out, examined first in the park clinic then transported to the capital. An alert was raised, and our team was quickly put together. 'We sent out photographs and a provisional file. Don't tell me you didn't get it?'

'You can get us copies now,' I said. 'And the clinic – can I talk to the examining medics? Toxicology reports? The more information we have, the better.'

'Absolutely,' she said, making several rapid nods of her head. 'I'll have the details brought over. You're having your medicals this afternoon anyway.'

'Great.'

'Though that's with Dr Andrews. Dr Andrews wasn't involved in the autopsies. None of us here, actually, were privy to them.

That was all taken care of by the team in the capital. You were supposed to meet with them. It was all in the file.'

'But we haven't seen anyone. We have to at least speak with them, ideally see them, before we go in.'

'They told us,' Alice said, lowering her voice, meeting Selina's eyes, 'we couldn't see the bodies. They didn't say anything about a meeting. Here,' she scrolled through her phone, 'I'll bring up the email.'

'I can't believe this,' Selina said, almost under her breath. 'I know how this looks, honestly, but I promise you, no-one here is trying to make things difficult. I probably shouldn't say this, but ... it's incompetence. The problem here is there are too many departments, and no-one's clear exactly who's doing what. So things get missed. That's why you didn't get the file. It's inexcusable, I know, I just want to reassure you it's not malicious.'

'Have there been further casualties?' Jane said.

'No. Not that we understand. The rangers weren't able to make a full census, but they didn't report anything else amiss.'

'You do, at least,' I said, 'have the blood kits we need to do our work? We've heard nothing further on the doctor, so we have to assume his absence. And if we don't have the kits ...'

'Yes, of course we have them – didn't they tell you that either?'

'I wasn't sure, that's all.'

'The equipment is ready for you in the clinic. It's all arranged. Not the new software, obviously, but everything else you'll need. All samples will be analysed here after you come out. We'll go over everything later just so we're absolutely clear. We'll replenish your food supplies after the third week, as discussed. Frank will arrange the drop-off and set it up by phone. But you have everything you need – food, gas, et cetera – for the first three weeks?'

Strict communications protocols were in place. Signal was scrambled inside the park, part of a wider effort to discourage poaching and trespassing. We'd still bring our phones – a legal requirement – and a two-way channel would be set up between us and the admin centre. Every second evening, we'd send a brief update on our progress, a summary of the latest work. Again, Selina seemed to make an apologetic expression, implying she knew conditions were awkward and unreasonable and that she was almost embarrassed at having to explain. I appreciated that she seemed, in this respect, relatable, but I found because of this I didn't actually press her as hard on certain issues as I could have done.

I watched Jane sit on the canvas chair outside. She put herself down awkwardly, as if uncertain of the fixity of her environment. Her whole behaviour suggested someone so surprised to be there she thought she might still be about to wake up. I reminded myself of her lack of experience, that I should try to go easy on her, but I kept finding little things she did irritating. On the hammock she'd check the netting, back

herself up in front of it, pull out the near edge and let herself
go. Same on the leather sofas in the hotel lobby, dropping down
with sudden acceleration. She hit it loudly; I wondered if she
wanted us to say something, if she were doing it deliberately. If
maybe she just wanted us to notice her.

It was obviously difficult for her, all this, and she was wary
of how quick we might be to resent her. She'd said already,
more than once, she had no idea why she was asked to come.
Hopefully that would become clearer once we arrived inside.
Alice told me in confidence Jane was by no means the first
choice; several senior mycologists had turned the offer down.
We should be grateful she was there. She would have to help
us directly, especially now we were without the doctor; she
would have to interact with the animals. She was still going
over all the material we'd sent. Alice was instructing her on
the basics, which seemed to be helping, but for the moment
she was understandably having trouble adapting and finding it
difficult to be herself. I often thought I saw her stepping back,
removing herself, as if the only way she could get through this
was by projecting a near future, a time when it would all be just
a story, the most bizarre story, and she could share it with her
friends and the other people in her life, and it would have its
proper place.

The medics assessed us one by one through the late
afternoon, general and comprehensive health checks with
a particular emphasis on finding viral agents. If we were

infectious, if we were likely to become infectious, we could not enter. Obviously, there was interest in declaring us fit and well enough to spend up to six weeks in trying circumstances, with a limited and repetitive diet. The hike in, carrying our supplies and equipment, over two days through difficult, uneven terrain and at a steady incline, was the most demanding part, and we had to be physically capable of managing this. Bryan made it clear there was no emergency route out of the area we'd be camping in. At best, it would take three days for anyone to be retrieved.

But the tests weren't about us, they weren't for us: the priority was protecting the animals. Ideally, we'd never have the opportunity in our lives of seeing them. Every time we saw them we threatened them; every time we breathed, stood, spoke in an area they communicated with, we threatened them. Literally so, Alice said. Our pathogens may be communicated, in certain circumstances, through our eyes as well as through our mouths. The eyes become irritated, fingers rub at them and dig out contaminants. Polluted water runs from the tear ducts, infectious material expressed from a naked eye, watching. So seeing them was explicitly dangerous; speaking of them, describing them, was even more so. In close proximity it was advisable to wear masks, and even then to cup your hands and deflect the sound when you said anything. People on research trips look away from each other, and from the animals, when they are talking, often kneeling, head down, as if pushing their words into the ground, burying the indeterminate material of what they're saying. People were always mishearing each other, whispering requests for repetition, and often the full extent of what was said was only picked up later, when the recordings were played back in the relatively neutral, safer environs of the camp. These masks – goggles, cotton white fabric pulled over the mouth – tended to surprise first-time researchers, being reminiscent of the emergency room or operating theatre. You saw, immediately, that you really shouldn't be there, that it was wrong, you'd trespassed. Bonobos, just like the other great apes, were not equipped to live on the edge of us, their habitat destroyed at the same time as their immunity. That picture, of researchers trying to look away, to not directly intrude on the animals, afraid of the power of a glance, of what might be carried by their eyes as well as by their breath, breath that reached further through acoustic reinforcement ('don't speak, don't say anything if it's not absolutely necessary'), was like an emblem of our destructiveness. A series of researchers in masks and with our eyes shielded, standing in a forest apart from each other, cupping our hands and talking directly into the ground, backs craned as if in pain, vividly destroying an environment by standing in it, speaking at it, acknowledging the fact in the manner by which we did it. All of this was healthier – unutterably healthier – before words had been spoken.

Our provisional interpretation of what might have happened in the park was straightforward enough. Increased development changed the habitat as fewer species, plant and animal, were able to survive. The food available to the bonobos – largely herbivorous – changed. As the animal population fluctuated, the symbiotic networks many plants relied on for defence fell apart, and whole tracts of the forest collapsed. We believed the present moment was on the cusp of experimental animal behaviour. This was potentially dangerous; we made this clear to Jane. We didn't know what might happen. The troop was trying different foods. The two mature animal bodies may have been among the first casualties of this new experimentalism. While Jane's inclusion in the group was suggestive, it was unlikely a fungus alone had killed them, but rather that the particular combination of foods had reacted to allow the toxicity to breed inside the animals. Hopefully, Jane would be able to confirm this. We had to analyse their blood; we had to watch them – far enough away not to directly impede them, close enough that we could magnify a clear image of where they were going, what they were eating, what their daily patterns were. Were the deceased animals an anomaly, two foraging partners whose activity was unlikely to be repeated? Did one or more of the present troop carry greater instructive weight, their own experimental diets at risk of spreading through the group?

The clinic's broad front windows looked down onto the park itself. From the early afternoon the thunder rolled across the sky. It seemed to drift in from several directions, splitting and charging the air above us. It was still dry, the density of the air high enough that the sun prematurely darkened, making the wide static flashes of the lightning starkly visible. I got distracted; on every flash I waited, tensed my back, leaned my head forward a little, counting the seconds, anticipating the sundering boom of it, communicating precisely where it was and how quickly it was moving.

I lay back as the blood was taken – Dr Andrews said something about the thunder, about it being a bad sign. He told me to press my hand firmly on the puncture mark on my left shoulder.

I'd been sent back from another park at a similar stage ten years ago, about to begin a short placement arranged by the university. I was distraught. I had a simple common cold, and I had had to return home. When signs of an infection were discovered, however trivial they might have seemed, and regardless of the importance of whatever work was planned or however much money was invested in it, there was nothing you could do. You had to apply all over again, a process that could take months. So I returned to the university, feeling I might have to recalibrate my life, that I had just lost the opportunity to make a career. My flatmate dragged me to a house party and that night I met John. It was a tired joke: the susceptibility of the chimpanzee immune system to deception, the open defencelessness of the chimpanzee structure next to a human, was indirectly responsible for our lives. All our past together – John and I – all our hopes, all of it was contingent on the threat I posed, as a person, a human, to chimpanzees and other primates. We should be thankful, I thought, we should be grateful that this other species cannot stomach us. When I picture late at night the brightest impressions from my life – the wide beach, first memories stirring in rock pools, bedding in plants with Ivan and Catherine in the garden, this enormous light; enough, in even this beginning, my first few recollections of life, to last forever, an inexhaustible source of pleasure, pure happiness – I thought I should be praying to these adjacent species and parallel lives for giving me this, giving me the opportunity to have this, to be alive and to know that I'm alive and to be able to treasure it, to realise how rare it is. I should give my thanks to almost the whole of creation – to all that isn't human – for allowing me, and my kind, to feed off it and to kill it.

III

Propped up in bed, two upright pillows behind him. Something was altered; something was strange. Going to turn, he was blinded by an internal light, a whiteness surging in his head. He reeled back, closing his eyes. His head was swollen, with an alien consistency; it wasn't all his own. It rolled, dipped, moving as if by itself, putting undue pressure on his neck. His shoulders ached, the nerves lining his limbs tingling. He had to move. He peeled the bedsheet away, watching the industry of his fingers, the independent scuttling motion as they clutched at the material. Adjusting to the darkness, he looked around him. He didn't recognise the room. A cabinet by the bed; past this, in the far corner, a chest of drawers. A bare, unused room, a room awaiting a guest. He watched his hands again – dull, swollen, insensate. Digging into the mattress, he heaved up onto the floor.

He tried to think of his most recent memory, the last thing he could recall before waking, but the pain immediately seized him and he backed away. Where was he? What had happened?

Planting one hand against the wall, he lurched forward in slow, collapsing steps. At the end of the room he pressed the door handle, turned and pulled. He came out onto a dim corridor. As the wood panels creaked beneath him, he experienced a rush of nausea, a revelation of unmeasured space, limitless distances opening up beneath him. It wasn't safe here. He grasped the wall with both hands. Ahead were three closed doors and a landing, a staircase. He needed to be back on ground level, a firmer surface, somewhere he could trust.

He inched forward to the first door, pushed it open: a bathroom. The second room was unfurnished, the third room empty except for curtains and an undressed bed. The rooms and the corridor were dark, gloomy; the light would hurt his eyes – he couldn't bear to press the switch. He approached the stairs, one hand against the white banister and the other holding his head to limit the jarring while it rolled. A pain burned between his jaw and ears, his teeth felt loose, something trickled down his neck. He went to call but his throat was rough, spitting up a bitter taste. Slowly, eyes trained on the stairs, some distant impulse keeping him moving, he descended.

Downstairs was pale wood, an open kitchen, a table, two chairs, a sofa. He covered his ears, waited for the nausea to ease, the imbalance to settle. He couldn't think. Constructions were remote and impossible. He was relentlessly quiet, hiding from the greater pain, the warning image of a thought searing across the cortex. He looked around, trying to find a familiar object, something meaningful that might let him know where he was, what had happened. He went to the window and moved the curtain aside. Thick grey fog; impossible to see anything. Again he had the impulse to call out, but his tongue was heavy, hard to shift. He went to the sink, turned the metal lever and clamped his mouth to the flowing water. He coughed, water spilled onto the floor. He tried again, lapping, gulping it back, sucking it in. The cool water flowed through him, branching out, filling his extended body.

He went past the stairs and found another door, pulled the cord automatically and the room lit up. He blinked, startled, his eyes fizzing from the pain. A larger bathroom. A sink, a mirror, white tiles, a shower. A torn white shirt, a bloodied neck, thick matted hair, an unfamiliar face. He stretched his mouth and the hole widened in the mirror. His arms moved to the top of his head, went to touch. He felt further across the hair until he found a depression at the centre.

His hands sprang back. He held the edge of the sink, waiting. Eventually, he opened the cabinet's mirror door and took a second mirror from inside. He raised this smaller mirror and lowered his shoulders, dipped his head. Between the two reflections he found it: a small shaved circle, a crater filled with hard black blood.

He made a cup with his hands, gathered water from the tap and released it over the wound. The crust collapsed, the blood spilled. He repeated the process until the water ran clear.

He cleaned the wound on his neck and then removed his shirt, trousers and underwear, noting how they seemed to gather the moment before they contacted the floor. He examined the rest of his body and found further cuts on his left arm and on his chest. He watched all of this distantly and with little curiosity. He appeared to be seeing through a camera lens, observing another person. He detached the showerhead, turned the water on and sat with knees raised in the small cubicle, dabbing at the places marked by blood.

He woke up with a start. He was lying on the sofa downstairs. There was a noise. At first it seemed to be coming from inside. Thumping, shaking, rattling. He closed his eyes, trying to hold it, and the pain stopped. When it resumed it was louder, more forceful. He opened his eyes. Someone was banging on the door.

He got to his feet. Another blow rattled the house. Each one hurt. Every thread and fibre inside was wrenched and pulled apart. Slowly he approached the first door and prised it open. The blows stopped. He waited, feeling the colder air in the connecting room, smelling something bitter.

The next knock was faint. Two further knocks followed. He saw his hands moving towards the key, placing it in the lock and turning with a loud, clear click. He pressed on the handle and pulled the door towards him.

Thick, cold vapour entered the house. A foot stepped forward, approaching the upper step. A long black coat, a hat, a case. An arm extended towards him, taking his hand, shaking it. He waited. The mouth moved – a sound came out, fluid and quick and impossible to grasp. The face looked at him expectantly. He stepped back, withdrawing into the house, gesturing for the figure to follow. The figure moved forward, paused, then entered. Quickly he closed the door. Already it was colder.

The figure looked around, still holding the case with a long, drooping arm. A new sound, a closer kind of pain, working from the chest and the jaw and the inside of the head. A movement like that when he was eating, fragments of nose and mouth shifting up and down. A dry floating sensation and an echo in the mouth. He was speaking, saying something. The figure lifted his head and replied, 'visiting'. Another word – 'understanding'. The final word – 'doctor'.

IV

We'd been walking only hours, sweating heavily, though protected at least from the direct sun, and already the compound – the other voices, the electricity, the sense of structure and willed domesticity – seemed almost impossibly distant. As I looked at Jane in front, I thought it was difficult to tell which came first: the introspection or the mycology. She walked with her eyes pointed at the ground. She missed the trees – we had to walk with her between us, Alice leading and me at the back, guiding her, pushing her on. She saw a different world than we did. I tried to recall any previous mycologists I'd known and picture whether they had had this pronounced stoop too. It made sense that the discipline selected for introspection and then that the pursuit of it, the actual practice of hunting mushrooms, accentuated the posture too. People would stumble into mushrooms, literally. It seemed to me Jane had known the ground better than most people would long before she began her study. Naturally, then, she wasn't the best communicator. She tended to drift away on her own, a different course, and I had to remind myself that when she looked at the ground it wasn't in distraction, that this was her work, that she saw something in it. Whether or not it was down to this stoop, this wandering, this appearance of unguided distraction, I saw Jane as considerably younger than Alice and myself and felt duly protective of her. She appeared anxious, preoccupied, didn't respond well to prompts, to comments that were intended to be light-hearted. I had tried to engage her about the stoop, about looking to the ground, about whether it came naturally, but she answered with a humourless laugh. Later – and expressed differently, oddly; she had clearly composed it, rehearsed it – she said it was ironic that mycology drew introverted people when the whole story was essentially about communication, about networks, about the conveyance, under the ground, of vast tracts of information.

These networks, miles upon miles of hyphae linking the roots of the trees all around us, were only as thick as a single cell. It was 'surpassingly fragile', she said, still speaking with her head lowered so that I had to strain in close to hear her, her words seeming to be spoken into the vegetation and the fungus we walked through, put directly into them, as if to offer misguided nourishment. This makes the hyphae hard to study. If you make contact with the lines – if you so much as disturb the ground around them – they can splinter and break apart: the observer effect, the experimenter interfering with and invalidating the results. It was all but impossible to gain direct, immediate access to these threads of information, which is why they studied the fruiting bodies, the mushrooms blooming and bursting over the soil surface, instead.

Every so often – twice, three times an hour, declining in frequency as we progressed, either because the fruits she saw were self-similar or because Alice's frustration with the interruptions was getting to her – Jane stopped, put on her latex gloves, squatted and picked a mushroom. She cleaned the bulb with her spit and then manipulated it with her hands. She showed us, once, the colour changing, a beetle-like blue emerging from the black. This was likely toxic, Jane told us, carefully wrapping the specimen and packing it away. It wasn't unexpected. The more the habitat was disturbed, the greater the variety of fungus we'd find. Environmental destruction was, for many fungus types, attractive. Fungus followed footprints, she said. We studied it and inadvertently we spread it more. Spores one-thousandth of a millimetre thick.

The first time I saw her visibly frustrated was when I mentioned psilocybin. 'No,' she said, cutting me off, 'that's not my area of research.' I backed off – clearly the question was familiar to her, along with certain assumptions. I apologised, tried to clarify my meaning – were there recorded instances of animals ingesting the psychedelic compound? Not many, she said wearily, few examples and little in the way of effects noted, although certain groups were said to feed the mushroom to their hunting dogs, possibly to sharpen concentration and sensory awareness. I let it drop, resolving to get back to it later. I would think of a more subtle way into it; I would have to. But it was difficult when the whole issue seemed lurid and over the top. On the connecting flight over, trying to prepare a little by reading papers on animals and fungi, I'd seen a note referencing a discredited theory that suggested psilocybin

– the toxic compound described as a psychedelic – might have played a role in cultural evolution, perhaps even in the establishing of certain religious beliefs, inspired by the visions it induced. I wanted to ask her about this, as in one sense it was the direct opposite of the prevailing theory I'd been exposed to in my own education. God, from my loose memory of the undergraduate classes, resided not in these bulbs sprouting in the ground but in the tall swaying trees around us. God, still, in both theories, a hallucination; a chemical inspiration or a face, a presence – a product of fear as much as awe – captured in the rustling movements of the branches ahead, in early light or in the last part of the day.

More generally, I thought, stopping occasionally not just for breath, water, relief but for a slightly prolonged vision of a particularly startling play of light and cloud whenever the foliage broke enough to grant a view beyond the foreground, I wanted to ask her, wanted to find a way of asking her that wasn't stupid and ignorant and that wouldn't undermine the seriousness of her work, just what she thought about the simple brute fact that these substances were growing around us, underneath us, with the capacity to affect an absolute and instant transformation of our minds. Wasn't it strange, still, I thought, mindful of my shortness of breath, of changes in oxygen levels and of possible dips in the lucidity of my thinking, that this was all here, around us, outside of us? The paper described the close structural similarity of psilocybin

and serotonin, so close it almost seemed – I gasped, lumping
the weight of my supplies up a brief but sharp incline – as if
little pieces of mind existed underground, created out of
the breeding and recycling of decayed organic matter. I was
distantly aware of overreaching, of exceeding myself, remotely
critical but at the same time giving in to the effects of the
sudden pale light reflected off the trees – Alice, but not Jane,
had also stopped to observe this – and of my tiredness, of the
upheaval and the risk and the excitement inherent in all of
this, and I felt, for just a moment, tender towards the ground
and all the different pieces of feeling, and even memory,
that were inside it, that continued to live and to regenerate
inside it. What did it mean? Was it any different from digital
information storage or from radio emissions that continued
to play out unheeded, unending, through space? Or from the
cliché, overused because true, that people do live on through
what they have done, what they have experienced, that is
transformed into memory and carried by others, remembered
differently and passed on by those people too? I heard the
remote critical voice again – what was this nonsense? Where
was the logic in this, the evidence in this? But I smiled as I
resumed walking, down the reverse side of the incline, sensing
a brief orange glow instructing us to stop soon and make camp
– there wasn't long left – and I thought of Ivan, my father, of
the light in my room and of the plants that he had put there.
I remembered the marks on the wall registering my changing

height and the areca palm potted on my floor that, through summer, in direct light, would ascend in a spiral, corkscrew design, a picture of energy, of urgency, of a vigorous kind of happiness in living. I continued, feeling a pleasant glow from the last, denser light breaking in through the canopy, shafts of sun revealing the air to be thick with spores and seeds and trails and breaking tissue that disappeared as soon as I took a single step into it. I felt good, strange but familiar, felt Ivan close and yet far, felt almost the urge to lie down immediately and press my head against this earth.

On the second day we separated further, far enough apart you could imagine you were alone but not so distant you couldn't focus and make out an unnatural colour or movement, another person. We stopped every four hours to rest and rehydrate. I was too tired to complain. I found myself, as well, blindly following Alice. We tried to minimise use of the mApp, wary of battery limitations. We used the tents as roof sheets when we stopped, spread out in the trees.

Jane, I thought, now seemed cool and remote, as if in denial, as if she were sure there had been a mistake and it would quickly be rectified and she would soon be sent back home. We were both a little unsure around Alice, who barely concealed her impatience and dissatisfaction with us. We should be moving quicker. Complaining about fatigue was redundant. Alice rarely laughed; I wasn't sure I'd seen her smile. It was interesting watching

Alice walk. Despite her pace I thought I saw a limp, or rather a conscious effort to avoid revealing a limp. The beginning of a grimace, heaving her rucksack up again.

It was striking to consider that she might, without ever admitting it, even be suffering a chronic pain. I hadn't picked up on her limp before we'd left HQ, but then we hadn't actually done much walking through the over-populated airport or the short, narrow corridors and softly lit hotel lobby. I couldn't remember exactly when it started. She could have hurt herself on the first part of the journey, fallen and decided she couldn't say anything because it would upset our rhythm and delay us, worried also it might prejudice us against her. Was that why she seemed irritated? Was she managing pain? She would hate it, I knew, if she had learned the speculative way I was beginning to pity her. She would maintain I had no right to do so, on the basis I knew nothing much about her, knew so little that my weak attempts at prediction were baseless.

Perhaps the injury was older, fully recovered and with a phantom trace, still hurting. She might have hidden the injury in case it was quietly used against her in selection procedures. The clinic's trials would have been an ordeal. Or she was unaware of the injury's effect on her, and what I was seeing, or what I thought I was seeing, this attempt, at some level, to pretend that something wasn't there, demonstrating it while covering it up, was an old habit, a hesitancy, a lack of trust built into her, doubting, maybe, after the accident some time ago, her integrity.

She had short hair, a muscular frame and was several inches taller than me. I had met her only once before, years ago at a conference, though when I mentioned this she expressed surprise and suggested I had mistaken her for someone else. She had published widely until about five years ago, and her work was highly regarded. I asked her a couple of times what she'd been working on since, but each time she managed to be evasive and move the conversation along. I was trying to tell myself the issue wasn't personal, wasn't directed at me in particular, that Alice was simply, and understandably, focused exclusively on the task at hand. I watched her again, walking in front, taking the lead. I now saw no trace of a limp and suspected I'd invented it, searching for a way of sympathetically undermining her.

Alice maintained an unwavering pace from the front. She wouldn't let us fall behind. She continued pushing us on. The longer we went the more natural the whole process became. Jane stopped complaining. We walked so far apart that talking became difficult. My feet moved by themselves; I felt myself drifting pleasantly, better accommodated to the place, and I sustained this relatively thoughtless, peaceful, almost trance-like state for as long as I could.

Only when I stopped and felt myself gathering again, a little dazed and briefly alert, did I contemplate some of the landscape around us. Torrents of secondary growth. A fallen trunk ripped open and carried by at least a dozen younger trees and vines. We passed through an oddly cold, quiet, gloomy thatch of bamboo stalks, bending towards their twenty-metre summit, creating an archway, a cathedral filled with shadows. Jane, for once, looked up. The stalks swayed, strained. Later in the afternoon we passed a stunning, dramatic collection of giant tree fern, vast and surpassingly soft, tinged with a sleepy cottony veneer, drooping and hanging high above us. For me this was the most transportive sight of all, putting me in mind of the outsize aspect of the Mesozoic era, and I indulged in childish play, imagining untold megafauna – gargantuan raptors; dragonflies as big as cars – concealed on the other side of it.

I looked at this and it seemed impossible there were cities, external regulation, imposed structure, that the overwhelming majority of my days were spent domestically, in narrow buildings, and that I had even been prone to both boredom and anxious thoughts about the immediate future. I tried to describe this fleeting sensation and I ruined it. We had stopped to rest and both Jane and Alice looked at me suspiciously, perhaps pityingly. My anxiety returned as I doubted the integrity and priority of the feeling, suddenly caught up in myself again, in my own local limitations.

'We shouldn't stay long,' Alice said, hurling her pack up again. 'If we push on we can reach the coordinates in three hours.'

The first sign we were close was the sound of flowing water. We were so tired, exhausted from the bulk we carried, and our impressions so confused by the lack of clarity, the infrequency of any notable vantage points from which to gather perspective, that we weren't sure exactly where the sound was coming from. We went separately, each trying to catch it. Twenty minutes later I heard something crunch behind me. I turned and Jane appeared, head low, apologetic, flushed. 'Found the river,' she said, her large protruding boots leading comically in front of her.

One of the advantages of making camp within distance of the stream, in addition to the obvious utilities, was the possibility of keeping our domestic space isolated from the troop. The animals took the bulk of their water from roots and from fronds and were known to be fearful of rushing water. The rangers identified the troop as being, on last sighting, nine kilometres distant from our present location. Of course, it was possible they had since shifted substantially, perhaps driven in some way by whatever had happened to their two deceased conspecifics, but Alice and I agreed this was unlikely, that the preponderance of fruiting trees nearby suggested they had not exhausted their time here.

I smiled, let my bags fall to the ground again and stretched out my arms.

'Not yet,' Alice said. I thought I saw a hint of humour in her eyes. 'We still have to choose the site.'

It rained; we had to hurry. We found a reasonably level spot to put our tents up but had no time to clear ground or begin other adaptations. We could worry about everything else in the morning. There was so much to do, even after establishing the site. Digging out the latrine, heaping twigs and leaves into a large pile beside it. Hanging the lime powder in a sealed bag on a branch. Building a lid of snapped branches tied with twine, covered with leaves, to lay over the hole. The latrine should be roughly a kilometre from camp, the kitchen too. The kitchen an area just big enough to hold the three of us under a tied tarp roof, reasonable enough protection from the rain. Rocks collected from the stream to hold the gas canister and the cooking pots in place.

I sighed, peeling off my bag for a second time, and took out my tent. After setting it up I began unpacking. I took the pile of ziplock bags used for storing samples as well as collecting any food that might break off from our hands. Leaving food behind was strictly prohibited. We could attract first one, then further members of the troop towards us, which would be disastrous. They would destroy our camp, breaking our equipment, spilling our supplies. Worse, we would artificially manipulate their diet, making the whole trip redundant. So nothing could fall on the ground. We'd have to measure our meals conservatively because we couldn't leave any scraps. Cans would be rinsed and packed in sealed bags too, our pots and cutlery immediately scrubbed clean. In theory, there should be no food waste at all. In reality, in my experience, there always was. Something always fell on the wet ground. It was important, I reminded myself, that we were patient, that we didn't blame someone.

We were supposed to be four and with an odd number the easy thing was to form a division, create a scapegoat.

Jane spilled her rice almost immediately, and I had to suppress a grin; she had turned quickly because she thought she heard something behind her. She maintained it wasn't a mistake – she'd definitely heard something, something was definitely there, behind us.

The next morning we bathed with a cup by the edge of the stream and gathered our drinking water upstream in a large pail. We let the sterilising tablet dissolve and attached the lid firmly. Alice and I went out to survey the wider area, while Jane continued to establish the camp, laying out the equipment and preparing the kitchen as I'd instructed. Alice was different, focused but calm, as if she'd relaxed into herself now that the work had begun. A tension had broken. The air remained humid. Alice had told us that on the verge of the rainy season we should expect long rains, three to four hours every day, usually through the afternoons. It would get worse as we went on. This first morning I was struck by the loud, startling bird calls attending the stream of small canopy pieces dropping from the weight of the previous days' rain. A thick, bitter smell enveloped us, and there was a fog, a whitish green opacity, and insects I mistook, at times, for birds.

We'd been warned about these. The insects around Westenra were especially virulent, another reason the park had closed.

We were being bitten all the time. I didn't know how they got under the material. A freshly swollen bite, cut from the needle-like mouth, seemed to have a stone inside, and I couldn't stop digging until I'd got it out. Already they perforated my shoulders, my hips, my ankles, my insteps.

The newly mutated vampire mosquitoes – named for their unusual longevity, an inadvertent effect of WHO efforts to control and limit reproduction by altering the genome – left a particularly irritable bite. There might have been fewer of the insects, but it didn't feel like it. Most estimates had the annual number of bites as unchanging, at best slightly down. Perhaps even the total body mass remained stable. This, after all the promises, was a disaster. CRISPR-X cut into the genome, adapting the germline so mosquito offspring were highly weighted towards males, non-toxic and non-birthing. The change was to spread quickly through and dominate the population. Malaria and other insect-borne diseases were to disappear entirely; the species would eventually reach a tipping point and collapse. Now that the failure of the project was clear, officials lined up to deny responsibility. They'd done everything they could, running simulations of extraordinary power, but not one had managed to conceive of what would actually happen.

Previous lifespans were short, typically two to three months; this was now massively prolonged. Several papers presented evidence the mosquito was now living upwards of a year. This had seemed highly unlikely, requiring structural changes to the insect body, fortifying the lower tear-shaped abdomen and altering wing speed to carry larger blood packages. They flew with a new dip in their arc from the extra blood. A descent, as if free-falling, the quick collapse giving further momentum and driving and launching them upwards through the air.

Bigger, the insects were at least easier to spot. Rather than striking both hands together, I tried to catch them by flexing my palm and snapping it shut, like a Venus flytrap or a serpent's jaw. Even if I did get one, it produced an explosion, a small balloon of blood popping. Alice noted it was becoming a problem in home and interior design in the tropics: how to mitigate against the likelihood of blood spilling. Clear plastic sheeting over all surfaces was the cheapest option, while the recent trend was for darker furnishings, better at concealing the blood colour. More expensive synthetic materials explicitly designed to be 'blood deleterious' were rolled out for sofas, carpets and bed-sheets, though its durability meant it was unlikely to become affordable for anyone outside the elite. The hotel, by the airport, was the first time I'd encountered it; it mimicked liquid qualities and gave me dreams of drowning in the room.

The literature continued to speak of CRISPR-X as surgery performed on a virtual body. Scientists removed or switched off attributes and were liable to leave coded English text inside, notes describing the procedure but also, according to rumour, incorporating unrelated, frivolous text as well – personal messages, jokes, puzzles, even whole novels spliced as code into inactive parts of the genome. Even the name implied this hubris. X: hollows, ex-spaces, caves put inside, absences resting like phantom limbs on the body-map. But something would grow, something would step inside the cave and flourish and breed there. Any change to the germline was perpetuated, becoming an indelible change to the ecosystem too. This was where everything spiralled, autocatalytic reactions launching at a breadth still impossible to predict, whatever the scale of modelling software.

It was microbiology all over again, the tired analogy of the 'battle' between differently scaled creativities, each driving the other in turn. The first toxic male mosquitoes had been identified in the past several months, another impending catastrophe. It was difficult to keep track. There would be another fêted solution, it would succeed briefly, another unpredictable adaptation would then render it redundant. I thought of the etymology of malaria, the belief that the sickness came not from individual animals but simply from air – a context, a general state, impossibly diffuse and resistant to all attempts at mitigation.

The single most disastrous effect of mosquito cutting was the inadvertent strengthening of a strain related to the Zika virus. This virus struck me as hard to believe, so monstrously elaborate and cruel you were almost forced to believe in its own agency and willpower. The virus works by vertical transmission, the infected pregnant woman giving it to the embryo and the infant then born with a miniaturised head. The brain has partially collapsed; the skull doesn't grow out. This can occur at any stage of pregnancy or even after birth. Seizures follow, patterns of severe brain damage; the backs of the eyes are scarred. The infant can't hear a rattle, can't track a moving object, may not be able to move independently or even feed or sleep. I thought about this a lot. On your own, walking for hours, or in your tent as the night stretched out, you can think the worst, become paranoid. Sometimes it felt like human generation itself was being targeted. Was this, now, the slow end of the world? I would imagine, or try to, the courage demanded by the most basic act of all, giving life. It was a problem for anyone working in biology, maybe especially for those who routinely confronted animal extinction – impossible to be naive about everything that could go wrong. It seemed a miracle, every time, that it happened, that someone could be born, could grow, could live a relatively healthy life. When I picked at the bites on my arms and insteps or when I clapped a whining insect dead and the blood parachuted out, I thought the odds against an unfettered life must be incalculable. And yet it goes on, I thought, it goes on.

I remembered, when I was young, being paralysed at times because of pure unknowable potential; I would stand, at the edge of the garden, looking at the beach, unable to move forward because anything could happen. If I stepped I could create a murmur, an echo, a wind whose consequences could carry forever. I should hold my leg still, I thought; but what if it was my immobility that created the danger, obstructing something I couldn't comprehend? I tried to think about it and in doing so turned my head. I also realised my mouth was open and that I had been absently flexing and opening my hands. All this, too, would have its effects. I didn't know what to do or where to go; I was stuck. There was too much of everything, unlimited pure potential in every moment, and I was affecting it even while I considered it. I couldn't step out of it; in not moving I was still creating changes to the air and the land and the water all around me. So not doing something was a decision too and made you equally culpable. I couldn't remember either how long I stayed there, frozen on the edge of the garden as the day turned cold, or how I got out.

Ivan or, more likely, Catherine, I supposed, must have found me eventually, dragging me back in from my daydreaming, pulling my deadweight and scraping my feet across the lawn until we reached the plant beds and it was impressed upon me that, now, I had to get up, I had to lift myself and stop playing. I had to grow up. I only found out later how concerned they'd both been about these episodes, this tendency towards paralysis. Ivan said he'd look into me and wonder at the effectiveness of trying to talk, wonder if I was really any longer there. So overloaded by the possibilities of the infinite number of things that I could do or say, only the smallest fraction of which I was able to foresee in any way and so be consciously responsible for, I thought that when I froze like this I was partly, briefly wishing myself out of existence, out back into the infinite independent parts that composed me. I remembered doubting if I was really the best possible use for this shoulder-length nut-brown hair, the constellations of freckles on my arms. I pictured car crashes desperately requiring blood transfusions and replacement body parts, and I imagined the billions upon billions of smaller animals that I could translate into and all the various kinds of living they could perform.

V

—Where am I?

—In your home, of course.

—But I don't recognise anything. What's happened to me?

—There was an accident. You're disoriented – you fell. But it's okay because I am here to watch over you, to oversee your recovery.

—What kind of accident? I don't remember anything. I don't know what happened.

—It's okay. Temporary retrograde amnesia is common in injuries such as this. Your memory will come back.

—No, I need to know. What am I doing here? Why am I not in hospital? Surely I have family, friends? Where are they? I don't remember anything.

—Don't worry, I'll explain everything later. You need to rest. I'll come again tomorrow morning – we'll establish a routine. Everything's been taken care of, John. Everything's fine.

When he woke it was light again. Almost a whole further day must have passed. The next thing he noticed was the pain. He seized his head, tried to still it, but the swell continued, a great liquid thrown, heaving across hemispheres. He breathed slowly, trying to create a controlling tempo. He felt as if he was going to vomit. Then he smelled it. Iron in rain. He saw the blood. He sat up, looked towards the door, searching for signs of another person, someone who could have done this to him. He looked behind and saw pillows caked in blood.

He felt his head where it had been shaved. Blood had hardened again. A bruise was forming under the cuts on his neck. He pushed at it, the flesh giving softly, and he flinched.

He needed to remove the blood from the bed, the associations of openness, of coming apart. He stripped the linen and gathered the sheets in a heap. The mattress was stained in long dark leaf-shaped patches. He walked to the stairs and then turned back. He imagined the crack of his ankle then his neck, saw his limp body sprawled at the foot of the stairs, waiting for the doctor. He had to be careful. He put the bulk back onto the bed so he could bring the first of it down safely.

He loaded the washer, noting the unpleasant foamy structure of the bunched sheets. Hearing the dull hum and whir of the spinning drum, he realised his hands had programmed the machine by themselves, that they had retained the information. He was watching his hands, the articulated joints and soft palms, when he heard the shuffle of feet outside, three sharp raps on the door.

The doctor unpacked his case and laid his machines on the table. He appeared older than John, though he couldn't tell by how many years. He worked busily and didn't say anything for some time. 'Just going,' he said quietly, 'to take a reading.'

Pulling out a chair, the doctor asked him to sit at the table. 'Open your eyes as wide as you can.' The first device appeared similar to a set of binoculars, only with a large square panel dropping at its base. The doctor peered through the sockets, studying John's eyes close up. He clicked on something, generating a humming sound. 'Just a moment longer,' he said, 'that's it, almost there.'

He brought out a tendon hammer and a stethoscope. He read John's heart rate, then he weighed him, then, asking him to take his shoes off and stand with his back to the wall, close to the window, where the curtain was still pulled, he measured his height. 'Okay, okay, very good,' he said, keying information into his palm-sized tablet.

It was difficult to retain what the doctor said. John watched the sink, the pattern of drips from the faucet. He went to nod, then stopped because of the pain, the feeling of something loosened, the lack of fit between brain and skull, the organ slipping in the case.

Pushing on the back of his neck, the doctor's cold hands sent waves of alarm radiating through him. He whispered to John, encouraged him to tip his head forward just a little. He held him in this position, made several noises, then stepped back, tapping him on the shoulder, indicating he was free to raise his head again and resume a natural position.

'It should have held for longer than this,' the doctor said. 'I'm afraid the initial stitching from the hospital has come loose. I'll have to see to it now. Is there a basin? A clean cloth?'

The doctor told him to find a towel and put it round his neck and then laid a second towel beneath him on the floor. He gestured for him to tip his head again, recommending that he close his eyes. At first the warm water stung. John braced himself, feeling his scalp being pierced.

'Hold still. It's important that I get this right.' Although the doctor was simply stitching a surface wound, it felt severe, as if his hands were dipping further, descending into the depression. He bit his lower lip, resisting the sensation of pins driven into him.

'Should hold now,' the doctor said, stepping back, cutting the thread, gathering the utensils into a white cloth, which he folded. He picked up the floor towel and mopped up the small amount of water spilled on the table.

'Are you going to tell me what happened, then?' John said.

Looking him in the eye, the doctor addressed him. 'As I've already said, you suffered an accident, Mr Harper. Something hit you, and you fell. You spent three days in hospital, where you underwent a series of tests. You suffered a moderately traumatic brain injury, but you are going to be okay. No midline shift, no notable enlarging near the ventricle area, no apparent diffuse axonal injuries. Don't look so shocked. This is good news. You were deemed fit to complete the rest of your recovery from home.' The doctor drew his hands together, making a suction sound as the air compressed. 'Listen to me, John. You're going to be fine. Just take care of yourself. Keep your head up wherever possible. Sleep on your back, support your head. Take particular care when washing not to split the stitching. Be mindful of the cut when you're dressing. So long as you adhere to this the wound should heal in a matter of days. I'll monitor how it develops, and I'll remove the thread when the time comes. Be particularly wary in descending the stairs. Rest. It's the only cure. Stay here, in the cottage; a low stimulation environment is essential. Leaving isn't a good idea; this weather is expected to continue for some time. Naturally, you aren't to drive. I'll be visiting daily and I'll conduct further tests.'

'But what happened, exactly? Look, I need to call someone, I—'

'Your phone was absent when you were admitted to the hospital. All you had with you was your identification.'

'Have you looked? Is it in the car?'

'It's not there.'

'Then can I use your phone?'

'But who would you call? It's too soon, you need to wait for things to come back. And this weather, John. You won't get reception for miles.'

VI

It was our third day at camp and already Alice had come closer to the animals. She had identified each of the three distinct sub-groups. I hadn't appreciated this source of anxiety until I felt the relief. Though we hadn't mentioned it to each other, and despite the staff's assurances, we were worried we might walk into an atrocity, the whole troop wiped out. We would track them again tomorrow, moving closer, signalling our presence, drawing their curiosity and hopefully, eventually, becoming habituated. Then we'd each attach to a separate sub-group and begin our observation. Start counting. There was no option other than for Jane to join us; it just wasn't possible for two people to give comprehensive data readings of three groups.

We went over this as we prepared dinner. Alice produced a hip-flask and we passed the bitter spirit round. Though I enjoyed it, I couldn't help thinking the laughter was a little hollow, that we celebrated in a slightly performative and premature way. We were keen to state things were going well – as if we could somehow control the outcome of the next five weeks or so through the manner by which we approached them. I left first; I had begun to talk in an overly enthusiastic, automatic way, and I knew I would regret it if I continued, knew I would wake early and restlessly hunt my displays of stupidity.

I was sick in the morning. Alice thankfully had already left, though Jane heard me retching, saw me staring at the small amount of stuff that had come out, disbelieving. She teased me, laughing. It boosted her – I tried to encourage it, smiled, accepted the mocking tone. But I knew it wasn't right. I had had just one, maybe two sips of the alcohol. The drink wasn't the cause. Jane, and presumably Alice, were fine – it wasn't food either. This wasn't good. If I had contracted some kind of virus, I wouldn't be able to have contact with Jane or Alice. I would be ostracised. It would be a disaster – unimaginable, wholly possible. I wasn't equipped to travel back on my own. Should I contact HQ now? I thought. Send someone all the way here, two days' walk, by which time the worry would almost certainly have passed? I couldn't think about it and told myself I would have to wait for further symptoms. We were all still adapting to conditions and recovering from the walk. We were exhausted. Low appetite, given the food constraints, was a necessity – we were encouraging it. In these circumstances it was going to be difficult to identify positive signs of a virus before it broke out in full form. I didn't know what to do – separate myself in precaution thus knocking morale, as well as limiting our observation and analysis? If I didn't, I risked sabotaging the whole project. What if I had already passed the dormant virus on to Alice, who in turn had given it to the troop?

*

We were camped in a long valley, hills on all sides, huge evergreens around us and above us, a hundred feet high or more. The area was distinctly reverberative, especially in wetter periods, generally during the afternoons, when storm cells darkened the air, sent the palms stirring and unleashed torrents of water that passed on in minutes, leaving wisps of steaming moisture drifting over the vegetation. The immediate post-storm silence made the resultant calls – insects, reptiles, birds, our troop – even louder. Rain gathered in the thick, soft canopy, a vertical pressure I couldn't shake off. With the thinner root systems it remained a possibility the weight of especially heavy storms could affect the trees' integrity, upturning even otherwise healthy specimens. Sometimes in the storms I looked up and watched the trees sway. I was uncomfortable with the sounds that we were making, the din of our tin plates and cups as we prepared our evening meal, snatches of conversation, short laughs, occasional recordings played by Jane or by Alice. It was as if, with every sound we made, we contributed to the accumulating pressure weighing down the canopy. The water gathered there, drew our sounds in soft clumps, sent them echoing out and back again. The sound appeared suspended above us, a burden, something that at any moment might snap and break.

The troop used the reflective, wetter canopy to amplify their calls, pushing sound out further through the forest. Other animals exploited the quieter dry periods, typically mid-morning and an hour before dusk, to issue their own communications across more limited distances. We adapted to the mutable environment too, becoming more daring and moving closer to the animals at certain parts of the day, when our sounds, our footsteps, our arms pushing through the undergrowth, our limited speech, were at their lowest natural amplification. It was quickly apparent that many other factors affected our sound, from the flux of the temperature to the level of light to the relative density of the airborne insect clouds. Everything was significant. Each location in every separate moment gathered its own distinct profile, a certain audio character that would never be directly produced again. In order to actually listen to what was happening, and likewise to minimise the disturbance we made as we contributed to it, moving through it, we had to go slowly and with great care. Shifting, separately, along the forest, tracking our respective sub-groups, we tried to operate at a different acoustic scale.

Every single detail in the forest seemed to contribute directly to the resonance of sound. Not only the volume and density of the preceding storm cell, and the acid content and the weight of it pressing down on the canopy and the lower branches, bending them, coming off slowly in large thick globules, forming scattered pools across the forest floor, driving the tempo of the rushing nearby stream and creating temporary ponds almost instantly filled with the larvae of dozens of insect species, larvae that seemed, as well, to give off its own sound, early in the life cycle, a creaking, popping effect in the black ground-water, attracting other insects and birds, not only all this but our own composition affected sound too, the amount of moisture currently present in our bodies, influenced by our diet and our sleep, and then by our anxiety, our restlessness, the nature of the dreams we had been having, then the heaviness of our footfalls, the angle and height we raised ourselves to, the position we turned our heads towards, our optimism, the degree to which the entire history of our lives had led us to be confident that good things would happen – this defined, presently, the position of our bodies and this too conducted and issued sound. In order to learn anything about where we were and what was around us we had to think like this, in an increasingly fine-grained manner. Every single thing, regardless of size, was significant. Everything mattered and in those first several days, tracking and, the more I learned, coming incrementally closer to my sub-group, I felt a sense of urgency, purpose and vitality such as I had never previously experienced anywhere.

Crouching under palms, secondary water filtering down to me, my stomach contracted and I remembered waking the previous night to an audio hallucination, a sense of movement, the feeling of someone or something present directly outside the tent. Where was this coming from? What had caused this? The effect was that I placed a hand over my stomach, tipped back my head beneath the palms, closed my eyes, sighed, each of the movements being instrumental and decisive too, in the way sound carried. It struck me as ludicrous and impossible that the sound, here, in Westenra, of larvae shifting or of a virus unsticking from a hard surface, was altered – was relatively changed – because of my physical reaction to a recent nightmare (itself harking back to long, intense and recurrent dreams I had had as a child). Every moment of my life, every single thing I had seen, dreamed, believed, affected my current position crouching under the palms, altering the sound of the rain falling indirectly and thus the distance and direction of the surrounding animal calls. However many times I tried to consider this or appreciate this, the resolve passed.

Like mycologists, primate researchers also had to learn to speak to the ground, but as field research took up such a negligible proportion of our time it came less naturally to us. There simply wasn't the same risk with zoo animals, whose immunity had flattened through prolonged contact and direct medical intervention. There was a limit, as well, to how feasible it might be to look down when the objects of your study were forty, fifty feet above you in the trees. We were aware – as Jane was in speaking of the impossible fineness of hyphae threads and the impracticality of it from a research perspective – of the violence of our observation. Too direct a contact kills. Our observation then had to be both intimate and indirect, rigorous, long, even constant. The fact Jane was aware of observer threat was at least promising, given we'd have to instruct her so she could pick up her share of the work. Essentially, we wanted to – had to, for our presence to be justified, to claim to be anything like useful – see everything, at least during daylight hours. It would seem daunting at the start, but she would learn. The reports would stack up, with some additional secondary video available afterwards to cross-check and ensure we didn't miss anything important.

––––––––

A crack in the canopy, a sort of liquid rustling, a burst of sudden sunlight entering through the swaying trees. Three individuals, at once, leaping and then calling, definitely juveniles. My heart thumped and I alternated my gaze, looking centrally, peripherally. They were gone; we heard nothing. This was the first meeting.

In their proportions they were closer to us than to chimpanzees, limbs shortened, thinner trunk, and they furthered this impression by regularly walking on two legs. They were unnerving when they were on the ground because they were so quiet; they appeared and vanished discontinuously; they knew how to measure everything around them so perfectly there was often no audible sign that they were there. But the trees were different: thinner branches bent and curved and creaked to them, leaves washed and rustled as they moved through them, while just the sound of their bodies carrying through the air had a particular quality you soon learned to identify. They exploited the fact that the ground carried them in a way we didn't. For them the ground was an option, it was a thing to be considered, it wasn't inevitable. If they were careful they could walk on almost any ground surface silently. If they're walking on the ground, it's because they want something. Their faces, while they walk there, take everything in. I almost wanted to say that this was one of the reasons they went with their mouths open – trying to absorb more of the world. It was obvious they were looking and planning as they went. They acknowledged more than we did – basic, important things, shapes and textures and densities and temperatures. And I had to concentrate, pay close attention, because I would so easily lose them. Intermittently walking in the forest, moving in a kind of temporally jerking way, there and gone.

When they were extinct – a technicality, a matter of syntax – I was trained to imagine they'd come back, that their movement had tricked and beaten my concentration, that they were effectively hiding and would reappear again. And I would stupidly keep waiting like that. I knew it was not necessarily interesting or significant or unusual that they were so aware when they were on the ground, aware of being on the ground, and that soon – I kept having to correct my thinking: not soon, already – they would be erased from the ground. There was something in the contradiction of, on the one hand, their fineness in being on the ground, their constantly monitored consideration of being on the ground, and on the other their sudden, irreversible, almost unacknowledged separation from the ground that I couldn't process, just as I wasn't able to properly understand their way of walking, forgetting them and losing them from sight.

We set up audio recorders at hundred-metre intervals based around Alice's measure of foraging patterns and favoured food sources. Bonobos had an extensive vocabulary, mild differences in pitch denoting a range of meanings. The call we heard more than others was this quickly repeated 'weeah-weeah-weeah-weeah' sound, used at various volumes according to proximity. It was casual, a simple expression of presence – 'here' – alerting individuals who had become lost from the sub-group or announcing the discovery of something of interest, most likely food. To me, this close, it sounded artificial, sort of rubbery. I pictured practice CPR, chest compressions on a doll torso, the air wheezing out of the plastic body, though the animals' sounds came twice as fast.

They had thin larger necks, delicate heads, giving them an almost studious appearance. They had been observed pointing and throwing items into a specific location. Their quieter somatic communication was breathtakingly elaborate and capacious; you could watch a group all day and observe the constant subtle interplay of gesture, transmission and reception from the slightest cue, the smallest movement

– a turn of the head, a shift of the arm, a look in a significant direction, the silent extension of the mouth, each pregnant with information.

I remembered reading about researchers' attempts to teach them human speech, doomed because the animals couldn't close the velopharynx and form consonants. Insane imperial fantasies, believing the only thing obstructing them was a difference in anatomy directly below the chin, that with prosthetics or an altered, vowel-heavy language they could bring out familiar and intelligible sounds, that the vast space of the animals' lineage could flow unimpeded from human symbols.

We prepared as much as we could in advance but there were certain limitations. You couldn't, for instance, apply the alcoholic solution to your hands before the animal went under, as the scent drew its curiosity, making its movements unpredictable. The gloves we wore were fresh, but these had to be treated too. We couldn't be too cautious. We would apply the tranquilliser remotely, through a dart – Alice had the best aim – then wait to see how well we'd judged the animal's size and the corresponding strength of the compound. It was imperative that the three of us performed this task together; for the period of the blood extraction we had to leave our groups unsupervised. We decided to limit ourselves to a single instance of bloodletting each day, starting in the early evening, the dip time when activity was at its lowest among the waking period. For this first extraction, we chose an adolescent male – group B, position 6 – not young enough to still be under his mother's protection, but not so large as to challenge the volume of tranquilliser.

Leaving camp, we ensured our masks were fixed in place – I rarely saw the others during the daytime, and this vision of their faces obscured surprised and fascinated me. Jane, in particular, seemed to have become something else, and I barely recognised her. She was strident, attentive and not unnerved. Alice led us to sub-group B. We tracked the animals for forty-five minutes, waiting for B6 to become isolated from the others. Quickly, we moved. Alice released the dart; it thumped into the skin. We watched, waited. After the animal had gone, falling backwards onto the leaves with a slow rustling as it tipped and a single soft thud as it landed, we removed our gloves from the sealed container. The animal lay peaceful, as if dreaming in front of us, and we worked quickly. Size was only so reliable an indicating factor. Alice brought out the syringe while I looked for the most promising entry, directing Jane where to shave the hair. Once the syringe was safely inserted and the blood drawn, I asked Jane to prise open the mouth and set the teeth apart. The warmth of the animal came through in our hands as the bitter scent of masticated plant stung us from its opened mouth. I examined the tongue, palate and teeth, recording images on the micro-camera. I removed any external matter for later analysis, indications of dietary behaviour and/ or parasites we might have missed. We were quiet, wary of external interference, curious conspecifics gathering, possible hostility or, more pressingly, of the animal prematurely waking.

This first bloodletting was performed on our sixth day at camp, considerably earlier than our best hopes. From first shot to filled syringe took nine minutes. We retreated, monitored the prone body, timed its period unconscious. We were buoyant. Everything had been a success. In the evening, after we'd eaten, the flask was passed around and I found myself mimicking and only pretending to drink, dipping my head back in a way that was surely evidently inauthentic. My memory of the nausea earlier in the week remained clear, but I was too much of a veteran of these kinds of trips not to realise the importance of the group's unity and the instrumental role played in it of passing round and drinking from the same cup.

Jane was given responsibility for transcribing the night sounds. This was Alice's idea. We found ourselves waking up in the night with the sense of something passing over us. The mass of flowing ink looked more like a painting than a data transcription. I hadn't expected that the group's mycologist would have musical training, nor that it might prove more instructive for her time here than her knowledge of fungus types. She was locked into the recordings, completely absorbed. The more I watched her, the more I thought she was almost another person. She rendered everything she heard in great detail, pages and pages of marks for every two to three seconds of sound. The device auto-recorded once sound reached a certain level, and we typically heard cries lasting sixty to ninety seconds. Something was disturbing the animals in the night, and Jane was attempting to find out what it was. She didn't just transcribe each recording once: she tried meshing and overlaying the various nights' recordings, using separate ink tones. She took me through the transcriptions, playing one, two seconds of sound, stopping the recording and then opening out the sheets that corresponded to it. She wasn't just transcribing the bonobos' calling, she was attempting to pull out the peripheral and secondary sound – bird call, the insects, the moving trees – the counterpoint, she called it, which could be instructive itself. The more she listened and brought out different aspects of the recording, the clearer picture she got. She kept describing what was happening – both what was in the sound and the way that she approached it – in visual rather than aural terms. She nodded, said something about relative constancy, stability, variation and differential pattern. I was staring at these sheets, pages and pages scored minutely, aggressively, and I must have been exhausted because I felt I saw something moving in the pages, an object, underneath the graphs and illustrations, an identity, a face, I thought, behind the scrawls and sounds.

*

Effects from the mining were difficult to measure; it was an open secret that even direct fatalities were statistically adjusted to average levels. Alice spoke about 'remote motion sickness' brought on by the constant juddering of the ground in deep drilling and blasting, affecting populations many hundreds of miles from the source and which could result, after prolonged exposure, in brain swelling, loss of balance and other kinaesthetic defects, haemorrhaging, even death. Additionally there was the problem of valley fever, where the disturbed soil displaced harmful spores that became airborne, shattering immune systems, creating problems in breathing and provoking disease. By far the biggest problem was exposure to excavated heavy metals, which were absorbed into the wider environment. WEBG, in a statement, denied the problem, claiming uranium was 'a natural trace element found in the great majority of living things'. We collected plant and soil as well as fungus samples and rainwater and water from the stream, we gathered stool pieces and urine, though we were cynical about our chances of taking any of it beyond the gates, and though storing some of these materials carried a risk, any escaped odour liable to draw in other animals.

Uranium was brought into the park by many routes. It was possible we introduced it ourselves, just by being here. Tailings discharged from the mines were incorporated into water, soil, plants and invertebrate animals, consumed in sequences of larger animals – birds, reptiles, mammals, ourselves

– who further spread the element through the movement and breakdown of their bodies. Jane described uranium leaching directly into hyphae and travelling rapidly over the great extent of these organisms, hundreds, she said, even thousands of metres. One of the things she was looking for in her fungus samples was malignant growths, signs of mutation and distortion in the white filaments, altering toxicity levels in the fruit it spawned.

I thought there was something awful and awe-inspiring in this sudden, rapid dissemination of elements, the mass turnover of affected plant and animal bodies. Insects, in their hundreds of million, breaking down into soil mulch then growing out as the basis of trees and fungi, producing fruit and seeds consumed by unfolding animal sequences, finally collapsing to recompose the forest, everything turning over again in a sweeping regeneration. The forest itself left no record; humidity prohibited fossilisation. In this sense, and counterintuitive as it might seem, given the palpable digestion all around us, the forest was deathless. I managed, in spite of all this, to routinely walk on the ground without ever considering it, without ever thinking of what it was made of.

Jane attempted to shock us with night stories of fungal rapaciousness and the possibility of reconstructing prior events from resultant growth. A community struck down by famine then, in a morbid but, she said, perfectly natural sense, resurrected in the effusive growth of carnivorous fungus, these saprotrophs draining the collagen and keratin from the bodies, bulbous white fruit emerging overground in excessive quantities; an apparition of the village, ghostly bodies illuminated through trees in the moonlight.

I pictured a time-lapse display of the soft drift of human civilisations and considered the vast power of the trace uranium presently inside us. From this, everything accelerated, beyond perception, beyond control, the smallest, most innocuous act blooming out into something incomprehensible, unfathomable. I saw dense spiral patterns, exponential increases through simple logarithmic progression – 1, 2, 4, 8 – quickly gathering a number greater than all the atoms in the universe. I saw the uranium mines – the opened earth – as the source of a dreadful unfurling, an autocatalytic reaction consuming all life, all information, in an unseen nuclear detonation, a brief, vivid white light flaring soundlessly in a small pocket of our solar system.

VII

It was afternoon, he had eaten, and though he felt drowsy following the morning's work he was determined not to sleep. All he had to do to drift away was close his eyes but he knew he shouldn't, he should stay awake as long as he could. He made himself get up from the chair in his room, approaching the stairs. He hadn't been able to answer the doctor's questions. He couldn't describe the pain. *Not just cloudy, but as if... my head is occupied, strange, far away, physically remote from me.* He walked uncertainly, sceptically into the kitchen. He smelled something. Another symptom, he thought dismally. What had done this to him? But he stopped by the fridge and reached an arm out and opened the door.

The food was beginning to spoil. That was it. There was an electronic display inside but he couldn't make sense of the readings. He made a mental note to ask the doctor the next day. Wary of his tendency to forget, he resolved to write it down. He wandered through the house for several minutes, searching both levels, every room, every cupboard and every drawer, finally realising he was looking for his laptop. An external repository holding his information. Everything would be stored there, a record of his life. If he could find it it would all make sense, everything would come back. But his search failed; he assumed it was being kept somewhere safe, maybe even temporarily removed to save his eyes from strain.

The doctor had mentioned something about avoiding high-stimulus objects; he needed to ask him about this as well.

Rifling through the drawers, the cupboards, he skimmed over the contents, irritated by the unfamiliar and unreadable objects. Where were his things? Who did these belong to? Not for the first time, he suspected a level of organisation above and outside of him, a malign influence controlling things, watching him and moving him around. Paranoia: another 'post-concussive symptom'. It was easier, and demanded less of him, to think like this. Still, he clearly wasn't being told everything, though he could see no reason for the doctor to withhold information from him.

The house was sparse, thinly populated, and nothing he found gave him any information he could use. Given the size of the house, he surely didn't live there alone, and yet nobody else had come. Sometimes he listened by the covered windows, by the doors, waiting for the sound of feet approaching, a key turning in the lock. He was restless, tempted always to turn, to look back over his shoulder, imagining the approach of an unknown figure. He continued searching. Eventually he saw a small paper notepad and a pen, but when he sat at the table he felt a fatigue, a torpor, an overwhelming reluctance to begin writing. Something about the refrigerator? But he didn't know how to begin. Putting the pen down – odd, alien in his grip – the pressure lifted. He packed the notepad and the pen back into the drawer and tried to recall what it was he had been doing.

The smell. It wasn't limited to the fridge, nor to food items. There was a quality, a low ferric musk, he'd encountered before. It was strongest by the kitchen and the bathroom downstairs. He stood at the sink, reminded of the feel of the warm water dissolving through his scalp. He shivered as he pictured the wetness seeping into the wound, the doctor's hands inside.

Before he stepped into the shower cubicle he glimpsed his body in the mirror and saw the scratches on his chest, his arms, his neck. He leaned in at the sink, prodding the wounds. Though it was impossible, they seemed to be deeper than before. He didn't know why the doctor had said nothing about these. Surely they were written up in the notes from the hospital. It didn't make sense. He stepped back from the reflection, watching it fade. It couldn't be real. None of this could be happening to him.

He pulled open the fridge door and saw a faint grey puff grown over the fruit and vegetables and meat. Milk had turned in the carton, grouping into thick, tumorous lumps. He put his hand to his face, covering his nose and mouth from the smell that issued.

'John, what is it?'

As the doctor walked towards the fridge John stepped away, leaving the door open.

'This should have been seen to earlier,' the doctor said in a low voice, adjusting the settings inside. 'It's the weather, the network failures. It's knocked the fridge controls. It's too warm and the food's expired. Whatever's rotted first has spread.'

The mould wasn't confined to the refrigerator. Two parallel dark lines, beginning from the door and reaching out onto the vestibule wall, had appeared overnight. It was almost a relief that he had not imagined the smell. It was not another symptom; it was a simple, natural, routine process. He found further lines by the windows downstairs and in the bedroom above. As he preferred to keep the curtains closed, it was possible the fungus had entered earlier, hidden by the material. The view outside remained unclear; whenever he pulled back the curtain he saw the heavy fog. The insulation was flawed and the vapour found a way in, drifting through the house, dry rot beginning on the exterior door and by the windows. It wasn't significant, but he told himself to monitor it, to keep checking, to watch how it developed.

The doctor made some notes on his tablet and then gestured for him to sit back at the table. 'Okay, let's leave this for now. I'll dispose of the items when I leave. If you give me a list I'll bring fresh supplies. Anything you need, it's not a problem. For the moment, I think it's clear we can't rely on automatic delivery, that this is our best option. Now, tell me what you remember of the tests, John. The hospital.'

He thought for a moment. 'I don't remember the tests,' he said, facing the covered window, the dim light, 'or the hospital. Just this white mask, a plastic shield over my face, gaps for my mouth and eyes.'

'Yes, that's right. It's a less intrusive form of analysis. We're developing new forms of measurement all the time.

Craniocerebral trauma can be quite resistant to interpretation. Later, if necessary, we can use the full-body scanner.'

'The magnet? To draw out what's wrong?'

'Yes, the magnet. But I don't think it will come to that.'

'You're sure the damage isn't more serious? That I'm going to recover fully? I'm going to get my memory back?'

'I've no doubts. You wouldn't have been released otherwise. As I've said before, the worst thing you can do is spend time worrying. Now, John. What is this?'

'I'm sorry?'

'Would you open your collar, please.'

He tugged at his shirt, struggling with the buttons – he was still having trouble performing certain manual tasks, holding a pen, opening packaging. Eventually he exposed his neck, showing two long scratches and the large yellowing bruise underneath. He pulled back his sleeves and unbuttoned the top of his shirt, displaying the two further marks, one on his left arm and the other on his chest.

'This is everything? Nothing on your back? Open your mouth, please. Your mouth, open it wide, and hold until I say.' He lit a bulb on the end of a silver pen and aimed it inside. 'Right, right,' he said, 'okay. One last thing. May I see your fingernails? If you just lay your hands flat on the table – like that, yes, thank you.' He recorded several images on his tablet, talking quietly to himself, making no further direct contact with his eyes.

'Now take your hands back, relax.' He turned from his case, clipping it closed and, facing John, seemed to reset his expression. 'These are fresh. Do you know what that means? You are breaking your wounds, John. You are responsible for these. Don't worry, we can treat it. It's not so uncommon following physical trauma. During your sleep, you have been replaying the attack, making an active, ongoing attempt to counter it.'

'I don't understand.'

'Your arms are thrashing during the night. You're responding to something, responding to what happened. You're trying to claw at something, something which you deem to be a threat, but because there is nothing there you are applying this violence to yourself. The skin and hard blood beneath your nails, you're digging it out.'

'And my mouth,' he said, his voice trailing away, 'why ...?'

'Yes, I've found evidence of tension and applied force upon upper and lower molars. You wake, sometimes, with a sharp pain in your jaw, extending to your neck. A really quite severe pain. You have a dry, powdery taste in your mouth, persistent, difficult to shift, yes?'

'Yes.'

'Those are nightmares. You are grinding your teeth during nightmares. Mr Harper, may I ask you something? It's important. Now, do you recall anything about these nightmares? Anything at all?'

'No.'

'Nothing that could give us an insight into the attack? The nightmare may feel real, it may seem as if it is happening now.'

'Nothing's come back. I remember only a field, a large emptiness, this sound.'

'You're certain? When you do remember, I'm confident this auto-violence – these renewed lacerations on your body – will cease. But for the moment, we do need to do something about them. So I'm going to issue you with a mild sedative to be taken once every twenty-four hours, in the evening, directly preceding sleep. This will help us with the immediate problem of the physical symptoms, ensuring minimal activity during the night, so you'll no longer be subject to the cuts.

'However,' he continued, taking a pair of scissors and a small ornate wooden box from his case, 'as an extra precaution, I recommend we see to your nails. What I'm going to do is cut the nails just a little further, thereby precluding any additional self-inflicted tears. I'll gather the clippings in here.'

The morning visits from the doctor anchored his days. Otherwise, his experience remained shallow, automatic and provisional; he walked from the bedroom to the kitchen, he cleaned up after a meal, he showered and dried himself. The moments didn't connect, instead repeating, stuttering. Frustrated, he waited for everything to link up, for one action to lead into another, for a through line to emerge, taking him forward. He was uncomfortable and restless because there was no guarantee the phenomenon would change. He had to trust that it hadn't always been this way, it couldn't have been. He flitted between rooms, observing the stiff, rigid motion of his arms and legs, sometimes forgetting what had brought him there and where he was going. He observed himself sitting and waiting and he had an urge to express a violence that would shatter this dull equanimity and take him out of it, take him forward.

As he found little instructive evidence in the house, he determined to watch himself more closely. Everything had come from somewhere; every action referred to something prior. The automation in his behaviour had been learned, trained. His habits, obviously, told something. Everything was encoded with the past.

Waiting for the water to heat he stood at the side of the cubicle, the showerhead pointing the other way. Too close to the jet and the stitching over his head might break. He was protecting his head, reacting to the attack. Much of his behaviour followed a similar pattern. Support and carry the head. No sudden movements. Rise slowly and carefully from a sitting position, watch for the first signs of blood rush. He walked tentatively, raising his chin, conscious of having to put the head somewhere, to give it a position, conscious of the fact he was still prone to dizziness and imbalance and that the position of his head contributed to this. It was no longer inevitable he'd remain upright. Only a fine balance permitted this – it wouldn't necessarily hold. To walk you had to move your feet a certain way, exert a certain pressure and produce uplift off the ground, assume consecutive motion in the knees, form a largely straight line through the rest of the body, the spine branching out into packed nerves. Noting the effort involved, the deliberation in setting his head this way, he gathered that his habit was otherwise, that he would ordinarily have walked with his head low, his neck arched.

He understood this while he washed his limbs, dabbing at his neck wound, and while he carefully washed the hair around the shaved part of his head. He thought about it more. He could discriminate behaviour that reacted to the attack from behaviour that preceded it. It occurred to him that if he could chart in sufficient detail every single action he took in response to the attack, every one of the numerous ways he tried to make himself comfortable, safe and protected, then a picture would emerge showing exactly what had happened, a picture of himself and whatever it was – most likely a bird of prey, they had reasoned – that had struck him. Taken to its logical extreme, this kind of bodily charting could develop even further, predating the attack, could ultimately reveal the whole of his life. Perhaps then he would feel himself again, and everything would be okay.

Getting up the next morning, going for a glass of water and returning to his room, the light dim, the sheets spread, he was struck by the fetid smell, musky and thick, a product of the consistency of his breathing in this one confined space, the slightly weaker pulse during sleep, the lowered body temperature, the activity and industry of his digestive system, all producing a distinct odour, a closeness he returned to and which he didn't recognise at all. But this was him, he thought, lying there, eight, nine hours, the sheets tighter to keep him fixed, as much as he could be, in a single position, precluding him from turning and from irritating his head. He was embarrassed and ashamed, wanting to distance himself from this evidence, the openness of his exposure in the air of the room. Even worse, he couldn't open the window, sure if he did so the mould beginning to appear on the wall beneath the sill would spread.

He was noticing a keener sense of smell and touch. Gripping the handle of a drawer in the kitchen, opening a door, holding a plate in his hand, the feeling would become immersive and enduring, and more than knowing he had performed these actions before, countless times – of course he had, he was grown, he had aged – he *felt* that he had, he remembered, haptically, the more extensive nature of his life, felt a warming familiarity in moving and gripping and holding things, felt an appreciation for the weight, shape and size of the objects around him.

Don't press it, the doctor said – at first he thought he meant his head, the wound, the cut – don't push it, the memory will return itself, of its own accord. Let it happen, the doctor told him, let it continue to happen.

He continued to divide himself up, feeling pity and sympathy for the person on the cusp of the attack. He wanted to warn him and if that was impossible then collect him and gather him and tend to him, settle him, make him feel better. He had been struck in such a personal way that he had forgotten much of his ordinary memory. Whatever had done this to him had reached inside and known exactly where to look. It was only natural, he supposed, that as he moved around the cottage, pulling open drawers hunting things, turning on the faucet, opening the fridge and unwrapping food, walking through doorways, over pale wood and linoleum, that he was watchful, as if he had to be especially careful, as if ordinary life could no longer be counted on to continue quietly and by itself, as it might have done before.

Five days after the doctor arrived he found his laptop packed away, hidden beneath towels in the storage closet. He must have done this when he had last gone out. He couldn't remember. He stared at the screen as if at an alien artefact. His fingers, assuming a claw-like grip, made no impression, the screen remained resolutely black. Even if he could restore power and find a network connection, he would still have to enter his pass codes. It seemed like so much. He put the laptop away.

He felt a lack of trust in the neutrality of objects. Something real, something with mass and structure, texture and weight, had collided with him. Something had done this to him. There was no reason it couldn't happen again. He had to be careful and watch the ordinary objects of the cottage, monitor them – the fluid way the kitchen drawers ran out along their tracks, how the weight inside was partly suspended and partly evident, the contents of the drawer and its floating emptiness presenting at the same time. He had to watch everything, monitor everything, feel every moment and gesture, appreciate it and inspect it for change, difference, for the earliest warning, perhaps, that something terrible was about to happen.

Sometimes he felt he was being pushed to certain parts of the house without having consented. He heard the noise he made preparing his meals, hitting a knife against the chopping board, blasting water from the faucet, steaming pots on the stove. He kept turning round, as if expecting someone. By habit he cut vegetables to the left of the sink, never to the right. He sat at the same seat at the table, facing the wall, though it meant he had to turn to check the door. Watching the flow of his hands pushing and lifting pieces of food, it appeared that they were weaving, building, stitching something together rather than taking it apart.

The previous evening he had been distracted, and when he looked down he saw that he had set an extra place, that both chairs were pulled out, two plates laid, and that food had been prepared for another person. He waited a moment. A voice seemed to approach from outside, and he veered away, dismissing the thought. *Who is it? Who is there?* But as he packed the unnecessary portion into a container and left it to cool, he thought of the familiar tributes left for the dead, the meals prepared and deposited at gravesides, the anniversaries on which an absent person is accommodated at a table.

VIII

North gate communicated with us sporadically, a curt acknowledgement of our brief reports every few days. Selina had suggested that there remained a remote chance the doctor might join us, and though naturally this should be a good thing – it would help speed up blood analysis, for one thing – I instinctively disliked the idea. An addition to the group, at this point, when we had worked hard at achieving a kind of balance, risked upsetting us. Food distribution would also be a problem. I dismissed it – it was an unnecessary and unlikely worry.

After the first week of contact we were well practised in our routine. We had thirty-one individuals, an unnaturally small troop which still split into three fluid sub-groups foraging in the day, maintaining regular vocal contact, then regrouping in the evenings in defensive alliance to build new nests and sleep. Each of us followed our sub-group from 'bed to bed', noting blocks of activity at fifteen-minute intervals and building up a thickening profile in our small digital devices. Later, in the evenings, we went over our data, trying to infer meaningful patterns. Generally, we observed food gathering and repeated various sexual encounters. Incidents of genito-genital rubbing were, as expected, close in number to those of male–female copulation. Sometimes we heard them laughing. It was distinct from every other vocal sound,

wheezy, chesty, sparked when grooming turned to tickling or
when the juveniles played. One of their favourite plays was
mock free-falling, dropping from a height near the canopy
and rushing through the air until, at the last second, they
reached out a limb and grabbed at a branch. However many
times you saw this gravity-play, you couldn't look away, heart
in mouth, sure that this time they were going to misjudge
and hit the ground, and that you needed to watch, to monitor
them, as if your presence was somehow reassuring.

Though they had little curiosity about us, they remained
extremely sensitive to cues in our behaviour. This was
defensive. They would rather not watch us but couldn't help
being aware of what we expressed. Part of the reason, perhaps,
I was so drawn to my group was the solicitation and concern I
read in them after exhibiting my illness, two of the matriarchs
coming towards me, inspecting me. I had the feeling I had never
been read so rapidly or exhaustively. They didn't like change,
wary of anything that might have been a beginning, that might
have led to new, unpredictable courses of events. This was
why initial contact was so fraught. Moving forward, we had
to act, to put on a front, to try to be the same person every
day to reassure them. Regardless of how we felt, whatever new
anxieties were moving through us, we had to appear uniform
and unchanging. If on one day I walked slightly faster than
on others, I might inadvertently antagonise the troop, who
could read a purpose I didn't intend, thus invalidating the day's

reports. It was difficult to maintain this front and also unlikely to work; fooling them wasn't so straightforward.

We couldn't move abruptly, and we had to keep measuring and re-evaluating our position – too close, we interfered and disturbed them, too far and they might wonder what had happened to us, whether our absence signalled something portentous. To the amusement of Alice and myself, the older matriarchs in Jane's group were becoming especially protective of her, displaying maternal gestures, on one occasion even supplying her with food. When we mentioned it she dismissed us in a fit of awkwardness, shaking her head, her face obscured beneath her fringe but not entirely concealing the red glow.

One of the useful things in having Jane with us was precisely what we had been most concerned about, namely her naivety. Because she didn't know much about the animals her eyes were fresh, and she saw some things Alice and I, more habituated, failed to notice. And she wasn't afraid to risk open, disarmed questions. She was surprised how much, for instance, the animals smelled each other, touched each other, independently from grooming. Two of her group were particularly interested in smelling opened mouths; Jane was recording this behaviour in depth, tallying each incident and looking for patterns. Was it more frequent first thing in the day, did it follow food consumption, did it tend more often than not to develop into brief acts of intercourse? She matched this smelling with the relationships she had charted in her group, seeing how it correlated with seniority. I asked her to keep me informed of results – there were obvious potential applications regarding health and diet: were they measuring food consumption; were they inspecting the development of an infection in the mouth? – but I was wary of pushing the hypothesis too strongly. Obviously we would pay close attention to these animals – to their mouths – when we took samples of their blood.

One of the frequent actions I noted was an animal approaching a conspecific while the latter was occupied in a task – eating, rubbing itself against a favourite tree bark, intercourse – and putting its hand over the other's hand, simply for the feel of it, the sense of the second animal's activity running through its body. It was difficult not to see such behaviour, historically, as instrumental to the development of empathy. This wasn't an original observation, though seeing an animal press its hand first on the chest, then the throat, of a conspecific who was calling out, thrilled me with possible implications. Alice, when I shared this with her over the evening's meal, was careful to stress the importance of objective, impersonal observation, how vital it was we remained detached at all times. As soon as we go in looking for something, as soon as we approach the work in anything other than a neutral frame of mind, the work is compromised. Obviously I knew this; obviously Alice didn't need to tell me; and though she might have claimed she did so for the benefit of Jane's education, it was difficult not to feel deliberately slighted.

The one thing, predictably, Jane had known about the species was that they were extravagantly and innovatively sexual. As with most new observers, however, she was surprised, even a little disappointed, at how ordinary, quiet and lacking in drama the sexual dynamics could be. Sex was casual, both in the lack of any lasting attachments and in its mundane functionality. The phrase Jane used, after a week's observation, was 'social hygiene'; it kept everything going in more than just the biological sense. Sex as greeting, sex as confirmation and reaffirmation of bonds, sex as a means of calming, defusing and recovering from a slight elevation of tension between two or more individuals. Duration was frequently a matter of seconds rather than minutes, and this brevity, together with the naturalness in which any of various non-sexual activities would transition into intercourse, made it unclear, sometimes, when sex was actually taking place. Intercourse was something like repeatedly interrupted but enduring activity, in the way that sleeping is, or eating, or defecating. Sometimes the acts stood out – Jane had skipped the part in her preparatory reading stating bonobos frequently assumed the missionary position, and that from various other positions too, in fact from any position in which it was possible, they would maintain eye contact for the duration, increasing, or heightening, the intensity of pleasure derived.

Everything was going well. We continued to hear signs of disturbance in the night, calls from the troop suggesting alarm, but finding no evidence of any external source, we put this down to repetition, the memorial of a prior event. The animals appeared relatively healthy, certainly with no obvious signs of illness. This was when the miscount happened. We assumed it was caused by a simple transfer between sub-groups, a younger animal probably. This could happen daily, sometimes hourly. There were now ten instead of nine in Jane's group (C). In counting the other two groups, one of them should reflect this and be down a number. But the numbers were constant. We went over this at night. We couldn't blame her – she had virtually no experience and was doing the best she could. I'd been surprised how capable she was; she observed patiently and recorded simply and directly. Alice said she shouldn't worry, it was the easiest thing in the world to miscount, they move so quickly, she would get the hang of it.

'Start with identifying marks,' she said, 'soon enough you won't have to try – you'll know them by the way they move.'

'No,' Jane said. 'I was careful. I know how to do it. I didn't miscount. There's one more, a new one.'

We went through all the checking procedures, counting and recounting, defining each individual with as much detail as we could. It was difficult, laborious work, irritating, and it set us back. We noted attributes by hand and recorded more video. In theory, the easiest time to make a total survey was in the night, when the sub-groups fused together, aligned in individual nests. But there were practical difficulties: too close and the whole troop scattered; too distant, in this darkness and obstructed by the foliage, and you never saw them to begin with.

I stopped, crouched, held my breath. It was late, that thick, heavy last light, almost gone. I'd been about to move on when I'd heard a snap and realised he was, not directly above me, but close enough for me to see, even in the poorer light. I'd lost him an hour ago. The trees between us were thinner, recently stripped, though I was evidently concealed from his position. With my lenses I could see up at him, his shifting black fur, close to the top of his tree, preparing his nest.

He was quiet – all I heard was the one branch snapping; the nest was tall and almost complete. He was young – perhaps he'd only been building one or two years. He shook the stems loose and gently, firmly popped the leaves from the branch so they came away intact. He scattered the leaves around the circular rim of the nest's upper layer. He had come to the end, stopping but not yet lying down in the nest. He turned to his right side, and I was able to see, through my lenses, that he had stored a bundle of large, soft fig leaves along the rim of the nest. I'd never seen this before. He spat onto the bundle and pressed down on it. He was pasting the leaves, making a parcel. When he was finished this – only a few seconds; he had judged in advance how many of these leaves he needed – he sat back, peered at it and looked out beyond the forest at the sky. Almost dark; I could just see. He carefully placed the pillow inside and then, awkwardly, turned his body round, shifting it in the narrow enclosure of the thicker branches around him, and lay himself down inside.

My mind was racing. I tried to take it all in. Before building, he looked around him and projected the amount of space he would occupy. The same embodied self-knowledge the animals used in judging which branches were and were not strong enough to hold them. He looked around him, and in the base where three strong branches met the trunk he envisaged himself in it, blended with it, dark fur and wide bridge of nose set into the looping strings of leaves. He then stripped enough from the tree to model himself, making a bowl, a container, a place to be held in. But this wasn't the end. He built a new object for his head and put it inside the nest. He carried an image of his head – its size, weight and texture – and modelled the new object on it. He looked around him – earlier, while foraging – and picked out the softest leaves he could find. He prolonged the foraging, risking the irritation of the others in his group, expending more of his energy, searching for the parts of the ground that best matched his perception of the demanding sensitivity of his head.

I had never seen leaves sought out and collected in advance for the particular purpose of soothing the head. This was extraordinary. I crouched, now in darkness, which either made the insects seem louder or was the signal they took to amplify their call. He had displayed tacit acknowledgement of some special need to protect the head. I found this, presently, affecting: the determination of the gesture, the extra effort in fetching those especially soft leaves. He had carried them, even with difficulty, retained them; this was self-kindness, an effort towards a small satisfaction and a pleasure. Had he enjoyed even anticipating it? Displaying this care towards himself? Did he look forward to lying down, to the sensation of tranquillity and of the world drifting away?

We were more wary tranquillising mothers of dependent-age infants. Those under four years were practically inseparable from their mothers, so we had to dart both at once. The process for a single animal took between nine and fourteen minutes, depending on constitution and the effectiveness of the dose. Around half the time, after shooting the dart, we'd also need to shave a small area in order to find the vein. It was more likely in mother–infant lettings that one of them would wake mid-operation. Though the process could take twice as long, equivalently heavier doses were considered dangerous and weren't permitted.

Jane's words, her clipped manner of talking, her accent and the softness of her voice, made it particularly difficult to hear her underneath her mask. I was irritable because of the time sensitivity. I had the feeling, possibly having picked up some series of small details subconsciously, that this adult might wake sooner than the others, and that there was extra pressure to finish quickly.

'Wait,' she said, speaking up. 'We're sure we haven't sampled her before?'

'Of course.'

'But look at this.' She directed us to a neat circle of exposed skin on the underside of the infant male's neck.

'What – is that shaved? Can't be.'

'It's recent, look, you can just feel the beginnings of the regrowth.'

'And here, look – those are syringe marks?'

Inside the shaved patch, in the centre of a purple bruise, were two small red incisions.

'The marks are too thick. It's not us.'

'The patch is circular, looks like it was trimmed by a machine. But not ours.'

'It's a bite, isn't it?' I leaned back.

'Some animals do that,' Alice said. 'Vampire bats, I've seen them. They use their canine teeth to shave hair and help them lap at blood.'

I remembered the rumour, claiming piercings on the cadavers' necks. 'You've seen them?'

'Not here, I don't mean. Anyway, it's not fatal.'

'It must have attacked it in its nest, when they were both sleeping.'

'Best time to see them would be at dusk. We should try. From the bite marks, I'd say they're big. Look for prints by the stream, where they drink. Angled hind-prints from the curved thighs.'

'They walk? Bats? On the ground?'

'Rarely. They're actually capable of running, too.'

'The infant's in your group?'

'I'll watch him, sure. You think something might happen?'

Our time was passing – there surely wasn't long until the animals woke.

I passed Jane the file and she scratched out fungus from the molars, tapping it into her bag. She'd now found fungal residue in three animals, none of whom were showing any ill-effects. This residue was hard to age, but at least indicated they'd been eating from it recently. We finished up, packed our things away, and as we left I noted the animals beginning to stir.

Walking back, we discussed the possibilities. We agreed the bites were unlikely to be fatal; more of the group would have been affected. Our favoured thesis hadn't changed: if the fungus had poisoned the two animals earlier, then it had happened indirectly. What additional agent created the toxicity? And why would only some of them suffer?

'What if we're thinking about it the wrong way? What if it's nothing outside?' Jane walked more easily through the thicket than either myself or Alice. 'Like, it's not a diet thing, but it's the way they eat it. Would that be possible?'

'How they chew?'

'Maybe if it's digested too quickly it can become toxic?'

'Or the opposite, a long-term effect. If they don't scrape their mouths, say, the fungus turns, the stomach acid no longer neutralises it, it turns to poison?'

We'd arrived back at camp. Alice gathered a bucket from the stream and went to wash her vests. Jane retreated to her tent, bringing her samples. I watched her a moment and thought about psilocybin, the absurd hypothesis of fungus evoking hallucinations in animals. Though maybe hallucination wasn't so ridiculous; there might even be a logic. If the animals were denied real space – enough matter to live inside – then false space was an alternative. Similar ideas had been used in zoos for decades. Sculpted water features and fibreglass trees were inserted into primate dens, mimicking the extinct home environment. Attractive plants were electrified to stop the animals eating them. Psychopharmacological supplements became a large part of the captive animals' diet, individually calibrated according to behavioural observation and blood tests; the intention was to relieve visibly anxious and depressive states. Some keepers to whom individuals had become attached put ground Valium into the animals' food thirty minutes before they left each morning to lessen the volume of their shrieks on departure. The animals couldn't bear them going. Groups had been recorded consuming urine and faeces from those individuals fed the strongest doses.

Rotterdam zoo was the first in the world to introduce interactive video displays, simulating an environment the majority of the animals had no experience of. Soon enough, video was upgraded to 3D holographs that responded to the animals' behaviour and to testosterone, oestrogen and adrenaline levels. The programmers boasted authentic background representations that changed in real time – weather systems, collapsing trees – and dextrous foreground simulations where other species appeared unpredictably. Trials involving virtual reality headsets were a great success, inducing false memories of emotional and physical satisfaction – bond-making, courtship, genuine exertion – with the effect that the animals showed lower levels of depression and anxiety.

Zookeepers tried to stop the primates exhibiting damaged behaviour: dragging from one end of the enclosure to the other, regurgitating and reconsuming their favourite meal, in deadening boredom, even eating parts of their own body. Visitors found it worrying and alarming, apparently because it seemed to suggest unhappiness, specifically an imaginative capacity and the total frustration of the desire to act on anything within it. Those animals that didn't pace, that didn't demonstrate, affected by the feeling of a past inside them, a planted satisfaction, were less harrowing to watch, more lucrative. The next step – the only available step – was direct electrical manipulation of the chimpanzee and bonobo brain.

For all the money spent on digital and pharmacological hallucination, one of the most effective primate stimulants remained a bowl of water. Chimps gathered around rain puddles. All enclosures were built to slope onto a raised base, forming a trough. Standing water attracted the animals, who stared into their own urine puddles. The water amplified the limited space, creating extra virtual zones through the angles of reflection. One of the observed changes in captive bonobos was their greater self-recognition. Research on this – a comedy of mirrors and dabbed spots of red paint – had been mixed at best, but the captive animals seemed unusually focused on their own reflections. This may have been an indirect effect of changed diet, over time. But it may also have been related to a reconfiguration of internal and external space.

I lay in my tent thinking in circles while the night drifted on, unsure again if I'd managed to sleep. I could feel that my thoughts were different, straying into odd territory; I now expected the nausea daily, just before the morning. I pictured things turning themselves out, a surface splitting open and curving back along an outside. I shuddered at it, this horrible amalgam of expressed soft tissue and whorls of harder shell. I knew that my thinking would become twisted and knotted, that I would see strange pictures that frightened me and came from me, but the anticipation didn't lessen the effects. I panicked every time. I worried I'd contracted a cerebral virus, a virulent malarial strain, that, haunted by tactile impressions of my own brain, my mind had turned exclusively upon itself, its own basis. I had no symptoms other than this – no aches, cramps, high temperatures or exhaustion beyond that which could be expected.

I left, I vomited, I came back in from the trees, stepping over the twigs and leaves, rinsed my mouth with water and spat out.

I did it again, but it wasn't enough. I washed my teeth a second time, but I could still sense the vomit around some inaccessible part of my mouth. I was too aware of my mouth, stretching it and toying with it. My teeth were obtrusive; my tongue was swollen. I worried I was going to choke. I turned to Jane's tent and in my headlamp saw her razor outside. I picked it up and turned it to my face. Attached to the razor, on its other side, was a fold-out pocket mirror. I held it to my opened mouth expecting to see something ghastly and amorphous, an outsize mass of tissue hanging from my palate to my gums. But to my surprise, and relief, the picture was familiar. Nothing was wrong. I packed the kit away and returned to my tent.

IX

Standing in the vestibule, he looked at the row of coats and at the boots and trainers lined up under the worktop. He ran his hands over the nearest item – a dark-green waterproof wax coat. He measured his arm against it and saw the sleeve was too big. He tried it on still; the material draped over his shoulders and dangled past the ends of his fingers. The zip made a rapid cutting sound; with a hurry he removed the coat and returned it to the peg. He was sure this didn't belong to him. He opened up the pockets and was relieved to find no effects inside.

Four further coats hung on the wall. Two of these seemed to fit, more or less. He found three different sizes of boots, additionally one pair of shoes so small they must have belonged to a child.

He was unsettled by the prospect of peripheral activity, events taking place while he existed far away in the dead state induced by the sedatives. He was still adjusting to the medication, one of the effects of which was to take away all sense of duration in the night, leaving him, when he woke, without the experience of any time having passed. He simply took the capsule, lay down and fell almost instantly to sleep. Suddenly his eyes were open, nine, ten, eleven hours later. At first he was so unsettled and disoriented that he sought out every time display in the house, checking there hadn't been a mistake. His body – especially on the right side – was stiff, his head remote, dull and sore, but other than that he remained alienated from sleep, with the uncanny certainty that no part of him whatsoever had observed it. Nothing had stirred or stretched, nothing had turned, nothing had listened to or reacted to the faint autonomous sounds generated by the cottage – the walls, ceilings and floors acting under the pressure of the sustained, suspended precipitation in the weather – to the faint humming of the wall heaters and the fridge and freezer, to the drizzle of the pipes, to the sounds outside too, sounds, in the nights before he was given the sedatives, he remembered as odd, faint, unidentifiable animal calling. He peered through the curtains – despite the doctor always reminding him he should keep away from the light – checking that the night had passed, that another day really had come, that all of this was enduring, when really what it felt like was that he had laid his head gently, cautiously on the pillow, closed his eyes and immediately opened them again. Under such conditions – prone, unwitting, anaesthetised – it was possible some other activity was performed in the house. The wax coat, the heavy and unfamiliar boots, the child's shoes. Had they been left in error? Why hadn't he noticed them before? Did someone have a key? Was the house being used, during the night, to host something, a series of events whose nature and purpose he couldn't imagine?

Sometimes, in the mornings before the doctor arrived or in the afternoons or evenings after he had gone, he experienced strange, unaccountable flashes – not memories, exactly, not scenes that he was able to identify and place as familiar, as belonging to him, but images which remained remote, unclear and hard to place. These, he thought, would be effects from the sedatives; the fact that for several nights he had slept devoid of all experience, all sensation, that he could neither say that he had dreamed or had not dreamed, the fact that nothing in the sleeping period came to him at all, must surely do something to him. These brief flashes – accompanied by dread, a paralysing fear, a frustrated inability to understand what was happening – would be like compressed slices of a dream, shards of subconscious material released during the daytime, in his waking state. Boiling the kettle, getting up from the chair, suddenly he would hear or feel something – a door thudding closed; a warmth on his neck; one or more voices whispering around him – and then freeze. It wasn't real; he had already accounted for the phenomenon. But still, spending all this time alone, having so many questions about what exactly had happened, he couldn't get away from the idea that these flashes meant something, that they might really be significant, that, even if they were prompted by his medication, that didn't mean they weren't instructive. Why these images, these sensations, in particular? Who did the whispering, chattering voices belong to? Why a door closing? Why a warmth specifically on his neck? He pressed lightly against the wound, sucked in his breath.

He tried to dismiss these strangers, the unseen other people with some claim on the house. Still, the unfamiliar clothing, the sense, as well, of a mild disorder in certain parts of the house when he went downstairs in the morning, the impression that one or two things – the lay of the cushions on the sofa, the fridge door left ajar, a chair pulled out at the table when the last thing he did each night was push them firmly underneath – were not as he had left them. He studied the two empty rooms upstairs, dreading the appearance of footprints in the carpet. He pictured someone faceless, unfamiliar and unauthorised, entering the house and living there.

But it could only be himself. He must have moved. He must have sat up in the night, got up, left the room. Walked slowly, unconsciously, down the stairs and through the kitchen. He had checked the food in the fridge; he had approached the table and pulled out a chair, looking ahead at the wall, the covered window, the lines of fungus reaching in, moving stiffly and slowly and seeing nothing. He observed the image with a combination of pity and terror – the lax muscles and awkward locomotion, the raised, swollen head, the unfamiliar features of his face. What was it that disturbed his sleep and took him to the stairs? The doctor had issued the course of sedatives to 'prohibit', as he said, 'unconscious, involuntary movement'. And so far, in the most obvious respect at least, they had; the wounds appeared to be healing. Perhaps the sedatives instilled a different, quieter, still dangerous form of automatism, bringing him to the stairs, where no monitoring system could stop his fall, taking him down to the chair, the table, where he waited, apparently, though unwittingly, for the doctor.

X

It wasn't long after sunrise. There had already been new flux between sub-groups, making it harder to count. I'd switched with Jane, now following her group. I focused on two animals whose interaction immediately appeared odd. The younger of the two walked directly into an older female. This female, estimated age around thirty years, had thin hair across torso and breasts, large laterally protruding ears and very little hair across her head, leaving her scalp exposed. The muscles across her wide, strong thighs were clear, standing upright along the water's edge. The animals didn't look at each other. This was the strangest detail, the identical lack of awareness. They walked into each other, as if not recognising the other was there. If something like this happened, we'd expect an outburst – powerful females were known to threaten and attack, even tearing and biting off body parts. But I saw no retribution: the older female stopped only for a moment, on the brief impact of the bodies, then continued, now moving with more speed, and launched into the trees, while the younger ape slowly ambled across the ground.

I was beginning to think that Jane might be right. Something odd was taking place in the behaviour of her group. She had insisted that Alice and I take turns watching them. The miscount remained, reaffirming the additional animal. Focusing on the younger animal now, it was clear something was wrong, and that she didn't correspond to any of the identities we had so far noted. She was malnourished and appeared to be engaging in self-harm, tearing large clumps of hair from her shoulders and her chest, hair which she chewed on, swallowed and regurgitated. We saw her do this again and again; I imagined she was replaying something, perhaps trying to capture something that had passed. Several of her nails had been broken off and she stumbled while she moved. Her head was cast down; she rarely walked bipedally, her arms only poorly supported her moving through the branches. She should have been easy to follow, but one of the problems I found, over the following days, was that she kept disappearing. She rarely vocalised or interacted at all, making only brief wheezy noises which the other animals ignored. You saw her – rather a glimpse of her – though the trees and then somehow, despite what was clear at other times to be her impeded movement, she was gone.

She was worryingly thin. Sometimes as she reappeared I would take her at first for some other animal, an unknown species. She looked younger than she was – closer examination showed her to be adolescent, nine to ten years – not fully completed, in some light partly translucent, as if manifesting before us through the air. Likely, of course, she was shifting in the other direction, un-forming. I thought the rest of her sub-group walked and swung in a sort of stilted way, as if moving through some difficulty or resistance. It was like she dragged them back. They tried not to look to her though they knew that she was there. The juveniles played, but with less abandon, and their mothers remained permanently close. And then there was the food. At first, this seemed like a breakthrough, a positive sign: her group had left two intact junglesop fruits behind, in an area easy to reach. This was the first direct communication I'd seen in three days observing her. She came slowly, gathered the fruits – long, yellow, each weighing around five kilograms, easy to process, with seeds the animals either spat or threw away – sniffed them, clutched them to her and shifted away. But nothing developed from this. Instead, the same two or three animals left her a small amount of food each day, at the end of their foraging. Unlike in more routine food-sharing, these fruits, nuts and leaves were given intact, a further suggestion of reluctant, ambivalent association. They didn't directly share. They didn't take from the same source. Each time, she waited until she was alone before gathering the food, inspecting it and moving off, refusing to eat in front of them.

Far from a sign of acceptance and integration, this strange behaviour seemed to increase her isolation. I was struck again, watching her move hesitantly forward, by the idea that they didn't know what she was. Sometimes it seemed the other animals – even the lowest subordinate male – refused to acknowledge her as living. In almost all aspects they acted as if she was not present. But there were signs. Despite casual sub-group fluidity, her own group remained fixed. For this reason, I thought they were broadly protective of her. Equally possible, and as their countenance sometimes suggested, they were afraid. Leaving the food could almost have been an act of tribute, a token left for a strange, remote thing that could not eat it. We were worried about disease – her diminishing stature, the hair loss and the way that they avoided her. Possibly a cerebral strain, accounting for the odd compulsive symptoms in her behaviour too. She cleaned herself obsessively and engaged in other ritualised behaviour, including patting her left shoulder three times when she prepared to pass a certain tree. Alice and I debated the extent to which we could call this magical thinking. Did she believe her rituals were effective? What was it, exactly, she was trying to control? We'd witnessed no sexual activity involving her – another extraordinary and exceptional observation. Most worryingly, we still had no adequate explanation for where she had come from.

I woke to a rising, thickening nausea, my head full of the sound of the calls above me in the trees. I was already on my knees and my hands were clawing uselessly at the tent partition. I found the zip and yanked it down too quickly – the sensation, of something rapidly and unnaturally opening up, gave me the awful feeling that the world had spilled over – and I vomited silently, capaciously, onto the black mud outside the entrance to the tent.

I wondered if this – the nausea and the fatigue – might be a result of the vaccinations. There were many possibilities, the pills too. Though I had never previously experienced physiological effects from the malaria prophylactic, that didn't necessarily mean I wasn't suffering them now. I brightened at the idea this was the entire explanation. I put my headlamp onto the lowest setting, and slowly and carefully stepped outside. The stench was awful. It had collected into a circular pool and, turning away first and drawing in my breath, I divided it in two, scooped my hands into the wet mud beneath it, lifted the mess up into both arms and carried it away. I walked slowly into the trees, turning my head to make a full sweep with the light, tempted to laugh at the ridiculous image, carrying this bundle in my arms, as if it were dear to me. But I was here to bury it. I dropped it on the ground and returned quickly with the rest of the loose, falling slop, now forcing it down lower into the ground with the topsoil and the leaves I sprinkled over it, now stomping onto the conspicuous mound with my boot. I finished: you could no longer see anything, and I wasn't sure who, or what – my colleagues, myself, the other animals in the forest – I was hiding the sight from.

Their ears were identical. Of course. This was a daughter, her daughter, and she had come back. She wasn't new to the troop – she was returning. Her malnourished condition and the unfamiliarity of her conspecifics suggested she'd been gone for months at least. The age was exactly right. She had left in order to join another troop, and she had roamed the park and come back because there was nothing else. After reaching menarche, females abandoned the natal group, the sub-group and the cluster entirely. The journey, travelling however far to attach to an external troop, was the single vital element driving bonobo society, maintaining affiliative relations between remote troops and keeping the species genetically viable by restricting inbreeding. Other than chance meetings when their roaming territories briefly overlapped, a daughter never saw her natal group again. This exile, or emigration, was definitive, had been ongoing for up to two million years. And now it was failing. The emigration was frustrated, and the daughter came home broken and starved, where she was no longer recognised.

We had no way of knowing where exactly she had been, how far she had travelled within the park, how her food sources had changed, what new potential predators she'd faced. Alice noted an awkwardness in her gait suggesting poorly healed limb fractures. We could expect this pattern to repeat through later females. The stress, even the shame of the failed journey, would affect health, exacerbating genetic defects brought on by the inbreeding. I'd imagined, before I came here, that some preparation for exile might persist, but hadn't considered they would still attempt a full journey. The longer we spent at Westenra, the more forcefully it was pressed on us that the troop wasn't at threat from any single agent. The animals were being attacked simultaneously from several sides.

It was understandable we grew oppressed, solitary in their company. Jane formed models and projections from the data gathered, staying awake to monitor activity in the nests. The troop continued to call out sporadically through the night. Alice and I tried to eliminate thoughts of more mid-term threats and concentrate on the most urgent crises. I considered the troop increasingly lost, shorn of and loosened from identity, and I wondered in what pathetic and creative ways the animals would compensate for the now permanently frustrated migratory instinct. The more I thought about it, the more it seemed that every interaction of mother and infant from birth was at once preparation for and expression of the central migratory instinct, that the instinct was crucial even in governing maternal care of males, who would not ultimately journey far from home. Carrying the young infant ventrally, on the mother's underside, allowing no greater distance than a metre to separate the two in the first six months, then slowly easing out, the infant prised apart as in an agonisingly attenuated gravitational pull. Her new larger body made her increasingly distinct from her mother, made her physically separate, and in parallel with this she continued slowly falling. Almost a year old, she could exist as far as four metres distant, though these excursions were still rare and brief and provisional. Every day, every hour and every moment was a scaled version of the larger, later emigration. At three years, bigger, approximately fifty pounds, her mother allowed her almost out of sight, as far as ten metres, and now carried her dorsally, changing the infant's perspective, pushing her eyes directly outwards rather than pressed in against her side. She was weaned at four or five. In the next two years she more obviously practised emigration, keeping to the same sub-group but frequently wandering alone. Then she left the sub-group and practised foraging with others. Finally, after all this fine-scaled preparation, she was ready, and without gestures or any difference in the preceding routine, she left her mother, her natal group and the whole cluster of conspecifics that was everything she'd ever known, and she exiled herself, journeying towards a new troop. And then she returned, months later, in the state we were witnessing. The identity of the animal was destroyed.

XI

It was midway through the second week of the treatment and John watched the doctor arriving, making his way through the vestibule, appearing to notice neither the raincoat nor any of the boots and making no reference to the mould that was spreading through the house. As usual he laid the case on the end of the long table and took his coat off and hung it on the chair. Under his coat he wore a fading brown corduroy jacket and a dark jumper, with dark trousers and a pair of immaculate plain black shoes. The shoes never had the slightest mark or drop of moisture on them. He never wiped his feet on the mat, standing waiting on the steps to be invited in, long arms drooping at his sides, deep case held not far above the ground. Despite the damp fog and the unpaved driveway and the track that he had had to walk along from wherever he had chosen to park his car, he never brought any dirt into the house; he never marked either the linoleum vestibule floor or the pale wood floor of the kitchen. He watched the doctor unpacking at the table, noting again that it was difficult to place his age; on some mornings he appeared significantly older, perhaps even approaching retirement age, but on mornings such as this he was a little younger, with more colour in his cheeks, a quickness in his step, the appearance, even, of a thicker mass of hair.

'How did you sleep last night?'

'Fine.'

'Any recall? Any disturbances?'

'No.'

'Very good. We'll continue with the sedatives. How is everything, from your perspective? How do you feel the treatment is going?'

'I don't know. The nausea isn't as bad, but I still don't feel myself, and I still don't remember anything, only these flashes, which I can't read. It's hard. It feels strange that I'm here on my own, that no-one has come.'

'What do you mean, John?'

'I don't know. My family, my friends. It's just strange, it isn't right.'

'John, all the evidence I have indicates an exemplary rate of recovery. I know this is disorienting, I know it's hard, but I promise you your memories will return, soon. You really are getting better. As soon as you're up to it, we'll look at making contact with people again. The important thing is not to strain or push too hard. When you least expect it, everything will come back.'

After checking on the fridge and on the condition of the fresh supplies – a meat-concentrated diet, which the doctor had introduced, in addition to the list of items he requested, and which he found difficult to follow, still lacking in appetite, still feeling a sort of grey insubstantiality, a greyness that he recognised, unpleasantly, in the tight cords of fat covering one end of the stretch of liver packed in a stained brown paper bag, a cut with a strong odour that filled out the fridge and beyond, distracting at least from the smell of the fungus – the doctor gathered up his coat, his case, and told him that he would see him the same time tomorrow. After he closed the door – he always waited twenty seconds before setting the lock, not wanting the doctor to hear him, thinking it might reflect badly, conveying paranoia, an unreasonable preoccupation with security – he returned to the kitchen and slowly pulled one edge of the curtain. The doctor, carried in the fog, which still showed no signs of abating, had effectively disappeared. On the sill, beneath his fingers, he felt the thick black-green webbing of the fungus. He closed the curtain and turned around. He hadn't eaten since he woke, and when he had mentioned this the doctor appeared concerned, focusing a severe expression and making him promise to cook the liver as soon as he left. He recommended frying it lightly, with the faintest smear of butter, allowing the meat to turn almost exclusively in itself, to progress in its own fluids.

Approaching the fridge, he considered what he'd told the doctor and wondered whether he had over-reported, or under-reported, his symptoms. Both his condition and his perception of it were constantly in flux. There were times – typically in the evening, after the doctor had gone – when he felt a little stronger and when he believed he might have unwittingly exaggerated his state in order to play the role assigned to him, justifying the doctor's presence. Other times he believed that the opposite was the case, that he was so determined to be better that he created false lulls, hallucinated spells of wellness that inevitably drifted away; unable to face the reality of what was happening, he turned himself away from it. It was impossible to know which reading was definitive.

Opening the fridge door, the smell hit him immediately, as if it had grown stronger in the brief time elapsed. The brown paper bag, smeared in blood and fat, had started to degrade and parts were transparent. Whatever the doctor told him, he wasn't going to eat this. The idea of consuming it, absorbing it, this thin sheet of grey pungent liver, was grotesque. But he couldn't leave it here, in the fridge, continuing to fester, affecting the other items and the fridge itself, which he had already emptied and scrubbed clean. He couldn't put it anywhere, equally, that the doctor might discover it. The thought of the conversation, everything he would have to explain – why he didn't eat the liver; why he felt he had to hide it from the doctor – was exhausting. He suspected, already, that the doctor, as he left each day, opened the bins outside as part of his ongoing 'survey', his 'diagnostics'. He had heard, once, the familiar light clip of the lid closing. He would have to wrap the bag well, conceal it elsewhere.

He searched for a plastic bag, put his hands inside and eased it over the liver. He tied the bag securely and entered the vestibule, where the freezer was kept. He took the other items out and packed the meat deep inside. Store it at the bottom, he thought, where it would never be seen. Suddenly, a vision came to him: an industrial park, a tall building, a strip of beach, the sea. And he knew that was where his things were. But why? Why weren't they here, in the cottage? He tried to let the memory flow, but his deliberate intervention had already petrified it. Frustrated, he let the freezer lid drop.

At night, after his meal of soup, vegetables and bread – which he was careful to inspect for any hint of rot – and at the first signs of tiredness, having taken his sedative capsule, he went upstairs to the bedroom. The bedroom was oddly free of personal effects; again he had the feeling he didn't belong here, being merely a guest. No mementos, no clear markers of time, no photographs or paintings on the walls, no books. As the tiredness rose he got up from the bed and slid open the wide cupboard doors. Clothes hung along the railing, and in the long shelf above was a series of large canvas bags. Inside these were more clothes, carefully folded and with a slight musty odour suggesting they hadn't been taken out for some time. He pulled out and unfolded a slim black vest top. He looked at the arms, the neck, and felt a sudden movement, a sense of animation, gone as soon as it began. As the room started to blur, he pulled himself to the bed, huddled under the duvet and laid his head down as carefully as he could. In his last moment of consciousness he tried to focus, willing the resolution, imploring himself to remember this thought the next night: *Don't take the sedative. Remain awake, aware, concentrate.*

*

He spent the following day searching through the house, more carefully studying the contents of the cupboards and the drawers, going over the objects he found, running his hands along the material. He laid all of his own clothing together on the bed and attempted to arrange the collection chronologically, imagining the cycles and routines of his days. He emptied out the kitchen cupboards, examining the dry goods and imperishables, telling himself that he contained this, that these foods were a part of his diet and likely had been for some time. This was his life. He was brief with the doctor, submitting to the questions and tests quickly and quietly so that he could sooner resume his search. In the evening, tired, frustrated, disappointed at being no closer to unpacking his memory, he prepared for bed. Although he hadn't taken the sedative – he'd crushed it with the heel of his hand and washed it down the sink – he still felt exhausted. He didn't think he'd be able to stay awake. As he undressed in the bedroom, he looked at the tops of his arm, his neck, the hard case of paler skin progressing, insect-like, over the wounds, wondering what he had dreamed of, what had done this to him. Lying in the bed and turning off the cabinet lamp, he knew he might be leading himself back towards the source. He wanted this; he also feared it. He didn't have a choice; he couldn't risk missing something important. He had to remember. Whatever the doctor said, he had to do this.

He climbed into bed, lying as usual on the left side, absently laying his hand over the empty part of the mattress. Adjusting to the darkness, he noted the small radio set on the cabinet on his side. Though the dial was turned off, he had the impression of hearing music, so faint it was almost imperceptible. He smiled, comforted. A sense of companionship, of no longer lying there alone. Another impression, an arm reaching over him towards the dial, the music again. Suddenly he could feel her, as if she were there beside him. The warmth of her arm rising, the material of her T-shirt brushing his skin, the statement of a languid, deeper pleasure, a comfort on the edge of sleep. He saw, again and again, her arm arcing, the pleasure she took in the act, the satisfaction in reaching for the music, switching off the dial, tumbling away to sleep. He wasn't alone. He shared his life and it was beginning to come back to him. He wanted to feel, again, her arm over him, her body against him, her warmth in the bed. He settled into his pillow, imagining the moment again, exploring it infinitely, savouring it and luxuriating in it, knowing in full the tiniest sliver of movement that composed each part. Nothing could rival its ecstatic significance, a whole life, a universe, contained in and expressed by her arm lifting over him in the last part of the night, gently, faintly cutting the audio, the music still, for minutes after, seeming to echo, and stutter, and continue playing.

XII

It was still most likely we were witnessing an enduring, extended initiation period, that her behaviour would eventually stabilise and she would become more or less reintegrated as part of the group. But I continued to notice bizarre, improbable details. Her nests were astonishing. Each night, she built it to more than twice the height of the others' – in Alice's words, 'exhibiting compensatory excess'. I considered that she was building in fear, trying to more fully banish the possibility of sighting her. Again, I wondered at what the animal had encountered, what horrors she had seen, what had happened on her journey. Beginning early and sometimes long into darkness she made a tall mound, a cone shape, inside which she was obscured entirely. Bonobos' designs were always interesting, as I'd already seen with the younger male, and though little research had been done, it was believed individuals stamped unique and identifiable 'prints' onto their nests, that no two nests were the same and that with enough care the individual could be traced back from the nature of its building. The species built more elaborate and dense nests than common chimpanzees did, helped, among other reasons, by the animal's frequent tendency to walk on two legs, freeing its forelimbs to gather. I hadn't seen her constructing her nest – she disturbed easily and quickly so we were careful to stay at a distance, and it was difficult to make her out through the foliage and the approaching darkness. Jane, however, reported seeing her destroy her nest one morning, showing unusual energy and enthusiasm dismantling it with teeth and arms, flinging the pieces aside. She knew I would be interested and, after the animal had left, gathered what remained before it eroded entirely and took the small fragments back to our camp. There were several clumps – dirt, leaves and twigs – still matted in with resin and saliva. These segments, vertical cross-sections, enabled me to see the layered, thatched design and to note in it the beginnings of a spiral pattern. A single fig fruit, squashed and hard to make out, was embedded into the wall fragment. I felt a sudden chill, in the heat and torpor of my dank tent. Was she starving herself? Was she gathering up the food offered to her and gluing it onto her nest each night?

From previous glimpses of the full height of her nests – she was exceptional, as far as I was aware, in destroying her nest each morning – I was able to sketch a reconstruction of the whole model. It was strange, completely atypical in the species. The concentric spiral pattern defining the walls seemed to adhere to strict mathematical constants. I was unsettled by the suggestion of mechanisation, of a designed, almost industrial elegance. We drew maps of the sub-groups' movements through the day, recorded the position of the troop's nests when they came together in the evenings and within this, night after night, I saw the same thing. Not only was she isolated within the troop, but she remained separated by an exactly constant distance.

Somehow her conspecifics were able to position themselves around her by this invariant distance, irrespective of where in the forest they were placed. She must somehow have communicated to them, expressing how far away they should stay.

I didn't speak about this, aware how it would sound, knowing that what I was describing wasn't strictly possible, but I continued to dwell on it. I thought of disease, something that appeared directly as shapeless and wild, unfathomable but which, both from extremely close and extremely distant perspectives, expressed certain mathematical regularities. I woke sweating from a dream image, the swirl and coil of a double helix rising up and revealed in global epidemiology maps charting infection rates from a super-virus. Did her conspecifics know to keep just far enough away to be protected from her? From the disease?

It wasn't just in her nest or her position each night: I heard it in her voice. Capturing this proved difficult, but one night we found the correct distance and in the morning listened back to her audio. Through the next day, it was all I could think about. Eventually evening came and the animals regathered and we returned to our camp. I took the device and lay on the hammock. Jane was standing in front of me, waving, smiling. She mentioned rice and I nodded, reattaching earphones. I kept playing it back. It was instinctively unpleasant to listen to, even after many repeats. I wondered whether it had the same effect on all primates, a kind of pan-genus sympathy. The cry wasn't panicked; it wasn't an eruption or a plea for help. There was control and restraint inside. She was alerting the troop to the danger, but not only that. I checked: the gaps between the sounds were the same, identical: 1.4 seconds, unwavering. I knew what she was doing – she was trying to restore order. She was terrified. Whatever was happening – around her, inside her – she didn't understand, and she was scared. She was protesting whatever was happening and enacting it too. She slowed down her pulse, drawing herself in; she was dying. At first I thought it was an effort to stabilise and control anxiety, to dampen the heat and excess of her terrified and quickly beating heart, lock herself into a slower rhythm, limit the heat and movement and noise she made in an effort to elude the animal, the predator. But there was no predator, there was just herself, in her nest, sick. Her voice was the sound of the rhythm of the disease, the vacillating heat and tempo of the fever. None of this was deliberate, it was just happening, all of it was happening, and I couldn't explain it. I felt my centre swaying and dipping – my body, my heart, my breath – and I recognised the rhythm. I was dipping and swaying in the hammock to the tempo she expressed. I knew what was going to happen but that didn't mean I was able to forestall it. As best as I could, I gathered myself up and launched off the hammock, bending and manipulating my weight and pressing onto the material so I was able to get down from the height. I ran, though as I looked down my feet appeared to be making no progress, to be going over the same spot of earth again and again, and eventually, somehow, I found myself vomiting in the trees.

I assured them it was nothing. I admitted it all, the sickness coming every second day, sometimes several consecutive days, but maintained I was otherwise perfectly healthy, that after each bout of sickness I was able to continue in a completely neutral frame of mind. Besides, what option did I have? We couldn't abandon the work. I am not stupid; I am not so irresponsible as to put you or the animals in any danger, I said. My symptoms don't conform to any known virus; I am sure of it, I repeated.

Alice was quiet, her head low, whittling a stick with her knife. She wanted me to rest and I could feel her watching. 'Too late anyway,' she muttered. 'We'd all be infected by now.'

Alice remained distant, disappointed. Jane seemed strained, torn in her awkwardness. The three of us split as usual in the morning, tracked and observed our separate groups. Alice suggested another switch, routine, she said, it will make us keener, but I refused; I would continue monitoring group C. I asked Jane and Alice to listen in particular for any unusual vocal communication, and saw them exchange a glance. The day passed, and as soon as I woke, early, I listened to the night's audio. I heard nothing from her.

I made my way to the nests. They weren't obvious from the ground. I had to keep my neck strained and survey the forest at a level height. Eventually I spotted a dark bundle attached to a trunk, high above. After this, it was a relatively simple matter of walking out in lines, noting the position of each nest. I soon found what I was looking for. She hadn't destroyed it. Nothing had fallen to the ground. This was significant. I tensed; something had happened to her. Intact, above me, I saw its large, imposing shell-like structure. I laid all my possessions at the base of the tree, stripped my boots to get better purchase. With the troop split several kilometres away, I felt unhindered as I climbed. I told myself to go slowly upwards, to survey each approaching branch before laying my hands on it. I was wary of routine dangers – stinging insects, fresh sap – any of which could make me lose my grip and fall.

Something wet slipped onto my forehead and blurred my vision. I went to wipe it but caught myself in time. I needed to find a firmer base before loosening my grip. When I did so I realised that it was just sweat in my eyes, that I was jumpy and nervous and easy to scare. I was inhaling sharply – I wasn't sure when it had begun. I smelled something but couldn't be sure it was her body. I supposed I had imagined a different smell. I stopped, rested a moment. I was thirty or so feet above the ground. I looked back at the heels of my bare feet, my legs opened to turn around the tree. Above me, through the thick mesh of foliage, I could see the dark sheen of her nest.

Through my hands I learned that I was shaking. I was unsteady on the tree because of my quicker pulse. I muttered something, shook some of the excess sweat from my saturated hair. I continued climbing until I was level with the nest. I considered the branch nearest to me, trying to gauge if it could take my weight. Finally, I stepped out. I repeated, my priority was my own safety; I had to ensure, before doing anything else, that on each new step I was secure. I took a breath – regardless of what happened, whatever I saw inside, I would remain calm – and lifted one leg and one arm out, making a small arc of my body and, twisting, stretching out from the base branch, looked directly inside her nest.

It was more than big enough to contain a body. The rotting smell was stronger here. I was lost in the nest's complexity, the repetitions and spirals inside, so much so I hadn't even paused to consider my relief that it was empty, that she was not there. She had gone. Neither Jane nor Alice would find her – they'd report her missing from the sub-groups. I doubted we'd find a body.

I felt calm. I hadn't wanted to be confronted with the body, not yet, not ever. We had already secured blood samples; there was nothing further we could learn from a cadaver. I had held myself in a rigid, awkward position for several minutes; now that I realised this, I felt my body ache. I tilted back and brought my core weight down onto the base branch. I brought out the micro-camera, looped the string of wire from my pocket and hung it on my neck. I swung round again, easier the second time. Through the lens, everything was clearer. I was able to separate myself from the nest. I examined it, filtering out the materials composing it. Berries and figs and masses of philodendron leaves. All her food, the fruits her conspecifics laid out for her at the end of each day. Dense packs of ambrosia beetles and rotting wood. Bright yellow butterfly wings and a patch of synthetic blue fibre. There was more. The walls of dirt were hardened not just from saliva and rain but from a thick, black filament-like matter. I released the camera and used my free arm to tear a thin twig away from the foliage above. I leaned back over the nest, and, after a moment's hesitation, an instinct telling me this was wrong, that I shouldn't be doing this, I shouldn't disturb it, I pressed against the black resin with the end of the stick.

I heard something snap below. Silence. I had the impression I was being watched. Turning around, far enough to see a reasonable distance, would be dangerous. I could lose my footing. If it was Jane or Alice they would have called. Besides, they were far away, tracking their sub-groups. I waited, heard no further sounds. The illusion of an observer was not uncommon; I had to dismiss it. I knew it was reckless and I shouldn't but I wanted to press on. I laid the stick down and held the camera again, hoping the same trick – creating an additional barrier, outsourcing my vision – would help establish clarity. It didn't. As I observed the nest, I continued to sense an observer.

Was I being irresponsible? Alice wouldn't have allowed it; therefore, my only way of seeing inside was by going up alone, unacknowledged. How far in advance could they have warned me if the animal really had come back? Enough time for me to safely get down, considering her size and, though sick, the speed she was still capable of travelling? But I knew she was gone. I had to stop being irrational. For some reason, making contact with the nest interior, the black matter inside, had made me feel I was closer to her. I repeated, it wasn't logical, it didn't mean anything.

I drew the stick out again and this time pressed more firmly against the resin. The structure began to give. I didn't understand – surely I hadn't pushed hard enough. The liquid, which had hardened and given solidity and structure to the walls, now loosened and began to run free. It disappeared inside the nest, neither spilling out nor visibly pooling in the base inside. The whole extent of the nest began to shift as the walls fell in, drooping and collapsing. It seemed to lose depth, folding into itself. In just a few seconds little appeared left, just an odd flattened mass of twigs, earth and leaves that would quickly become unidentifiable from the tree, being absorbed by it. Other fragments, whether fallen to the ground or caught on lower branches, would be gathered by birds, insects, as well as her conspecifics, and incorporated into their own nests, absorbed into their own bodies.

Descending, I saw the black matter caught in my hands, though it hadn't been possible to grasp it. The backs were marked, and I thought this was wrong, that it shouldn't be like this. I gathered up my things at the tree base then dropped them again. The stream wasn't far; I wanted to wash first. I looked up, back at the tree, imagining I could see the outline of her nest again, a symbolic structure rebuilt in a different place each night. A refuge, a place in sickness to retreat to, a protective enclosure to experience birth and death. General in primates, even – the tendency to be born and to die in the night. The hour of the wolf. I thought of Ivan, my father. Driving to the hospital after the call at 03.28, neither John nor I speaking for the length of the journey, John extending a hand to my back as we closed the car door and faced up to the entrance. I saw John, the cottage. I pictured our new house. All I wanted, I thought, was to be home.

XIII

He found, waking in the morning to the dim light coming in through the fog and the curtain, that he was bleeding. Not only had his previous wounds opened, spilling out into the bed-sheets, but new scratches were ripped across his body. He looked to his fingernails and saw crusted blood. The doctor, he thought, must be wrong; the tears and scratches weren't provoked by nightmares but by the return of memory while he slept. Perhaps he wasn't attacking an imaginary figure – this wasn't about violence or aggression – he was simply grasping for something, reaching towards the life that he remembered, trying desperately to claw back those moments, to dive in, to move closer, to burst through to that life again.

He was distracted through the morning's session, the doctor twice asking what was wrong, what it was that was on his mind. He told him no, nothing was wrong, nothing was on his mind. The doctor looked at him doubtfully, prolonging his gaze, before finally pushing on. The day took an age to pass. As soon as the doctor left he tried, systematically, to record the previous evening's memory, the arm arcing over him, hoping that in writing it down it would flow, the image would animate and more would come. But he was frustrated; transcribing didn't work. The table downstairs appeared sterile, remote. He struggled to connect with the memory that had affected him so powerfully the night before.

He retired to bed early, crushing the sedative capsule and dropping it into the sink. As he pulled the sheet over him, he looked to the radio set on the bedside cabinet, focusing on it, trying to recreate the same conditions, willing the memory to return.

He sat up. The room was dark. He must have fallen asleep. He didn't remember turning off the lamp. Without thinking he turned to the time display on the cabinet, and he murmured her name. Her form returned, her breath, her warmth beside him where he lay. He saw her hazy, remote expression as she went to switch the dial. Suddenly another scene appeared and another, and he saw, in snatches, the whole of their life together, the years and years by each other's side. He saw isolated moments, snapping forwards and backwards in time, and knew he couldn't let the action go, couldn't let it disappear. Preserve the act, keep it alive. Start from here, the kinetic expression, movement, the real effect, Shel's arm moving in an arc over him, her character, the fact of her life.

He pictured her travelling with work, adapting her hotel room in the city, forming a brief and temporary culture, making small adjustments, leaning on the formalities, pressing on the room, making it different from all the others. Enjoying the thimble-sized capsules of milk, taking pleasure in delicately peeling off the paper tops, digging her elbows against her lower ribs, the heels of her hands together, the thumbs and forefingers pressing, peeling the tops away. The tray, the jug, the tall sticks of coffee, the paper-wrapped tea-bags, the boots left at the foot of the bed and the clothes hanging in the cupboard and folded over the chair pulled out at the desk. Writing to her mother each trip, postmarks for every new city. Still captivated by runways, walking slowly to the retractable steps, delaying the walk, with the strange lights flashing on the tarmac, never the smell of fuel you would expect, the odd toy-like vehicles darting between the terminal and the planes, the theatre of the runway, the dramatic horizons, the mysterious systems of lights, towers and flags.

He saw her backpack stamped over her shirt in sweat, saw her cycling to the university, saw all the books she carried, arriving with her hair wet, her face red, always new ideas on the journey in, the beginning of the day, breakthroughs, strings of connections appearing by themselves, the rush of the air cooling her smile, the wet shirt hung over the chair in her office, the blinds open for the eastern light edging a heat across the dampness, always knowing where she was, quick to orient herself in each new place – the wind and the tide, the sun and the stars – grateful for space just in getting off a bus, delaying, looking around, seeing where she was, where she had come to, as if it wasn't inevitable, carrying the alternatives and watching, fixing her eyes on the driver, oblivious to the line forming behind her, the muted expressions and the curses, the confusion of the line coming in, and saying slowly, clearly, 'Thank you,' nodding and stepping off.

Refusing to drink from any wine glass with the faintest finger smudge across it, the smear of a person on glass, cannot bring this to her face, as if the identity remained stuck. Modelling her voice according to the company, the ease of taking her for several different people, the sense that this is not controlled, none of this is controlled, it just happens. The sound of her voice, unable to extricate herself from it. The scowl on her lips realising she is wrong about something. The quiet movement, murmur as she tells herself not to be transparent, to compose herself, to remain neutral. Stopping always when she passes a mirror, suspicious, doubtful, never willingly appearing in photographs, leaving discreetly to the bar, the bathroom, sensing a picture is about to be composed, stepping aside and creating problems in ceremonies, birthdays, weddings, work events – everyone should be recorded – watching the composition from the side, curious. Sitting on the sofa in the evening, back against the arm, knees raised supporting articles, books, reading-glasses on and hair up, one sock pulled halfway off, rolling back, relieving the tension but keeping her toes and the lower part of her foot snug. Little treats, to feel better. Long evenings reading in the half-light. The desperate desire for the consolation that these evenings together were somehow still held, they continued. That he could reach out and feel this world they share still happening.

Late to meet her outside a bar, slowing before he reached her, watching her pacing, reading signs, posters, awnings, seeking messages, information, writing to distract her, the outline of her body moving across the street and back, her feet agitated, seeing her and being unusually aware of the architecture, the form of the street in the dark, the flux of unfamiliar people passing, the materiality of the scene with her inside it. Now urgently moving towards her raising one hand and trying not to look any higher, the tops of the buildings. The moment of surprise and transformation on her face. The extension of her body, reaching outwards and taller, shoulders higher, her arms around him, chestnut smell from her hair, damp from hanging rain, the cold of her cheek from waiting, the generation and exchange of heat across them, the prolonged hold of the embrace, the suggestion of flux, fluid bodies, the defencelessness of the two of them together.

Coming in, coming home, locking the door behind her, hanging the key on the pin, standing an extra moment facing it. Bent down, crouched, tugging her boots off, laying them carefully in position with the gentlest of thuds as the heels knock the wall, sighing, commenting to herself, collecting herself, rising up again, turning, opening the inner door, stepping in, presenting herself.

XIV

I refocused on sub-group C, paying particular attention to the apex female and matriarch, mother of the disappeared adolescent, C1. C1 was one of the candidates for seniority throughout the entire troop, with those who approached her displaying noticeable deference and subordination. More than any other animal, we were wary of taking C1's blood. C1 had one dependent daughter, less than a year old, kept, as if by lengths of rope, no further than a metre from her at all times. I watched, absorbed, the daughter play, her hesitant forays into independent recreation, tolerated with unwavering severity by the vigilant mother.

Our voices assumed a different quality in the rains, both because we had to amplify ourselves in order to be heard and because the more reflective acoustics created odd distortions. Distance was deceptive and it was hard to adapt, turning round surprised by the location of the other person. The pools formed in the storms were no longer temporary additions but grew larger with each day, changing the acoustics further. The rain fell constantly but variously, speed and intensity driven by the thickness of the vegetal obstructions. We heard it bouncing in scattered pool clusters, creating an odd sensation of circularity, of the water looping around us, ensnaring us. As the rain came indirectly, coated in matter by the time it hit the ground, our speech was indirect too. There were few horizontal or vertical clearings beyond the small area we'd used to set up camp. Discussing with Alice a favoured fruit source among my sub-group, I had the strange impression, despite the fact that I could see her, and that she was standing right there mere feet from me, and that I could see her lips moving at the same time, that the sound she made was actually coming from behind me. I turned twice, trying to find the sources of the strange echo.

The rains came heavier each day. I smelled rot in my clothes, my boots, and my ankles were becoming blotchy, apart from the bites, and starting to swell. The masks, the protective coats helped only so much; if you remained perfectly still for the duration of the downpour underneath the sheet of tarp and the transparent raincoat, it might be possible, in theory, to stay dry, but we had to continue moving according to the whim of each sub-group. We dried a little in the evenings over the small fire, Jane initially, to our confusion, appearing tentative and coy. Alice muttered something at her. Jane was embarrassed about putting her clothes out because of the smell.

It wasn't just that she appeared so naive and frail that irritated us, it was the regularity with which she complained about conditions.

'It's just us here, Jane,' Alice said. 'We're experiencing the same world you are. No-one else is listening.' Alice somehow was able to be direct and critical yet not offend Jane, something I was yet to learn.

I worried about my own symptoms, my vomiting, my restlessness and nausea late in the night. Coming into the rainy season, we were entering the period the animals were most likely to give birth, though with such a small group, and given the relative infrequency of birth in the species, approximately every four years, we wouldn't necessarily witness any; none of the animals we'd examined displayed signs of late-stage pregnancy. As well as births, the season brought a higher risk of parasitic infection, with tapeworms a problem. The animals, certainly in other documented communities, practised a form of self-medication, adjusting their diet in the rains to take on particular plants whose coarseness acted as a detoxifier, cleansing the body, at least some of the time, of the parasitic invasion. They swallowed the leaves whole, dragging the rougher matter through their gut, breaking up the parasite body – exactly the kind of process easily disrupted by a genetic switch: suddenly the self-medication doesn't function, and the parasite increasingly consumes the gut.

Infection was especially fraught in the case of animals that might be carrying a fetus. Jane complained persistently about her own health, and I wondered, in my tent, in the late evening, trying to wipe down what I could, conscious of my smell, which I inhaled gladly – damp sweat, light, pleasant tinge of urine from my shorts, sulphur from the bites I'd dug out, small punctures glowing orange and red on my arms, legs and even on my neck – checking the seal on my collection of notes, whether my unsympathetic reaction was driven from a sense that Jane was articulating something I feared myself – namely, that I might also be seriously ill. The smell again. I felt a mixture of pride and pity for it, something that accompanied me – a record of the things I did – and something that was me.

The rains, in the brief slivers of direct light, gave a silver, lucid aspect to the vegetation, which seemed to grow out wilder in real time before us, to become, in effect, a single indistinguishable mass, everything around us in the forest interlocking, feeding on itself, gaining symbiotic nourishment and taking on, as it often seemed, an outsize, giant aspect. It was difficult not to be intimidated, overwhelmed by the scale, which seemed even grander in its deceptive uniformity. In its adaptation to the rains, to the power and excess of them, to the relative lack of light and to the new patterns of behaviour in all orders of animal, the forest seemed to become transformed. Fungus attached to scale insects clamped sucking the life from stalks and leaves, parasites on parasites. Giant junglesop fruits appeared, an abundance too great for the animals in our sub-groups. Half-eaten specimens were scattered through the foliage, quickly consumed by the legions of ants emerging the moment, as if anticipating it, the rain ceased. Jane, understandably, was overwhelmed with work. Mushrooms shot up every day, every hour it seemed, in new places. Every time we lifted one the resultant absence, the cup-shaped hollow in the earth, produced an instant sucking sound, the hyphae seizing on the new direct access to surface rainwater. The whole of our camp began to smell of her collections, strung out in her tent and in the kitchen area under the simple roofs we'd improvised, and I even started to dream of their texture, of the fine, dense patterns both in the head of the bulb and everywhere beneath us, around us, in the ground.

The growth, the activity of the fungi, was astonishing. In theory there was nothing in-built that would limit it. Single fungal organisms could, in the right environment, grow out perennially, indefinitely, infinite lines webbing under the ground, bubbling up as brief instances of leathery fruit. Some had lived two thousand years. They emerged in such quantities they must surely have been eating up the forest. And yet the forest itself grew, too. As soon as the bulbs emerged, they withered and decayed. The mushrooms right in front of us actively recomposed the ground. The hyphae ate plant and animal matter and recycled it as their own fruits broke and their spores fanned out, lifted in the new turbid streams created in the rains.

Living insects were swept into the mouths of rapacious plants as larger animals were eaten up into the great lengths of hyphae in the soil. Even Alice appeared impressed next to this torrent of activity, the stuff of superstition, the beginning of stories, these transformations around us that might seem too great, too vast, too inexplicable to put down to a natural order.

I thought of the fat bulbs growing out in the moonlight. Jane described accelerated rates of bodily decay in certain climates, at certain times of the year, seeming to imply movement in these dead things, an occult reanimation breeding new mythologies, curses, monsters invented from malign forces we can never understand and can do little or nothing to appease.

Immediately the rain stopped there was this dripping near stillness, a hazy silver effect, a light sheen of mist revealing threads of fibre apparently hanging directly on the air, endless knots of impossibly delicate line glinting in refracted light and supporting ever enlarging globules of water, fat like pearls or eyes and bursting open as they fell to the ground.

We hadn't heard from the gates in six days. Loss of communication in the storms. Alice had anticipated this and on her advice we'd been careful with food, leaving a surplus from each day's rations so we wouldn't be stranded if there was a delay with the food drop. We'd been in the camp for over two weeks and, not knowing how much longer we'd have left, we woke with renewed urgency and set off earlier in the day before conditions deteriorated further. We'd worked quicker than anticipated, with only six animals left to sample, after which we could think about packing up.

Jane told us more than once there were fungi inside us, there always had been, something I tried to forget as the growths bloomed out rapidly after the long rain, large blotches, wounds erupting on the trees, appearing, I thought, like graphic interpretations of the alien levity, nausea and sickness I was intermittently still experiencing. In the built hollows of the trees, the long excavations drilled by social insects, were dazzling honeycomb designs, fungal agriculture, fields and gardens painstakingly grown out by the ants, used to feed and fatten their insensate young. It seemed that everywhere we chose to look, something fascinating was happening. Every inch of matter, if approached slowly and carefully, seemed to fold out infinitely, to inflate rapidly, and I imagined pulling on a line, a thread, spooling it out and never reaching an end. The density of life here was such that every niche, every single pocket of space, was appropriated, developed its own rhythms and sequences, contained its original relationships and novel behaviours, producing, in total, an unfathomable variety. Each pocket was key, every action initiated a chain reaction, creating a dizzying array of nested hierarchies, and it was the quiet, autonomous, undirected nature of this total effect, the fact, broadly speaking, that ecology worked, that was the most humbling and interesting detail of all.

Now that our supplies had dwindled, and we had no means of finding out if or when replenishments would arrive, we had to improvise, to walk out further, to start taking things directly from the forest. In this, and given that as much as conditions allowed we had still to follow and observe our sub-groups, we took on aspects of the bonobos' diet ourselves, gathering surplus fruit after the animals had moved on. In sub-group C I observed two adult males carefully inspect a termite mound that was breaking apart in the rain. This cathedral mound, originally several metres tall, was now partly exposed on two sides, revealing the packed networks and channels of its air-conditioned interior. Though the vast majority of the insects had evacuated, the clumps of fungi they had planted still remained; the apes alternately pushed inside with a finger, scraping out the contents and bringing fungus drizzled with drowned insects to their lips. And while we didn't eat from fungi raised inside trees or in mounds – it was perfectly safe, but the fact it had been planted, been tended to, been raised by beetles, termites and by ants, by the fact, that is, that in this sense it was partly synthetic, seemed to put us off; I was aware this was contradictory as in our day-to-day lives, in our homes, in our cities, we routinely ate foods that had been subject to similar levels of care and husbandry by animals, it somehow not seeming to matter, not to occur to us, in that context, but the three of us were in instant, silent, automatic agreement that we shouldn't eat what had been grown – we did, under Jane's instruction, fry bulbs blooming wildly by the edge of the stream.

Losing myself in long investigation of a single tiny burrow produced in the soil by an upturned stone, a rotted fruit or by the prints of something moving, I eventually pulled myself back, lifted myself out. It took a moment to acclimate to the wider picture of the forest. For that moment, looking flatly to the trees and vines and the outline behind them of the valley we were in, I didn't see any of those things, wasn't aware of them, wasn't able to conceptualise them. Instead I saw something like an infinite series of distinct, studded iterations; a vast aggregate of separate pockets, each one unique, original, harbouring living events, microsecond by microsecond, that had never happened before and were never to be repeated again. I had convinced myself, at least, that I could see like this, see the area not as a single field but as an array, a patchwork of individual points whose multitudes seemed, in this moment, before my nervous system failed and gave up and it all became familiar again, to have dizzying, awe-inducing, even cosmological implications. I saw – I thought I saw – the vast energy and effort expended simply to sustain life from one moment to the next. A structure billowing out, unfurling exponentially, and in the same instant contracting back to zero, a complex, reiterative, non-linear growth – the creation of the universe – something over nothing – again and again. As I gazed at it time seemed to suspend, and in that one elastic moment I felt a sense of possibility and immensity that shook me with its force, brought me almost to tears, being really aware, for what felt like the first time, of the silent expanse of living, feeling matter all around me. Before it could mean something, before I could truly consider notions of privilege, responsibility, shame, the forest built itself up again, appeared to actively, visually reconstruct itself, fluidly reforming into unity, and there I was inches from a piece of felled and rotting trunk, Alice scraping the ladle against the sides of the pot, my knees, separating out from the ground where I'd crouched, creaking stiff and sore, the smell of the soup activating my hunger and reminding me there wasn't long until dark, and what I had experienced – the ongoing evaporation and consolidation of the forest – was only residual, was difficult to put into words, was undermined by doubt over its authenticity. I wiped the sweat away – we really weren't getting enough food – and I got up, stumbling on the first step I took.

XV

They were building their house. That's where he had been when the attack happened, waking days later in the bedroom in the cottage, emptied out, uncomprehending. The cottage was temporary. The unfamiliar objects, the cupboards, the drawers, the wax raincoat, the steel-capped boots, they belonged to friends, colleagues of Shel's, who had let the place and would be coming back. Their own things were in storage; they'd brought essential items only. He recalled the radio playing from the cab as the movers tipped their flat into a truck, Shel wrapping her favourite books and jewellery in bubble-plastic, anticipating the tight corners on the road. Everything now was stacked in pallets in a warehouse by the sea. Shel grew up by the sea and even locked inland she tried instinctively to stay on the tidal side, crossing roads, choosing one restaurant over another, still miles from water. Now the inside of their house was stacked there, vulnerable to the mould spreading in the fog.

The doctor knocked, standing formally as usual on the steps, waiting for John to invite him in; he led him to the kitchen. He had done his best to conceal the fresh wounds, washing the blood from his scalp and pulling on a high-necked jumper. The doctor couldn't know what he was doing, washing the sedative down the sink each evening, determined to stay close to the memories of Shel while he slept. Not only did it seem inappropriate to share these memories with the doctor, it felt dangerous too, as if exposing the stories might jeopardise them. He remained vulnerable, a little unsure of things. Whole periods were still missing – of the attack he knew only that he was visiting the building site, that he had sensed something and a sudden impact had smothered him. He retained no recall of waking, either at the hospital or at the site.

The doctor wasn't the only threat. Every day the fresh spread of the mould astonished him. It was as if the more he remembered – the more he thought he remembered – the more the fungus grew, taking nourishment from him, drawing strength from each lived moment and expanding. Again he sensed how vulnerable his memory was, how easily it might be brushed away. He had been hurt; his recall was taken from him. And now that he sensed it returning, he perceived the danger around him, on the walls and ceiling, growing in from the window frames, waiting, ready to prey.

'John? John, you're okay?'

'I'm fine.'

'You appear upset.'

He let out a sigh, shifted position in the seat. He pressed his temple. 'I'm worried about the stitching. I think it's come loose again.'

The doctor told him to bow his head. The inspection didn't take long. He stepped back and rubbed his hands. 'John, it hasn't come loose by itself, has it? You've been scratching at it. You are still taking the medication? You realise how important it is? The skin around the wound is becoming inflamed. If you continue like this an infection will take root. Look, it's time for me to go; I'll check on this again tomorrow.'

After he had seen the doctor out, promising he would continue on the course of sedatives, he wondered whether he should contact the university and have them pass a message to Shel. He could keep it brief, tell her he'd been involved in an accident and had been to hospital but was recovering well, recuperating from home. He tried to look at it from Shel's perspective: was it in her own interest to know this? She was far away on work, in difficult and challenging circumstances – a message coming from him, relayed through her employers, possibly distorted, would at best inconvenience and alarm her, at worst bring her out of the project. He couldn't risk such a misunderstanding. He'd wait until he could talk to her himself. Besides, how could he even contact the university? He had been told to stay in the house, away from the light, and driving was still off-limits. The router blinked red; he was without his phone, his contacts list.

She would be angry with him, later, for not telling her, for not finding a way, but this trip was too important. It was the culmination of her professional work so far, maybe even the culmination of everything she'd devoted her life to since she was a child. He saw her childhood home, a village of two thousand on a slope facing the sea. Catherine and Ivan – her parents – worked with film and TV crews, leasing out landscapes. The village gave tax breaks to the crews who came to film by the castle, by the sea. The beginning of Shel's fear of cameras, of being caught in a composition. Cameras and mics roaming through the streets. Shel hiding in her room, wearing a disguise, peering over the wall at the end of the garden. The large black parasols on summer afternoons, planted on the beach, visible for miles, ominous, beetle-like, as if emerging upwards through the sand. Worrying the tents would be swept away at high tide. That they wouldn't get out in time. Startled, distraught, coming home from school seeing nothing remained of them, no trace on the beach. Stirring in the rock pools, unresponsive and alone.

Her parents provided plants for filming, managing to convince producers they couldn't work with artificial varieties, that it had to be the real thing. Real and consistent for the film's duration. Tending to the plants, looking after them, a lot of work. Showing realistic development of plants across the time-line depicted in the film, the consecutive seasons. And the crews might need to build a foreign set, something that doesn't grow naturally in the climate. We can take care of that, too, Catherine said. Shel riding home in the back of the pick-up, holding on to her favourite plants, hugging them to her knees, retrieved from a film that had ended, a landscape, she said, that had collapsed.

It was, ironically, in thinking about the techniques of memory training that he recalled the nature of his own profession. He had been sitting at the table in the kitchen, the empty bowl from dinner still set next to him, when he realised the process of visualisation the doctor encouraged was a tool he used all the time. As a software engineer and coder, he would walk through each data structure he wrote as if it were a real place. The larger programs he coded, hundreds of thousands of lines each, were like cities, every part of which – every paving slab, every alley, every street – he knew intimately, exploring the topography day and night. Shel said his work was disappointingly non-dynamic – he never seemed to be doing anything, just sitting there, stretching back or leaning in, never the rapid blur of hands skimming keys that she'd imagined. Only a fraction of work actually involved setting down code; most of the time you were visualising it. Rather than architects, coders were more like urban planners, occupied less with the elegance of a single building than with the efficacy of a huge, sprawling city. Does it work? Are the necessary fundaments – plumbing, energy, transport – in place? How does each area of growth affect everything that preceded it? It wasn't that he was naturally cynical – coders had this wariness driven into them, they had to anticipate errors everywhere, flaws could arrive in the most unexpected places. A short shell program written years earlier could inadvertently counteract a new structure, creating a loop whose endless vibration brought the whole system down. So he was constantly watching for this, simulating the effects of each new line, each command, each character.

'Who has arranged all this?' he said to the doctor as he was leaving. 'Who is paying for it, these home visits? Is it work?'

'Yes, that's right, John. It's your employers. The cover is in your contract.'

He watched the doctor from the doorway until he disappeared. He wondered who among his colleagues had been told what had happened, and how much they knew. Had the information been passed to his friends? Did they think he was still in hospital? How many messages had he missed? He felt a warm glow at the thought of their concern, a concern exacerbated by his inability to respond, and he looked forward to seeing everyone again, to returning from this dramatic isolation.

He was excited by the progress he was making, becoming integrated once again in the world, feeling the freshly collected content of his life. How much more was there? What was he still to recover? This sensation of expectation, of anticipating unlimited stories, *his* stories, was inexpressibly strange; he wondered, nervously, what would happen if the stories felt unfamiliar, if he had changed irreparably and the memory no longer fit. He felt conscious of himself as a place, a physical expanse. He imagined, awkwardly, the data implications, the impossible volume of a whole life's return. How could it happen in a finite amount of time? One memory after another, piece by piece returning? Wasn't there too much, always? Boundless information upon limited space? He worked harder, hungry for more, inhabiting the memories, considering the perspective and wondering what it looked like facing the other way, what was behind it, where did this street lead to, and then this one, what would happen if he pushed it this way, then that way, rotating the globe. Pushing the images around, he imagined he was imprinting, etching on a space. He found that instead of simply trying to recall something, trying to remember what happened, he was simulating it, imagining alternatives in parallel forward lines, generating binary trees and nested interrelations that appeared to have no end – first his desk, his terminal, then the office, the projects he worked on, the clients he met, the colleagues he drank coffee with, going further and further, the fractals radiating out.

He lifted his head up, distracted by the humming of the fridge, the vibrations pushed along the floor against his feet. He recalled a news report that had been sent around the office sometime before the attack about a fridge of the same model, an 'auto-replacer'. The sensor – a single red line – watched all activity, and if a listed key-item was removed for more than three hours then another was sent. If a barcode was within eight hours of expiring, another was sent. If waste gas was detected, the source was identified and another was sent. In the news feature the fridge was ordering vast amounts of food, multiple repeat orders of the same few items, which piled up initially on the doorstep but eventually circled all the way around the house. The automated deliveries continued, the signal reiterating its command again and again, the new food wasting in the heat and rain. No-one had reported anything, and the security services ultimately came only because the account had run into debt, no longer able to pay for the food which was still arriving even as security broke down the door. She was lying on the tiled kitchen floor and had been dead six days. The official explanation was a flaw in the scope of the sensors; the fridge had picked up traces of waste gas from the body and read this as a signal to order more food, to replace the thing that had begun to rot. The story had drawn grim laughter – the company was humiliated; there had been terminations – but he kept thinking of the stuck signal, the repeat command to order more food. Shel said it was like one of those dogs that sits whining by its owner after they'd slipped and died, as if willing them to wake up. But he saw it differently; his understanding was that the mechanism was trying to replace the person. It picked up broken-down foods in the body's waste gas and ordered fresh examples. Because the rot remained, it ordered new material desperately, urgently, excessively. He'd been haunted by the idea that the mechanism was building up, around the outside of the house, a large store of the foods that had been inside the body, as if eventually, after a certain threshold had been reached, the person would collect herself again, stand up and only then, after the rot had gone, would the signal go silent.

A sharp pain in his scalp distracted him, breaking his concentration, and the memory tumbled away. He fidgeted, pressed his finger to his scalp. The wound felt warm to the touch, and he remembered the doctor's caution about infection. Perhaps he should put some ice on it, take some of the heat away. He pushed himself up from the table and entered the vestibule, heading for the freezer. The wall connecting the two doors was darkened by the spread of mould. Walking past it, he felt a new, bright pain on his scalp. He cried out, put his hand to his head. He instinctively stepped back out of the vestibule and the pain subsided. When he stepped in again, it flared up. He stood at a safe distance in the doorway and looked around at the mould, noticing for the first time how bad it had got. He was surprised the doctor had said nothing. The walls were covered, ribbed with dark folds. It almost resembled a neocortex, he thought, morbidly, the unpacked surface of a brain.

XVI

Jane asked if she could speak with me. Alice was off camp; I was using the last of the daylight, taking my things out of the tent, attempting to dry them, sorting them – clothes, documents, equipment – into a kind of order. It was a losing battle. I tried it day after day but there was never enough time, the darkness and rain coming suddenly over my shoulder. It was infuriating, distracting me; no room inside, no light outside.

'Still trying to unpack, I see,' Jane said. I turned and she was carrying something. She looked different, walking cautiously, uncertain. She was worried about something. I stood up. 'Will you tell me what you think of this?' she said, thrusting the recording device at me, as if eager to be rid of it.

At first, I heard what I expected to. A branch falling close to the recorder, leaves rustling, sporadic calls from the troop a distance away. Further calls, the first alarm barks. They got louder, no longer just one individual seeking a response. It became a chorus, more urgent than the earlier calls. Suddenly it stopped.

'What did you think,' Jane said, 'of the footsteps?'

They came towards the end. The first notable thing was that they were loud. The pace suggested two legs. I became embarrassed. 'Well, that's me, I think,' I said, trying to hide my face. 'I must have got up in the night.'

'Must have?'

'Well, I mean, I did. To use the toilet.'

'You walked that way? The latrine's the other side. At 04.35? That's the time stamp.'

'Well, I didn't go to the latrine, as such, Jane, I was practically sleeping, I don't remember exactly. I just wanted to get outside the camp. I was ... sick again. In the night. Obviously I shouldn't have walked past the recorder. I didn't mean to – I'm sorry.'

'You're sure this is you? I don't think it's you. Listen.' She played the recording back again. She paused it. 'Look,' she said, 'I've isolated the footsteps. They're louder, they suggest more pressure than yours. You're, what, five seven? Listen to the gap between each footfall – it's not consistent with your stride.'

'Maybe I was just walking oddly. Like I said, I wasn't feeling myself.'

She shook her head vigorously. 'No,' she said quietly, as if hopelessly. 'You're not listening. It's something else.'

XVII

He was jolted, snapped awake. His head thudded and a dull pain throbbed in his neck. There was something wet over the pillow. He reached for his neck and flinched as he touched the open wound. Pressing it with one hand, he found the light switch with the other, briefly blinding himself by the illumination. When the bright white spots had settled in his vision, he saw the blood seeping through his hands. He climbed out of the bed and went into the small adjacent bathroom. Hesitantly, he stripped off his T-shirt and looked into the mirror. His neck was bloodied and three long narrow scratches were dug into his chest. He wiped and padded his neck with paper and, after managing to stem the flow, made out a new pair of short scratches, almost like punctures. Opening the mirror door he found dressing and a bandage. He noticed his nails were clean – the blood and broken skin must have washed off in the sink. He leaned back and held his head. He was destroying himself. He should have listened to the doctor, continued on the medication. It had seemed wrong, turning away from consciousness in the night, when the memories were strongest. He'd thought he'd be safe from open wounds, cutting his nails back until they bled, but it hadn't been enough. He had continued, blindly, tearing through.

He turned off the light, and as he stepped into the corridor, a capsule and a glass of water in his hands, he heard the firm, unmistakable sound of a door closing.

At first he assumed it was a car door, somebody waiting outside. Perhaps the sound carried differently in the fog, especially so in the night, in silence; the vehicle could have been hundreds of metres away, by the farm. He listened for an engine, footsteps, voices. Perhaps it was the doctor arriving with some new crucial information and, with no other means of contacting him, coming directly to the house. Had something happened to Shel? Was it Catherine? Was it a representative from Shel's work coming to bring him news?

He retreated to the bedroom and laid the glass and capsule down on the side table. He saw his hands shaking, the hair rising on his arms. He breathed slowly and carefully, whispering that everything would be okay, pleading for everything to be okay. Whatever happened, let her be okay.

He heard the same sound again, a soft thud, only closer this time, as if inside the house. He turned off the lamp, covering himself under darkness. He knew, now, that this wasn't a vehicle. He must have forgotten to lock the door. Perhaps the doctor had not closed it properly, and now it was swinging, hitting off the frame.

He waited by the bedroom door in the dark. He didn't want to go down, didn't want to see. His eyes turned to the sedative capsule and the glass of water. He could sleep, let it all drift away, wake in the morning, wait as usual for the doctor and for the pattern of the past two weeks to resume and repeat.

The next sound confirmed that it wasn't the wind. Though he knew it was familiar, knew he'd heard it countless times before, he struggled to place it. A loud, prolonged screeching, like something being dragged. His heart thumped; the room grew colder. It was the table, downstairs. Someone had pulled out a chair at the table.

He panicked, tried to settle himself, tried to think. Though his instinct was to stay, he knew he couldn't hide there, trapped if the intruder ascended. He had no option but to go downstairs. He had to confront this, whatever it was. He looked around the dark room, hunting for something, anything, that he could carry as a weapon. But the room was bare. He took a steadying breath and crept towards the landing. At the top of the stairs he smelled the familiar iron odour from the walls. He strained his neck, trying to see down into the kitchen. He froze. A single chair was pulled out. A figure occupied the seat, facing the wall. Slouched, arms on the table, calm, oblivious to his own presence on the stairs.

He didn't want to alert the intruder. He pressed gently onto the banisters, and slowly, agonisingly, he began to descend, making his way silently down the wooden steps. He kept his head lowered, watching his feet, moving deliberately, avoiding sight of the table and the guest. His mouth remained closed; he focused on his breath.

Reaching the last step, he looked up. The table was before him, the chair pulled out. A sense of movement around him, a rush, a sudden shift, a change in the atmosphere. The seat was empty, the door was closed. He wheeled around, trying to locate the figure, but whoever it was, whatever it was, was gone. He slammed the bolt across the front door, locking it securely, and he let out a shaky breath. He went around the table, inspecting each of the chairs. He went through the corridor and checked the bathroom. He looked out the window on to the driveway. He couldn't see anything in the fog. Had he dreamed it? Had he not been fully awake when he came downstairs? He knew he should stay in the safety of the house, but he needed certainty. He took a torch from the kitchen and put his coat on and laced his boots. He took the key, opened the door and, for the first time in over two weeks, stepped outside. The raw cold startled him. The fog was visible in shafts of moonlight cutting through the darkness. The conviction, still, that someone was there, that someone had been inside and that they remained close to him, concealed in the fog. He recalled Shel's warning on the drive to the airport, saying everything is different in the fog – speed, sound, distance, it's all distorted; everything is unreliable. You can't trust your senses, she said, you have to be careful. She told him he was going faster than he realised; the scene outside only appeared to be unchanging. He heard her again – you can't trust your senses, John.

Whoever was there, whoever had been inside the house, could emerge without warning, appear instantly out of the vapour. The construction site again, the whirring sound, the air rushing, the blind impact of something shattering coming out of the sky. He listened for external breath, looked for unnatural shadows. He inched forward, shone his light, swept it in an arc. The driveway; the car; the trees ahead; the beginning of the fields, insubstantial through the fog. He approached the car, tried the door; it opened. He stood a moment holding the door, feeling the unfamiliarity of his own car after all this time. He considered the space inside, the two front seats. He leaned in. Blood on the passenger side, on the headrest and on the seat cushion. He shone the light further; no blood on the driver's seat. Nothing in the back. He was about to shut off the torch and return inside when he noticed an object beneath the passenger seat, something reflective, glimmering as the torch passed over it. He searched again with the light, caught it, reached in and gathered up his phone. It was smeared in blood. Smudges of a fingerprint over the screen. He must have tried to call at the site. He had been awake at the site; he had tried to find help. It didn't make sense. What had happened immediately after the attack? Who had taken him? The screen was cracked, but he pressed the power switch and was surprised to see blue light bursting out, sending its own beam, lighting a channel through the fog.

XVIII

None of us heard the buzzing at the time. It might have been a drone, probably one of the security drones that had gone off track. It was sometimes hard to appreciate the real volume of the recording, after you'd tuned into it and started to adjust the settings on the device. But this seemed louder, faster than a drone, and later in the day, walking through the forest, I thought it was closer to that of a light aircraft.

It came at the beginning of the night's recording. Alice suggested it was internal, a mechanical fault, but after several checks we couldn't attribute it for certain. It began as a wide fluttering noise, becoming louder, closer, as if travelling at great speed, and seemed to come from different points, each driving towards a centre. There was an odd high-pitched whistling, wavering around the point of audibility. I thought of the doctor again – a simple association from the first real thing the recording reminded me of, the low flight of a light aircraft. The doctor stranded, continuously unaccounted for within the airport zone. The conflicting simultaneous messages claiming his presence in disparate locations. The insistence of various staff, who, as far as I could tell, absolutely and vehemently believed what they were saying, that he had landed, he had returned, he had never been there.

*

Somebody had left food out. One of us had not been circumspect in cleaning. That must be what had happened; someone must be to blame. They had to be. Alice stormed back to her tent, Jane sat vacantly on the ground, I went over the prints again, marked on the small clearing in front of our tents. Look at it, analyse it, what is it, what does it indicate. I squatted and put my face against the mud. Cloven hoofs, toes two and three large, pressing firmly into the mud, with the flanked claws, one and four, skimming the surface, suggesting either a boar or another unknown animal moving at speed, its ankle joints giving way, flanked claws descending and skimming as a light impression. Despite the large number of prints there was a pattern, clearly tracing the movement of a single animal. Prints from the fore limbs were larger and heavier than the hind. This suggested that the animal was accelerating. But how, in the dense, thick vegetation all around us? Where was it going? The tracks overlapped, printing over each other, as if the animal had got stuck, going round and round in the same space. I imagined it moving quickly, in a storm, imagined its enclosed, limited galloping, its too much purpose taking it nowhere.

How could we not have heard? What had brought it here? The night's audio recorded several alarm calls in the troop and we were a little unnerved at the coincidence. The prints were not produced by anything that should have scared them. It wasn't feline; it wasn't something that could get up in the trees.

It must have been dazed, scared by the same thing, possibly, that had terrified the troop.

There were silent episodes of sheet lightning, white electric charges that began to hurt my jaw. It was easier not to speak. I wrote a lot. We were yet to find any further signs of a real threat, either on the ground or on the animals' bodies. When I couldn't sleep, I imagined the animals were warning of something imminent, something which hadn't come yet but they could sense around them in the forest. And I tried to imagine what this thing could be.

XIX

He didn't sleep, he locked the doors, he kept the lights off. He didn't understand it: the doctor had assured him he had checked the car for the phone. It wasn't possible he could have missed it. Why would he lie? Did the doctor somehow not want him to recover and to leave the house? He remained as still as possible, alert to any sound, listening for the slightest tremor in the air. He removed his phone slowly from his pocket, carrying the soft blue glow in both hands. His fingers stumbled on the keypad. The numbers were loose and fluid, and when he went to key in one number he pressed several others as well. An error message appeared, telling him he had entered the wrong code and that his identity could not be verified. He waited for the shaking to subside, the excess energy to slip from his hands, then the combination to come back, the keys he'd pressed a million times.

The blue glow of the phone had an odd chemical appearance, as if marking a volatile substance. Feeling the pulse of information moving through his fingers, he thought of how tantalisingly close everything was: contact again, the wider world, Shel returning, their ongoing life together. Open the phone, check on messages from Shel, contact work, request updates from the agent on construction of the house. But even being this close, he was still so far away. Even were he to remember his code, he could see the empty signal bar at the top of the screen. He still couldn't call anyone. He couldn't drive anywhere. He was bereft. He realised, as if for the first time, the extent of his isolation.

He woke slumped on the table, the stitching in his head infected, the pain constant. There was a dim light settling through the kitchen; the stillness felt unnatural, artificial, as if poised and on the point of collapse. He imagined the effect of several people concealed in the house, stilled, controlling their breath, waiting to emerge. Would he hear them? Would he know for sure? He got up slowly, unsteady while the pain radiated from his scalp. He felt the wound on his chest and removed the bandage from his neck. He examined each room methodically, ensuring nothing else had been disturbed. He powered on his phone again, trying not to think, to rely on reflex action in his fingers, but still the pass code wouldn't come. He laughed humourlessly; he had retained the information to set the washing machine, but not this.

Perhaps he had a fever, the infection worse than he realised. It might explain what had happened the night before, the intruder at the table. No-one had been in the house, of course. He must have dreamed it, agitated with fever, made unreasonable inferences from the sound of distant doors closing. What mattered was the car, the blood on the seats, his phone. The fact that the doctor had lied to him about checking the car.

From that one deception, a whole concatenation of questions appeared, branching out one from the next. How had he got to the hospital? What exactly had the doctor told him about his condition when he was admitted? Who had authorised his release while he was still at such an early stage of recovery, barely able to care for himself? Why had he still not been shown any paperwork? Definitive proof of the results of the tests? He needed to think clearly, needed to decide what to do. The one thing he knew was that he couldn't continue like this, couldn't stay trapped in his own home.

XX

The prints returned the following night. The impressions were clearer and I was able to study the animal in more detail. The animal, this time, was moving cautiously, as if to avoid detection. The marks indicated anticipation, intent. The fore feet were placed on the ground separately, consecutively. I pictured the hind legs appearing to will contact with the fore, the animal seeming almost to step into itself, suddenly arriving further along the ground. The walking stride was approximately eighty centimetres in length. The short stride and clear straddle implied that, counter to the previous prints and to my earlier speculation, the animal was hunting.

Were it not for the cloven hoofs we would have been confident we were dealing with a juvenile leopard, perhaps on one of its first lone hunts. This would have explained the repeated alarm of the troop. But the marks we saw were more like that of a boar. Was it a single, isolated, perhaps wounded creature we were facing? A dangerously unpredictable boar?

We had to be better at clearing our signs. We built over the latrine with piles of fresh heaped earth, put leaves and stones gathered from the stream on top. We urinated further downstream, shared the trowel and dug a foot down each time we needed to defecate. At meals we wrapped remains into second bags and buried them. Rather than taking a bucket to wash, we went singly, directly to the stream, so our cleaning would wash off too. Without renewed contact from the gates we wouldn't be able to communicate our new position. They wouldn't find us when they came in. So we couldn't move. I was more worried about the other possibility, that, having moved to a new site, the animal would follow us. We would then know that we were being hunted. I tried not to think about the rumours, the animals strung up in the trees, the skin of their necks flayed. We couldn't leave the park, not yet. The storms were making it harder to isolate the animals and take our samples, and we still had three to go.

The hoofs returned a third night. Again, the nature of the impressions indicated the animal was stalking. There was no advantage, at this point, in pretending the situation wasn't serious. There was no doubt we interested the animal. However unlikely it might have seemed, I felt the animal was measuring us, surveying us. An attack may yet be imminent. We had taken turns to stay up, and though on several occasions we had shone our light into the darkness, on hearing what appeared to be a branch snapping underfoot, a light splash in one of the new pools, we were yet to see a definitive form. The prints had appeared, impossibly, in the slow daylight. We groaned, cursed, began packing our first things. I wrote what was intended to be a brief account of what had happened, covered it and tied it down on the most prominent tree by our camp. We were close to the given coordinates and the rangers would almost certainly find the place. We didn't know how far out we'd have to go. I'd have to return here, to the present site, to amend the account as soon as I had the new coordinates. I briefly surveyed the rest of our things, imagined carrying everything. As we'd consumed most of our food and gas supplies, it should have been easier to transport it, but the opposite was the case. Our stuff seemed, if anything, to have grown. The temptation in these poor conditions – lack of sleep and diminished diet, isolation both from ourselves and from all others, worries about illness and, of course, the unattributed nature of what was continuing to happen around us – was to believe we were cursed, that it was all hopeless, that we were bound to fail in this and the best, most honest thing to do was simply stop, lay ourselves on the ground and admit that we couldn't carry on. I controlled my breath and forced my eyes open. We could not leave the park, could not flee like this, our work incomplete, nothing resolved, unable to account for what had happened. We were just weaker, that was all, and it was natural that everything appeared heavier now.

XXI

It had spread to other objects, appearing on two of the plates on the draining-board by the sink, on the still damp linen and on the clothes hanging in the vestibule. It reached further across the wall, on which the first cracks had started to appear; unchecked, the damp would bring down the house. He imagined he could hear the popping of thousands of spores released each second, amplified in his brain, the yeast budding in his open scalp, the infection poisoning his blood, making his body weaker, the manner of his thinking more frenzied.

He wasn't sure how much time had passed since the doctor last visited. Everything was covered in a fine layer of mould, like ash after a fire. He had even found it reaching into the cupboards, searching out the things he held most precious. Mould on Shel's winter coat, working on the seasons' dust stored under the stiff collar, which she had liked to wear up but which had fallen over time, hanging unused. The mould, in growing over her collar, made a claim on her, as if it knew her, knew her history, every place she'd been to and everything she'd done, every time she'd turned her head in interest, every time she'd become distracted, every reverie, knew this and knew how she walked, how she'd learned to walk, who she watched when she crawled and took her first step, the smiles on Ivan's and Catherine's faces as they saw her move, attempt to stand, and falter, and go on trying, climbing over furniture, pushing against the wall, lifting herself up again. All this, he thought, was recognised by the thousands of spores budding and developing in the hard compacted wool collar of her coat.

He took the collar in his hand, felt it give, felt it, everything that was acknowledged in it, the uncountable iterations of Shel's identity, to be on the verge of collapse. Powder soft, the black-green smear carried away in his fingers.

The spores turned under his nails. As he looked down from Shel's coat he saw his feet and felt a great pity for them, for the weight that they carried. Each piece of chipped skin, every scar, every deformation in the outgrowth of a nail, every blotch, every asymmetric hair growth, formed a transparent record of his life. He remembered, what seemed so long ago now, being out in the open, running, thudding again and again off a hard surface, then not thudding but springing, moving lightly and making only minimal contact with the ground.

Kept to the cottage, confined by the fog and by his illness, he missed it, missed it all, even the rough feel of the wool socks on the base of his feet as he ran, the fibrous, sweaty crunch, hard skin stretched over the bone. He missed it desperately, sensation, real sensation, the most ordinary and unremarkable experience of life. Attached to the cottage, the mould around him a kind of company, he saw the growth taking nutrients wherever it could, taking pollen, vapour, taking himself, his own body and all its ongoing processes.

Taking his mind, his memory, his thoughts – energy intensive and attractive – every shard of perception and awareness more material for its growth, further proof of his confinement in the smallest room and the room closest to the outside, an outside he thought he might never see again. It seemed remarkable, incredible, wonderful that he had ever been anywhere else. He tried to keep remembering, to recall his whole life, the most fleeting impression onwards. He continued, another sensation, pain first, pain strongest, recalling the ache in his head after the attack, the tenderness in his mouth, his lower face, the rawness and the sense of that part of his body being unsupportable, recalled the way he lay in bed and his efforts to find the least agonising position to set himself, to be himself, to have himself continue in, felt unbearable tenderness for the person laying the body down and trying to manage pain, trying not to panic, to be reasonable, to go on living with it, shifting position by increments, felt astonishment towards this level of perseverance and optimism, trying every new position, putting the body here and then there, shifting millimetres further one direction and then another, a grotesque form of what he had been doing his whole life – walking, moving, taking himself from place to place, this impossible companionship, this ceaseless accompaniment, bringing him always somewhere, seeking out old places and invariably returning to the familiar, carrying on, always, he had to, there was nowhere else, adjusting the position by increments, millimetres, seeing how the new arrangement felt, how it fit.

There was a sudden noise from outside, close. A dragging and a thud, repeating. The vestibule door was open. The sound was coming from the steps by the door. The sharp retort of three knocks. He stayed where he was, listening, hearing feet shuffling on the doorstep. The doctor called out in a bright, cheery voice, a tone that felt rehearsed.

'John? Hello, John? I know you're there. I can hear you. Is there a problem? Is anything the matter, John?'

He didn't answer.

He flinched, hearing a rattling sound as the doctor seized the handle. The door shook in its frame – the whole downstairs level seemed to rattle. He was dizzy again; he thought he might be about to faint. He put his hand up to his scalp, feeling the heat beneath his fingertips. He thought perhaps he should let the doctor in, let him attend to the infection, but he wasn't sure he could trust him. Silence from outside. He crept closer to the door, entering the vestibule. The pain in his scalp worsened, but he ignored it as he approached the panel of frosted glass. He peered through the warped glass, seeing if he could make out any shadows. The doctor must have gone.

The door shook again and he recoiled, saw the doctor's silhouette against the glass, his long arms, his hat. His face was pressed against the door and his words came out distorted. He thought he heard water in his mouth, hanging saliva, as the doctor struggled to get his words out.

'John, it's me. John? I just want to check you're okay. I just want to make sure there aren't any problems, and that you've not had an accident. Don't keep me out here, John. Let me in. If you don't signal to me then please be aware that I will return. I will come back throughout the day, and at a certain point I will be left with no choice. Do you understand? Mr Harper? John? Are you there?'

'I'm here.'

'Open the door, John.'

'Not today. It's my throat. I think I'm coming down with something. I don't want to infect you. A day on my own would be good. I'll see you tomorrow.'

'I don't think that's such a good idea, John.' His head turned on the other side of the glass; the doctor had seen something, was considering something. 'John,' he said, his tone more measured, 'I have certain responsibilities I need to attend to. I really do think you should open the door. John?'

He heard his breath, a quick panting noise, something expressed through the nose, a note of desperation.

'I really think it's in your best interests to invite me in. Don't you agree, John?'

XXII

Death most likely occurred through the night, adjacent to her mother in their nest. Alice had found her, and despite the previous nights' prints no wounds or marks indicated an attack. The coincidence, however, unnerved us. I said I would investigate; Alice and Jane should continue monitoring the other groups as best they could. We had to continue working, had to occupy ourselves. Waiting, huddled in our tent, was the worst thing we could do.

I determined to record everything. The mother (C_I) carried the deceased infant, the dependent daughter she'd been keeping such careful watch over, while the sub-group formed at the beginning of the day, and both were included in core group activities. The infant body was carried and passed between four central adult females. C_I groomed her repeatedly, as did an older male, possibly a sibling, and several other females, until lack of reciprocity drew all but the mother away. Younger animals indulging later in play behaviour attempted to include her, persisting without apparent frustration, possibly reading her stillness as a new form of recreation. C_I remained proximate to the body at all times. Food continued to be gathered and provided. C_I alternated between attempts to nurse and attempts to feed from external sources. Husks of partly eaten, decaying fruits gathered around the body and were not removed.

C1 propped the body in a seated position against a tree base. She turned, stretched, then waited, as if testing it, imploring a reaction. It wouldn't move. She appeared to be practising the most basic animal movements, preparing it, encouraging it, as if she could instruct it back into life through repetition. The body fell. Several conspecifics expressed sharp cries of irritation and displeasure, quickly re-fixing it. They didn't like it when the corpse's face became hidden from view, planted in the ground, responding with urgent corrective behaviour. The face itself seemed an essential prerequisite for social inclusion. It would be interesting – if a wider sample base were available – to investigate the average duration of this behaviour. How long will an animal typically persist in looking to discover the face? When, and by what signal, will it ultimately abort, and no longer lift up the infant body, when it falls, in expectation of a face? Is there a specific identifiable point in the decomposition process where the face becomes untenable, definitively strange?

The evenings passed quietly, without sustained shrieking and with no further appearance of unidentified tracks in our camp. I continued following mother and child. A rotting odour appeared. C1 swatted flies away, evidently frustrated and inconvenienced by their interest. The humidity of typical bonobo territories is likely another factor defining the period in which group members fail to realise the body as non-viable; the period is limited by the great speed at which the body softens and carries away. The rains, additionally, speed up the process. By comparison, the common chimpanzee can spend weeks routinely interacting with the cadaver, mothers in particular continuing to express their own understanding of the body's viability. This phenomenon was observed, once, in the drier uplands to the east, over one hundred and eleven days.

The foul odour disturbed the group. The animals were more cautious and, following C1's example, began paying especially close attention to any fruits gathered, opening the case and distributing the seeds by hand, looking into the vacated space with apparent scepticism. The animals seemed to search for the source of the odour throughout their foraging. On four occasions members of external sub-groups appeared, curious, drawn by the odour, but these were lower status males and C1 comfortably repelled their advances.

Throughout this period C1 attempted, with increasing difficulty, to maintain normal behaviour, carrying the body dorsally, on her back. She folded the infant's limbs into her own, pushed the small hands and feet in at unnatural, unsupportable angles, bending them in order to fix the body temporarily in place. As the body diminished it began falling, loosened from the unnatural grip, a source of audible displeasure to C1. C1 then adapted her movements in an attempt to compensate for this new precarity, moving slower both arboreally and terrestrially and avoiding sharp and sudden turns.

Conspecifics were making fewer efforts to engage with the infant, but confusion reigned after C1 made a radical shift, re-fixing the position of the body and attaching it ventrally, on her front. This led to several adult females approaching and inspecting for the first time in two days. One possibility is that the infant body, smaller, noticeably diminished and now carried on the mother's underside, where she could be nursed, was taken by the others for a newborn animal. After smelling and licking the softening, rotting body, the conspecifics moved away, displaying agonistic behaviour, screeching and crying out. C1 affected an aggressive posture in response, briefly standing bipedally and extending her arms as wide as possible, with the inevitable effect that the infant body came loose, and she was unable to catch it.

C1's behaviour suggested she too may have become uncertain as to the infant's identity. Her renewed solicitations and attempts to nurse, the more regular periods spent removing the body and considering its status, indicated the belief that the infant really was newborn. On first glance, this behaviour appears distinctly counterintuitive. Carrying a prone body ventrally is, for simple gravitational reasons, impractical, clearly a poorer option than the dorsal alternative. Should C1 maintain quadruped locomotion and dorsal carrying then her back is presented almost as a horizontal unit; gravity attaches the child to the mother. Ventrally, though engaging the infant in a more intimate position, the body is much more likely to fall, costing C_I greater energy as she attends to it and tries to lift it again.

Again, the existence of a wider sample base would allow opportunity for further investigation; we could only speculate. But the action – superficially costly to the mother – must have been purposeful, and I focused on the projection of the infant as newborn. Was the change from dorsal to ventral part of a strategy to draw greater reserves from the mother, an attempt somehow to revive the infant, inspiring greater attentional levels? A plea for help from others too? Was she simply tricked by the change in size? Was the renewed intimacy really in aid of increases in heat transmission produced by ventral contact? It was an odd phenomenon to witness, regardless – a brief period of something akin to imaginative time travel; various efforts to wake the body up imparting radical chronological jumps – and I couldn't help wonder what the experience was like and how much the mother was reminded of the genuine postnatal period.

By now, C_I and infant were existing in a different zone of the forest, completely apart from the troop. I continued to follow them, bringing water and biscuits and a tarp roof so I could stay for extended periods, even during the night. I listened out, wary of the predator. Occasionally I heard distant footsteps, the slow, deliberate gait of Alice or Jane leaving their tent. I had to stay close to the mother – the lenses weren't good enough; the picture wasn't clear. It was important to find out if the infant spilled anything black from its mouth. The troop remained quiet; in some ways this unnerved me more. It was possible this change signalled not the abandonment of the predator's interest, but rather another phase in its activity, perhaps leading to an acceleration. Alice was worried. She said I should remain at the camp. I shouldn't be out alone; it was irresponsible. We didn't yet know what we were dealing with. Jane came in in support of me. She gave me a look I may have misread as understanding. I wanted to stay near to the mother, and the infant, and I didn't want to have to return to eat with other people each night.

My sickness in the morning was more sporadic. I seemed better able to brush off the nausea, able to contain what came out of me, gather the bulk of it directly in a bag. But every time I vomited I felt helpless next to the possibility that what would come out would be black.

The body was hung on Ci's back again, the small limbs tucked inwards. I kept thinking I had got it wrong, that my attention had been lax and this was a different infant body. It was so small. The body kept falling down, but she never let it stay there. As more of it was lost, the head, pressed in against the mother's shoulder, became relatively larger, so that it was easy to make the mistake, again, of confusing the motion as positive, as growth. I had the stupid thought of sitting in a train with another train parallel to it and mistaking its motion for my own, of believing – even when you knew it wasn't true – that something positive was happening.

As the body became particularly brittle it was only with great effort that she managed to fold and weave the limbs without breaking them. The folding movement – linking and binding the limbs – reminded me of something else, some basic organic process. She stopped offering food. There was now little possibility of recovering traces of anything from its mouth. I continued watching, suppressing challenging thoughts.

When the rain began, lightly, just before the morning, I panicked. I realised I couldn't find her. I slipped on the wet roots and fell and hit my face hard. My lip was bleeding on the ground, thumped with increasing force by the new rain. I made myself get up, and I heard a noise above me but behind, in the direction I had come from, and I followed.

I found her by the water. Her size was different. The infant, the body – tiny skeleton, matted clumps of black hair, sickening illusion in the movement of the worms – had gone, had washed off in the rain, had been carried in the turbid, deafening flow of the stream.

She finished drinking, climbed the bank, called out – her first call in several days – and a sound came back at her, and then another, and another, and I had lost her somewhere in the trees, thrashing and leaping and playing in her troop again.

Though none of us articulated it, I thought we shared the feeling that something dangerous had come close to us and had passed. The rains returned in earnest. Nobody expected them to be so prolonged, so powerful. Before we left we'd gone through detailed forecasts at the gates. The season had come suddenly, prematurely. Alice dug trenches around the camp, diverting water – a short-term measure only. A bigger problem, which we'd avoided raising as long as we could, was our ability to get out. Already, in the area immediately to the south, to make any progress at all we had to wade, with the water level at points as high as my knees. Should the rains persist, and the levels continue to rise to the north, exit might become impossible.

At this stage the work we could do was limited. We were unable to get close to the animals, the water restricting our movements and loudly announcing our presence. We had a single animal still to draw blood from – C_1. This was my fault. I had made the decision not to intervene, not to get close, in the days after she let go of her child. The rain had appeared to decline but only briefly, and it soon became clear it was the wrong decision, that we should have tranquillised her while we had the opportunity. Had her daughter died from the same illness as the two others, and was she infected too? Was it an unconnected death? I'd insisted, when I'd returned to the camp after tracking her, that we had no choice; C_1's reintegration with her group was the priority. I didn't want us doing anything that might jeopardise this. She rejoined her sub-group but relations remained demonstrably fraught, with her conspecifics evidently uncertain of her status. Moving in at this time – shooting C_1, incapacitating her briefly, drawing the blood – may, in these exceptional circumstances, have had severe consequences, possibly ostracising her from the group indefinitely. This, in turn, could have a disastrous effect on the health of the group as a whole.

We had deliberately waited until the end to target C_1. It had seemed sensible to postpone analysis of the senior matriarch until we had safely gathered blood from all the others, by which stage we'd have established routine practice, far less likely to make mistakes. We couldn't have foreseen what would happen, the early rains and the broken contact with the gates.

We continued to disagree over what to do next. I said I wasn't leaving until we had analysed her; otherwise the whole trip became invalid. We had come this far. Alice accused me of losing my objectivity, said I was too invested in this sub-group, and in C_1 in particular, that I was being weak and irresponsible. Our priority was our own safety.

'Even if you don't agree, which would be ludicrous, can't you see that at this rate we'll have to leave our things behind, that everything will be lost?'

'Just two more days,' I said. 'Give it two more days and if conditions don't change then I agree we should go back.'

I could see from the way she stared she didn't believe me.

Jane, to our surprise, took my side. Or at least, she didn't actively support Alice, her passivity endorsing the status quo. She remained in her tent longer every day, her sleeping bag tied up all the way around and behind her head, leaving only the lid of her face uncovered. I wondered briefly whether I shouldn't be worried about her, but dismissed these thoughts as relatively insignificant.

It was an unwritten rule, and living at such close quarters it was essential: don't look into another person's tent. Give them this privacy at least. And yet I couldn't help it. Something, I told myself, must have caught my eye. Jane, running through data with Alice, had turned her back and for a second her tent was open right in front of me – both Alice and Jane were looking away, and so I peered in, just for a moment. I saw a thick mass of paper stacked, dozens, even hundreds, of pages. How carefully was it all protected, I wanted to ask her, knowing I couldn't, knowing how severe the repercussions might be, how a single thing like the admission that I'd looked inside might easily be enough to shatter morale, damage the dynamic irreparably. I could say – I turned and proceeded away from Jane, hearing her zip her tent, though I was sure I'd been discreet – to the group as a whole and not to Jane in particular that we should perhaps review anything that wasn't stored digitally, but it seemed weak cover. What was more important: that we were able to continue doing our work or that we had legible records of everything when we left?

Alice was still trying to resume contact with the gates. Jane and I were silently preparing dinner, water running off the tarps above us. Suddenly I heard something strange – remote voices, a cloud of static, yelling. Alice emerged from her tent with her phone aloft.

'They're coming. We have to take a different route out. They'll show us the way. They'll be here the evening after tomorrow. So we might still have time, Shel.'

She'd kept the call brief to preserve the battery. She relayed the details – the apologies about the masts, astonishment over the storms, the excitement about the material we'd been able to gather, deep relief over both our general health and, with exceptions, that of the troop. Bryan would lead us back, Frank and a second ranger accompanying him, directing us and helping with our things. The rain was supposed to break later this evening, with the next few days forecast to be drier; water levels would dip, and in taking the new, longer route out, they should be able to bring us back in without too much difficulty. Forecasts, as we'd learned, weren't always reliable, but this wasn't going to dispel our new enthusiasm.

I walked out uncovered in the rain. Everything was going to be all right. I felt renewed affection for my colleagues, an almost desperate tenderness towards them. I looked forward, tempted almost to tears, to the following weeks, months and even years, the time the three of us would devote to making sense of what we'd gathered here, of what had happened. When I came back into camp and saw Jane, her head bowed, diligently chopping tomatoes, my instinct was to hug her. She heard me, and by the time she'd turned around I'd composed myself.

I felt unspeakable relief, not only because of the confirmation of our exit and our renewed contact with the outside world, but because we'd almost certainly have the opportunity to analyse C_1 and thus complete our survey. Alice produced the last of her bottle, and under the tarp, listening to the noise decline until it was no longer rain itself we heard but water falling secondarily, dripping from the trees above us as the birds shook the branches, we watched the silent, flickering sheet lightning, heard the last distant calls of the troop that night, and savoured the first feelings of satisfaction, completion, the feeling all of this, at last, was coming to an end.

XXIII

When he woke he noticed a change: a quiet, a sense of stillness, a difference in the air, the light. He felt hungry. He pulled open the curtain, and he froze – the fog, overnight, had disappeared. He put his face to the glass. The fields stretched on beyond the driveway. He heard the chatter of the jackdaws in the trees. He opened the window, realising he hadn't done this simple thing in so long. Sunlight entered the house in thick, stunning shafts. He could see a distance of hundreds of metres over the fields. He watched the farmer attaching something to a piece of industrial machinery. And on the far west of the field he saw a figure walking slowly, with some difficulty, moving in an interrupted, stumbling manner, finally making his way to the small patch of trees. The scene, through the window, in the dramatic and unfamiliar light, framed like a painting, appeared almost too vivid to be real. He waited, watching the trees, expecting the figure to emerge through the other side at any moment, but he didn't. After several minutes, moving back from the window, he descended the stairs.

Entering the vestibule, he saw the mould wasn't nearly as bad as he remembered. He opened the door. He went to his car, unlocked it and looked inside. There were small patches of blood on the front passenger seat only. He remembered a more dramatic blood spill glimpsed through the dark and the fog, and with only the faint light of the torch to see by. He shifted away from the thought, unsettled by the memory not only of the fear but of the sense of a collapse of logic, a barren, abject resistance and hopelessness. He would get a bowl of water, some soap, a sponge and begin on the car seat, which shouldn't take long. Then he would start on the wet areas of the house, the sinks, the bathroom, leaving the windows and doors open for the sun, the fresher air, the sounds of the outside. He kept stopping, smiling, involuntarily closing his eyes, enjoying the sun's radiation on his body. Leaving the car doors open, he went back inside, lifting the phone from the countertop. Without thinking, his hand flowed over the screen and the colour lightened, the phone unlocked. He waited several moments, feeling an almost unbearable sense of anticipation. He almost laughed when he heard the familiar tone registering renewed network connection. Quickly, without thinking, he typed in the number and waited while the long tone repeated.

It took several minutes for the switchboard operator to put him through. While his call was held, he removed the phone from his ear and looked down at it. The object was warm in his grip; he enjoyed lifting it and feeling its unusual heft, the compressed weight inside, the impression of a dense system of nested layers. The line clicked. 'First of all,' the receptionist said, 'your name?'

'John Harper.' There was a pause on the line. He heard the keyboard tapping.

'Can you confirm this was the name you gave when you were admitted to the hospital?'

He supplied both his date of birth and the date he'd visited the hospital. He was confident, he told her, the date was correct, though there remained a chance he was off by a day or two.

She apologised. They had been having some systems problems recently and some of their data was inaccessible.

'Ah, here we are,' she said at last. 'We had a different spelling. Okay. I'm sorry, let me see. What was that?'

'My doctor – that's what I was phoning about. I don't want to make an issue of it – I'm not comfortable with him any more, that's why I'm calling directly. I want to find out when I can come in for more tests.' He thought back to yesterday, his refusal to invite the doctor in, the last he'd seen of him as he backed away from the door, out of the vestibule. Though he had kept his eyes trained on the silhouette, he'd failed to notice the point it disappeared; there was no transition, no sound either while the doctor stepped down from the steps to the gravel driveway.

'Hmm. Okay, okay, John, why don't I call you back on this number in a couple of minutes? I just want to check a couple of things this end first, and I can find out what's happened. It would be helpful if you could source your own papers too, yes.'

'You'll call back, soon?'

'In just a couple of minutes, John. And then we can schedule an appointment, okay?'

He stared at his phone as he ended the call. He couldn't put it away. The weight seemed to grow with every moment. Images started to flash, the phone vibrated, an audio tone played loudly, repeating. A list of calls and messages. Shel: call after call. His chest thudded. He found the first message, put the phone to his ear, pressed play. It took several seconds to connect, then he heard a rustling sound, raised voices in the background. Someone sobbing. At first he didn't recognise her.

'John?' she said. 'John, are you there? John? Where are you? I need to talk to you. Something terrible has happened.'

XXIV

The sound was more distressing for its distance, for the fact the animals were unusually far from us yet their calls still carried with this much force. I woke almost unable to bear it. My stomach was turning. I felt wretched.

It had come back.

The shrieking had finished and I remained still, listening, waiting to hear the rain filtering down to the tent. But I heard nothing. No dripping water, no falling foliage, no birds.

I decided to leave the tent. To my relief, I found no new prints on our site. The troop's alarm may have had a different cause, unrelated. I looked around, the darkness edging away. Through the canopy I could only just make out the sky. Not long until sunrise. Something tall passed in front of me. I heard a splash, saw in the white glow of my flashlight a shadow slipping through the trees. I waited, held my breath, tensed my chest and heard it thudding. My arms were cold, lightly convulsing. I told myself there was no cause for alarm: the form was upright, bipedal. It wasn't the animal. I was not in danger. I breathed out, shook my head. I turned slowly and shone my light back on the two tents behind. Both were closed. The temptation again to give in to fear. But no, it could still be Alice or Jane; as a precaution, ever since the prints had appeared, we sealed our tents when we got up during the night. I walked on. I moved my light in a slow arc, signalling my presence, continuing into the trees.

Finally, a little spooked, I decided to call out. My voice was unrecognisable. Light, wavering, barely above a whisper. 'Jane? Alice? Are you there?'

I shone the light again. I knew the last thing I would appreciate, getting up to relieve myself, was a torch shone onto me while I squatted, but at the same time I thought it important I didn't turn back.

My heart beat faster; my mouth was dry. Could I really have seen something else? Was it possible that both my colleagues remained asleep in their tents and I was inadvertently pursuing something unidentified? But the height of the form, the manner of the movement ... Had one of the rangers arrived early, travelling overnight? Perhaps the forecast had changed and our exit had become more urgent. But then why hadn't they called out? Why hadn't they got in contact first? I was confident what I had seen – its size, its speed – didn't correspond to an animal. But how reliable was a shadow in the beam of a low flashlight, caught in thick foliage and reflected in the pools? Could I be certain it wasn't something else? The boar, a leopard, even? Was I certain that something really had been there? The reflection of my light on the water, a snapped branch plunging and splashing – it was enough to create the illusion. Even so, there was no pressing reason to continue walking out alone.

I had just stopped and was in the process of turning when I felt the temperature drop. I heard what sounded like a popping or sucking noise. I flinched, instinctively reeling from it, and moved backwards rapidly, turning around. Silence. The forest seemed devoid of activity, waiting. I lit a circle around me, then switched off the torch. I peered into the black, the dark swaying leaves, the lightly stirring water. I heard it again, that sucking noise, coming from the ground ahead of me. One, two. One, two. The sound – footsteps in the flooded ground – coming louder, closer to me, though I still made out nothing in the darkness. I went to call but my mouth didn't respond. I felt something heavy, cold and unfamiliar grip my neck – I sprang back again, dropping my light as I collided with someone directly behind me.

'Shel, Shel, stop, it's me, Alice, it's okay.'

I stopped to find my flashlight, searching through the sodden ground, squatting, trying to regain myself. I took a deep breath. 'I'm fine. What are you doing here?'

'Shel, why didn't you respond? I followed you for ages – I was calling you. Why didn't you respond?'

'But I – I've only ... I don't know. It doesn't matter. Let's just go back.'

We went slowly and in silence, the air bleaching around us. I switched off my light. It felt like we'd been walking for a long time, longer than we should have. I was tired. Had we missed the camp? Unsettled, still tense, confused by the floods, it was possible we had gone the wrong way. I imagined the tents lifted and removed, the camp dismantled and grown over. Eventually the ground-water thinned and I noticed my prints in front, leading away from camp. The area was familiar; there wasn't far to go. Alice had stopped behind me. 'Shel,' she said blankly. 'Shel.'

You could see the blue of the tarp and the three tents ahead through the trees. I tried not to look at the ground. Already I could smell something. Like the mushrooms, but stronger, worse. Unpleasant to breathe.

Coming into the camp, looking onto the tents directly, Jane's was the first. The front was ripped off. Pieces of the blue material lay limply in the mud, stained with red. I was distantly aware of a piece of the same blue above us, in the trees.

The camp was silent and as if deserted. We carried nothing to defend ourselves.

Alice stood behind me. I approached and looked inside the tent. The samples had come loose. Black mushroom everywhere, erupting over the scattered paper sheets. Blood smeared over the tent walls and the paper, over Jane's tablet device and the few pieces of her clothing. A warmth, a stench like dissolved metal. I saw Jane's bag first, where she had lain. I looked for a long time at it, the sleeping bag which she had worn tied all the way up to her head, comforting her, limiting her movement. She had liked to hug herself inside it. The bag was now empty. Jane lay outside it, several feet behind the tent. She had been thrown. She lay unnaturally on her front. Her limbs jutted at unsupportable angles, the bones snapped. Her head seemed to descend into the ground, as if she was tunnelling, fleeing, escaping. It was like there was a little hole there, in the ground, and she was looking into it, transfixed and held there, the earth set into the perfect shape to hold her. How had it been prepared, I thought. Who had prepared it like that for her. I coughed. The air was unclear. I felt a movement in my stomach and heard retching from behind me; everything disappeared.

PART THREE

Place Beyond the Forest

'It makes people look closer,' he said after he got back in, kicking the snow off his boots on the mat, his face red like it had been seared, clipping the door closed behind him, 'the ice – you have to pay more attention so you don't fall. And I'm finding more people are saying hello, when just going to the shops or something. I think it's partly that you can see people breathing.

'Come here,' he said, laying the bags on the table, turning to her.

'Don't,' she said quietly, gesturing down at the Velcro sling, 'she's only just gone to sleep, and already you've made the room at least two degrees colder.'

———————

There was the problem of how to collect, how to preserve, how to remove the body. The rangers – Frank, Joseph, Bryan – came splashing in from the trees only hours after they had found her. Shel and Alice were in shock, guarding either end of the scene. They could explain nothing. The rangers took out their guns, circled the site, silent. The smell of all that blood. Already new activity in the ground, in the trees above them. Wings beating, beetles creaking. An interest, a response from the wider environment, intent on soaking up what remained.

Everything would renew; nothing would remain. The whole of the tent an opened wound, an exposed person.

Joseph walked between the tent opening and the body, studying the ground. 'You found her like this? You haven't moved her?' Shel shook her head. Frank murmured something, pointing at the blood tracks; Bryan waved his arm dismissively. They were dehydrated, they needed food, they were shivering in the wet heat and their eyes had a glazed, absent sheen. Bursts of radio static sounded through the camp as communication continued with the park authorities. They couldn't leave the body unattended. Bryan would stay with it until they had executed the extraction plan. There was a limit on how close air transport could get. A rise in the hills eight kilometres away would have to serve as a landing area. Somehow they would have to bring the body up to it. It would take three days at least to have a vehicle arranged and delivered. Shel and Alice had to leave before then; the message was that they could not remain at the site. The park was sending a team and with Jane too the loading weight would be at capacity. Bryan repeated, they had no option, they had to walk out.

She flinched as the trowel smacked the mud. Bryan couldn't hold her gaze. They had to wrap the body in a tarp and lower it into the shallow excavation. A temporary measure, just to hold the body, just a little longer, until the team arrived. He would wait by it, it wouldn't be long, he had a weapon, he would be okay. They couldn't risk the provocation of leaving the body outside on the surface. It would invite further attack. I'm afraid this is just what we have to do, he said.

———————

She was born early, her bones still soft. The nurses spoke of *pre-age*, as if she wasn't really born and they still had time to prepare. References to negative time – *minus four weeks* – suggested an error, a countdown, a terrible energy inside her. Soon she would be minus eight weeks, minus sixteen, they would drift beyond the point of conception, beyond where their own lives began. Aware of the danger, the nurses then worked urgently, rapidly, reproducing and multiplying and ratifying her. She was too small to be enough so they made more of her, made images of her, which they hung along the corridors in protest, in refusal. She does exist. She will grow stronger. He walked out into the corridor and back into the room, switching between the test images and the body, trying to find out what was happening, what it meant. There were grainy prints that seemed to show the surface of a planet but were actually her brain. 'In ultrasound,' the nurse said. 'We can do it because of the gap in the acoustic barrier.'

He must have looked blank.

'The fontanelle. Soft spots.'

'It isn't hurting her? You're sure it isn't hurting?'

'Of course not. She doesn't feel a thing.'

It was an old, brute method, using echo to measure. 'They don't use their eyes either,' Shel said later, back at home, 'not at first. It might be one of the reasons she's crying – the sound gives her pictures too.'

'Pictures?'

'Of what's around her. Of us, distance. You know – like bats do.'

As she began to see more, and as everyone was telling them they needed high-contrast images, that newborns responded to monochrome, to binary, and as they didn't have anything else in the new house, they used the ultrasound scans, hanging them up in the cot. Catherine looked down, hands on her hips.

'No. I don't like this.'

'Why not?' Shel demanded.

'It isn't natural. She shouldn't be seeing it.'

'Why? It's just a tone contrast – her eyes are barely open, Mother.'

'I don't know. I don't like it.'

'Well, she likes it and it's helping so we're keeping it.'

He put her down in the cot and switched her position after an hour. He checked she was comfortable and measured her breath. Though the paediatrician assured them everything was fine, he watched the slightly raised front, the soft dip in two places at the cap, the flat area at the base of her head. The temporary openings were a little more pronounced and would take longer to form over. *The skull is more fragile so the brain can grow.* Could they really know, for certain, something wasn't wrong? The tests, the measurements, establishing what they could and couldn't know, were part of the problem; pressing in at her, taking from her, pushing sound against her, they shaped her too.

All this worry, Catherine said, was unremarkable, being simply what they had to live with. 'You focus on one day at a time, and you manage. You will never be more creative than in the conspiracies and nightmares you imagine now. You'll see the end of the world everywhere. But you'll get through it. She is much stronger than either of you realise.'

Alice had taken leave and she visited often, bringing drawings they hung alongside the scans, black charcoal sketches on paper – Dorothy sleeping, animals playing, a tall city skyline, figures in silhouette at windows. In directing Dorothy's growing attention, they influenced the way she moved her head. They changed the position of the pictures a little every day, and she rotated her head in sympathy. If they maintained this, ensuring her head wasn't static, then the flattening effect would disappear sooner. Carrying her in the sling – 'like an injury,' Shel said – helped too, adjusting her position through their natural walking motion. Part of his focus at home was in varying all movement, finding a counter-position for each activity. When he fed her, he had to remind himself to rotate, to use his left arm as well as his right. If he thought about the implications for any length of time – the direct correlation between this rhythm, over the surface, and the extension of her skull; the plastic exposure of her learning brain – it was unbearable.

Shel helped wrap her, lift her and lower her. Staring at the ground. They filled the earth in over her. Alice waited a distance away, unable to retreat to her own tent, which was identical to Jane's and thus a reproduction of the nightmare, but reluctant to go any further into the forest on her own. They worked slowly and carefully with the body, compromising forensics. They must hide the evidence they needed to retain, and in doing so they altered it.

The late morning darkness grew heavier, the sky snapping in thunder. Whatever the conditions, they were to leave. The park was explicit about it. The rainfall should not create undue problems, they said.

The walk was staged in prolonged twilight. Shel couldn't recall stopping for any length of time. Following the feet in front – Joseph a peripheral presence, an edge of safety, leading them, ushering them out – she put her arms into the wet undergrowth, hands running along the vines. None of it felt real. She welcomed the fatigue, welcomed the draining of her body, encouraged the pain. With the pressure on her back from the packs of samples and equipment, she was reminded of the first sensation in picking Jane up. She ate nothing and they had to intervene to make her drink. It wasn't that she didn't want to, she told John in the cottage, later. It was just that she had forgotten. It simply didn't occur to her that this was the kind of thing she might do.

Sometimes she stopped and looked up, and when the others looked to her and said, what, what is it, and she said, really, are you sure you don't hear it, you don't hear anything, she began doubting herself, doubting all this, doubting everything she had seen. This can't be happening. She heard a mechanical fluttering sound, like the audio they'd recorded earlier. Joseph assured her it was impossible, that the helicopter couldn't have been shuttled in so quickly. As they continued in silence, she thought back to the airport, an eternity ago. Jane slumped in the tall-backed chair, her fringe surely irritating her eyes, going through document after document in preparation. Would it have been different if they had been able to locate the doctor and bring him with them? How much sooner would they have gathered the blood and left? Her nausea peaked again, something turning and folding inside her. Something was wrong, inside her.

———————

They moved in three months before the due date. The new house was small, box-shaped with two bedrooms adjacent on the front side and a kitchen and living room on the reverse side, a narrow corridor running across it and a bathroom at one end. The second bedroom had functioned as a guest room – Catherine stayed frequently in the first weeks while they were settling in, unpacking the boxes from storage, and as the birth drew nearer – but now they put Dorothy's things in it. They washed and changed and fed her there as often as possible, trying to make the space familiar. At the back of the house, the broad kitchen and living-room windows looked out onto a small grass patch with the beginnings of a hedgerow and fences at either end. Beyond the hedge was a field they were told wasn't immediately to be built on, and beyond this the remains of what had once been several hectares of forest. Six houses had gone up almost at the same time; theirs was the first street in what would become a larger development. For the first time in their lives they had a house that would be their own.

Shel left for work at 7.45; Dorothy would sleep for up to one and a half hours, usually significantly less. He began cleaning during this first sleep, keeping her at or near eye level, placing the cradle on the kitchen table. He swept, dusted, disinfected the surfaces. By nine o'clock he'd given her her first change, laying her on her back on the waterproof mat over two towels on the floor. After this they continued playing, and he was often so surprised by the ringing alarm that it took him one or two moments to understand this signalled she was due another feed.

He tried to get outside not too long after midday, checking the cupboards and going out to buy any items that wouldn't be auto-replaced. The rhythm of the car on the road usually put her to sleep within four minutes. He drove a longer route to prolong her sleeping. By two o'clock they were home. He sat directly on the floor, supporting her on his chest and holding the bottle across her in his left hand. Then they read, played appearance games – he directed Dorothy's face tracking side to side. She saw him three feet away, her sight extending all the time. He tried to keep in that ambit, on the edge of her. She signalled when he left it, pulling him back into appearance. If he sat at the table he placed the cradle in front of him. If he was on his feet – making something to eat, searching for his keys – and couldn't attach her directly then he placed the cradle on a clear part of the worktop, from where their eyes were closer to level.

Her yawns occupied her whole body, from her closed eyes down to her toes, almost as small as spokes on a hairbrush. Another change, a sleep, usually the longest of the day. He cleared the bedroom, put laundry on. Tried again to make some progress with work, brewed coffee, washed his face. Her next cry was the signal for their walk.

The cold was a problem both directly, in its sharpness on her skin, and through the long, elaborate process of putting her into the various protective layers, which she protested and countered, cried at and tried to turn over against. He kept the afternoon walk under thirty minutes now that winter had arrived. When it was especially cold and she was against his

chest and he hadn't heard her cry or make any other sound in
the previous ninety seconds, he stopped, took the support off
and studied her sleeping. He watched, tried to learn to feel, as
well, against him, the faint pulse that sometimes issued from
her head. He was bathing her the first time he saw it, something
crawling in her head – he'd almost panicked but thankfully it
was evening and Shel was home. Still, after putting her down he
opened his tablet to medical dictionaries, one definition drifting
into another, each time he said this is it and I'll close it but there
was something else he had to know, and then something further.

————————

He arrived at the neurology department, after he'd phoned, in a
state of anxiety. He was still reeling from Shel's news from the
park. But his swelling had gone down and they were satisfied
with the results of the scans. The nurse told him it wasn't unusual
for symptoms to continue, in some form, for months. He may
never regain clear memory of the attack and the time directly
following it. If he was worried about anything in particular, or
if he noticed strange, unusual developments, he should have
someone drive him to the department. It was highly unlikely,
she said. He was in good shape. Other than certain temporary
prohibitions – he wasn't to drive for another two weeks, and he'd
return to work gradually – he was essentially ready to resume
his old life. She smiled; apparently he'd looked shocked.

He spent the following days cleaning, resting, regaining his appetite, walking further all the time. The doctors told him under no condition could he fly. Shel was being checked and debriefed and she said it wasn't a good idea for him to come out anyway. They spoke on video every day, long, halting conversations, peering in at the screen. She had become clumsy – he watched her misjudge distance and drop things. She wasn't herself. She put her arm out to the screen as if she would enter it. Her voice was blank, slow. She said they would have left camp earlier if it were not for her. She was worried about Alice. He downplayed his own accident; it seemed insignificant now.

The area around the cottage was still unfamiliar and he enjoyed, each walk a little longer than the last, discovering what was around him. At first he went slowly, bracing for the slight jolt inside his skull. A lot of it was in his mind, and if he didn't think about it he could move without too much discomfort. He greeted the few people he passed, spoke briefly about the pleasant weather, smiled at the farmer and at a neighbour walking her dog. Day by day, the slow buzzing around his head, the tenderness above his eyes and behind his ears, and other symptoms such as his occasional loss of balance, his sudden extreme thirst and his nausea, all began to subside. Soon enough, he was relishing the walks. Something was peeling open in front of him, the outside world slowly coming back in a gathering clarity. The light, which he had grown almost afraid of, wrapped behind the fog, felt warm, and good, and nourishing on his skin. He felt stronger, eager to make up for lost time. The seventeen days of the doctor's visits felt like something from a nightmare. It was a period in which he had lost autonomy. He was so grateful, now that it was over. He had walked a distance from the cottage, and as he turned and looked back, he saw the city's depth behind, carried in the clear light. He saw the colour in individual houses that must have been over a mile away. He made out details on the facades, saw tiny figures coming in and out. He had a feeling of unprecedented possibility and opportunity. He was well, and he couldn't believe his fortune. Shel would be home any day now. When he thought of her, of how much he missed her, of the danger she had been in, he almost burst with longing. His relief, now that it was over, was overwhelming

He walked back to the cottage, forming a list of everything he needed to do. He phoned the agent; when he explained what had happened she immediately told him she would pick him up and bring him to the site. He was in luck: building had resumed that morning.

———

He set Dorothy in her cradle on the table and she watched him preparing the evening meal, always at least double the quantity he and Shel would eat so they could store the remainder and heat it for lunch the next day. He avoided spices and anything with seeds, easily lost on the floor or on counter and table surfaces, hidden under appliances. He imagined Dorothy getting pepper seeds in her mouth, a sudden inflammation and the sensation, inside her, of burning. He changed her, fed her, lay her on the mat – she twirled her limbs like a turned beetle – and fixed the mobile into position above her, a fabric arch with pictures of birds and with a lever she could reach that had a rattle, three sound effect buttons and a small mirror.

Shel returned from the university not long after six. She crept into the house so quietly he didn't hear. He was surprised how suddenly the end of the day had come and resolved to plan things better the following day, to get a better measure of time, to be more productive. She inched forward and kissed Dorothy's forehead. She teased him about the excessive heat – he always had the house warm – and asked how long she'd been sleeping. While she heated the food he lay down for fifteen minutes, and after they'd eaten she bathed Dorothy and he tried to stay awake, looking blankly at news sites and reading over his code.

'You remember Mum's coming tomorrow? John? Around ten.'

He focused on the screen. He had forgotten. 'How long will she be?'

She tilted her head. 'She wants to re-pot the plants. It will give you a bit of time away. I thought you'd be pleased.'

*

The smell of garlic spread through the house. Catherine repeated they'd get used to it; he could hear her three rooms away. Four terracotta pots lined the sill in the kitchen for the southern light. Perfect, she said, for growing green garlic and bulbs too. The cold bright skies gave them the six hours they'd need each day. 'Just remember,' she said, 'and be careful washing so you don't get suds in the pots – the chemicals kill them.' Catherine came with fertiliser twice a month, tending to the green shoots, the first of which had come in in under a week, and to the cloves, bedded at a safe distance inches into the soil. 'These will take longer,' she said. 'Look for the leaves turning brown, around eight or nine months I should think.'

Every time Catherine saw him she gave him a big long hug – cardigans and scarves, thick grey curls bouncing on his shoulders, the smell of chamomile, earth, plants. At first, whenever she held Dorothy – Doll, as she liked to call her – she had burst into tears. Shel was irritated, but then something had switched and suddenly Catherine knew what to do. She was there for them; she made herself quieter, kept to the next room or sat outside on a chair or worked in the small beginnings of the garden, seeds under her nails, a presence, a visible means of support, proof that it was possible, someone, unbelievably, who had done all this before.

She had pushed the garlic on them from the start. Good to have it around the place, good for the air, good for you both and good for Dorothy. She swore it reduced infection rates, strengthened immunity, that it would help 'firm her up'.

'Mum,' Shel had interjected, staring at her, 'don't speak like that, like you're describing cattle.' He wasn't sure. Maybe they should move the plants. Tell her Dorothy didn't like the scent, it irritated her skin, though he could picture Catherine's expression, shaking her head and telling him she'd seemed fine earlier.

He waited an extra moment in the bathroom. He was being unfair; she was just trying to help. She'd told him to go out, see a film, go to a café, take a walk, and he had thought he would, it sounded reasonable, but when it came to it he was reluctant to go. He didn't doubt Catherine – she'd be fine with her, of course – he just found that he couldn't produce the energy needed to go out and do something. It was an effort to even imagine it.

Catherine had used the garlic with Shel, as her own mother had with her, a tradition, but proven to work, she said. He entered the kitchen, watched her wiping strenuously along the sill. 'It's important in the first months, in any case, but especially with an early child. Look,' she turned to him over her shoulder, 'I know you're sceptical, that you think there's something alternative about this, but there isn't. You'll see garlic in all sorts of medications, John. I want to do the little I can to help, that's all.'

He quickly agreed, alarmed by the suggestion of emotion, then wondering whether this might have been the intended effect. 'Your mother,' Catherine said, bending down to Dorothy, in her cradle, 'had the same plants in her house when she was just as small as you are now.' He'd heard the story before; she enjoyed telling it. Shel's father lined her room with plants. Ivan was not expressive, but he insisted on this, insisted on giving her plants. As an only child she might appreciate the company, but he maintained this was incidental. What he wanted was to take advantage of his daughter's light. He told Shel the plants in her room were the most special and needed the greatest care. It was important they took light wherever they could; just her being there, thinking about something, even sleeping, unconscious, was helping them. She liked to sing, and hum, and talk to herself – all of this would help the plants. Shel wondered if he had got the idea after they first heard her talking alone through the wall. Commentaries and dialogues and experiments – she said she was testing whether the voice in her head had the same accent as her speaking voice – and the other earnest consolations of an only child. Putting the plants in, Ivan would be quietly endorsing her behaviour, supporting it, while giving her a kind of company. Catherine was sure – if she could have asked him – Ivan would have denied it, said it was all, simply, botany.

Shel's car was being serviced so she'd taken his to work and, because it was part of their routine, because he enjoyed it and it felt like the day would be missing something otherwise, he decided to take Dorothy to the shop by bus. Again, that extravagant sky over everything. Packed snow creaking under the tyres. The refracted sun glare slowed the traffic, light bouncing off the windshields and the frozen lake water. It was a small single-deck vehicle; he saw the driver's eyes in the mirror monitoring them, making sure they were settled before restarting the electric engine and inflating the carriage. He realised midway through the journey they were in Shel's seat, right-hand side, third from back. And not Shel's seat really, Catherine had told him. It was her father's seat – Ivan would take the bus almost every day, sitting in the same place whenever he could. 'It's probably not even a conscious thing,' she said. 'I doubt she realises.'

The bus drew in to the next stop and a passenger on the other side rose to leave. There were only six on the bus, an equal distance apart. No-one spoke. Dorothy slept. He held out his arm, shielding her eyes from the sun. He looked through his backpack, though he knew he'd forgotten his glasses. The sky was cloudless. The clarity indicated enormous vertical distance.

It was only because the passenger had got up, carrying his few items, walking unsteadily forward and then stepping off the lowered platform onto the pavement, that the sun now struck them. He watched through the window as the passenger gathered himself and looked ahead to the near cluster of houses. He wondered if, even for a little bit, just out of habit

– it was a small village they had lived in – people had continued to keep Ivan's seat free. The fresh, unoccupied space changing not just the light, but the balance, the distribution of weight on the vehicle. Maybe passengers had had to shield their eyes, like he was doing now, because of the new conditions under which the light travelled. The electric pulse struck up again; the carriage inflated. He kept looking at the seat below him, to his right.

––––––

It was an off-hand comment made during one of the long video calls in the days after the park, before she was cleared to fly back, a suggestion in response to the brief and diluted account of the attack he had given her, but it stuck with him. He told her only that he had gone to visit the site; he had wanted to find out what was going on, why work had been suspended, why nobody was answering his calls. The fog, he said, came back suddenly while he was down in the foundations and, climbing out, heading back towards the car, something powerful had blindsided him, hitting him from above. Shel leaned in at the screen and asked him to repeat himself and say again what happened. He wasn't making sense. So he adjusted it, reframed it, changed the terms, and found himself telling her that he was struck by a bird of prey, that it must have been the beginning of the nesting season and both the property

developers in general and himself in particular had disturbed
something, and the mother was attempting to drive them
away, defending her territory. Shel waited for him to say more
and when he didn't she said, 'John, none of that makes any
sense.' She seemed distant, mulling something over, seemed
about to say something and then abruptly changed expression,
almost physically removing what was anticipated on her lips
and shifting the whole setting of her face and saying, 'But
you're all right? You've had it checked? I mean, you've gone to
the hospital, they've cleared you?'

'Yes, yes,' he said, 'I'm fine,' already regretting saying anything
while they were still this far apart – he hadn't meant to.

'Anyway,' she said, an afterthought, 'I don't think you
disturbed a nest. I think it's more likely, if it was a bird, that the
developers brought it.' She turned round. She was being called;
another meeting was about to start.

What she was suggesting, he found out, was that the
developers were using birds of prey to clear nuisance gulls
during construction. Left undeterred, seabirds would disrupt
work and pose threats to the crew's safety. Along with
other measures – pyrotechnics, video, audio – firms were
hiring specially bred raptors to hunt and terrify the gulls,
driving them away. There was an array of dedicated falconry
companies, each offering specialist services ranging from single
'performance' hunts to prolonged, intensive ten-day courses.
Some firms stressed a single day's hunting was sufficient, the

gulls being so alarmed by the raptors' sudden appearance they retreated from the area and didn't return for months. Additionally, and as a contingency measure, the whole of the initial hunt was recorded, the audio played back during what had been peak daily periods of activity, the volume increased so the sound of the raptors soaring and diving was clear even at a distance, the gulls' shrieks played out too to an emptying sky. This initial hunt was also recorded on video, available, in deluxe packages, as a further preventative measure, with giant screens showing longshots tracking the raptors who, though they seemed to be in flight, never appeared to move position, never arrived anywhere. The copy on one company's website elaborated on the particular terror induced by the footage of such an apparently tireless, uncanny creature, always in flight and always pursuing, always on the cusp of striking. More commonly, a prolonged series of hunts was recommended, stretching from seven to ten days, enough to establish marked and lasting trauma in the gulls.

Though all this struck him as unlikely, and baroque, Shel said he was naive, that the practice, though it had become popular recently, had been in use for decades. Companies were not legally obliged, she said, to publicise or even admit to hiring birds, so he shouldn't be surprised if he got nothing from the agent. As he ended the call, he had a clear memory of the moment preceding the attack, a sound not only of wings fluttering but a strange, almost artificial whirring, and he thought of the possibility that at the same time as the bird was diving towards him a recording of a previous hunt was playing out, that the bird was antagonised and driven on by an exterior version of itself.

He ordered industrial cleaning supplies and watched videos instructing him on exactly what to do as, fitted with a mask and wearing inch-thick plastic goggles, he treated what remained of the fungus on the walls. He spent two days working, keeping the house ventilated, doors and windows open, spraying and scrubbing and chipping away at the remaining hyphae, exhausted but determined to do a thorough job, to complete the process and leave nothing behind to remind him of the preceding three weeks, the doctor's visits and the spreading rot. He was determined not to dwell on it and instead look exclusively forward, to Shel's arrival, any day now. He arranged for the affected clothes to be picked up and treated by a specialist company, concerned that it would take longer than advertised and that when Shel returned she wouldn't find even the few things that she'd left. But the items arrived the day before her flight; he hung her mauve coat back along the vestibule wall, noting the collar was upright and there was no sign of a mark anywhere at all.

The morning Shel arrived he was restless in the cottage, distracted and uneasy and only feeling better when he was in motion, moving towards her. Looking out the tinted rear window in the black car, he noted the morning's silence and stillness, the sharpness of the air, the distance in the light. Going over the marshes, he almost couldn't believe this was the same place, that he and Shel had made this same journey only several weeks earlier.

He clutched the complimentary bottle of water in both hands. The vehicle travelled at a constant level speed and, with the comfort of the leather seats, the sophistication of the suspension, the direct line of the route, he had the impression of being carried on tracks, of being conveyed automatically, of existing above the ground. The driver maintained a uniform posture, arms resting decoratively over the wheel. Earphones discreetly in place, eyes inscrutable in the mirror under opaque glasses. They continued over the marshes, coming into sight, for the first time, of the terminal's signalling towers, the road now parallel to the tall fencing setting off the lengths of runway.

He looked out at the airport complex, noting the absence of trees beginning several miles before the terminal, the lack of any depressions in the ground where water could gather. In looking into corporate use of birds he'd found several articles saying airports were designed explicitly with birds, or rather the absence of birds, in mind. Increasingly they incorporated special breeding centres for raptors. The layout of many airports, seen aerially, mimicked wings, while of course the whole thing was a monument to flight. But at the same time they had to repel birds. Aeronautics developed further after deviation from the instruction of wings in nature – in insects, in birds, in bats. Increasingly restless, thrumming with nervous energy as the car approached the drop-off point, he noted that airports were explicitly anti-nest, that specially bred dogs, with high muscle ratios and massive hind quarters designed for optimal acceleration, were also trained to hunt gulls, to locate their eggs, destroy their young, and he noted the series of giant hotels adjacent to the terminal that specialised in conference traffic, an industry and a way of life that was also 'anti-nest', given the prevalence of corporate boredom, restlessness, extra-marital affairs.

He continued waiting by Arrivals, trying to limit the number of times he looked at the screen. The terminal remained oddly quiet, almost deserted. A cleaner slowly pushing a brush along the reflective floor; a single server leaning against the café counter, phone nursed in both hands. The whole area seemed to have slipped into suspension. The time display on the listings must have malfunctioned; he got up and looked around but, unable to see anyone he could report the issue to, he sank back onto his seat. Finally he heard the distant rumble of an engine and, shielding his eyes, saw an aircraft gathering speed on the runway, lifting into the air.

This seemed to break the spell. The announcements began, he heard the tracking sound of luggage wheeled across the concourse and gradually the seats began to fill around him.

He waited on the row closest to the exit, looking directly onto the corridor where landing passengers would appear from. He closed his eyes, stretched and tipped his head back, breathed in. He extended his arms and set them arrow straight on his knees.

The screen confirmed she'd landed. He waited in a heightened state of agitation. Still no-one had come. He got up, checked the screen again, considered asking at one of the airline's desks but decided he couldn't move away from the spot. Finally the first passenger appeared, then another, now emerging in quiet drifts of threes and fours. He stood up, turned round, feeling something had passed him. The others waiting disappeared, merging with the airport's flow. He looked in all directions, turned to his phone, snapped his head back up at the listings. He trained his eyes on the corridor exit. Something was wrong. She was not on the flight. As he got up and stood by the railing it seemed inconceivable Shel would appear, that she could come out of this place. He tapped his foot on the ground. He heard a voice, two voices, heard her boots on the hard floor; he called out.

———

Her lips were open, her eyes shut tight, a flicker of movement beneath the lids. The dark, wet down of hair receding. She seemed very far away. He looked around the kitchen, trying to remember where he started. There was a routine, the same routine, which he followed every day. He wasn't making the most of his time with her. Already – four months – she had grown so much, but he seemed able to perceive it only after the fact. He wanted to acknowledge now, at the time – not later, not looking back – her presence, the fact of their being there, this extraordinary fortune. And the day drifted on and away. He made coffee and she slept; he opened up his laptop. One, two hours passed on the floor, feeding, then she slept against him, held in the sling. He checked the tightness and, in lifting the material at his shoulder, adjusting it a little, her weight was communicated quickening through one of his fingers, the faintest additional pressure, an almost imperceptible difference, heartbeat and the blood pulsing, the tiniest gradient.

They didn't leave the cottage for three days. They ordered takeaway and slept late. The oil-stained paper bags by the sink in the kitchen, the spices lingering in the rinsed foil. They didn't shower. This sense of extension, of accumulation upon himself. He trailed the smell of her, took her back to bed. He caressed her, pushed her hair back with his third and fourth fingers. Her slow, bare footsteps over the floor. She kept stopping what she was saying, inches from him. Reaching for him, pressing at him. Relying physically on the contact of the other person. All the times that she had stopped him, gently prodded him, pushed in at him, held him. The passivity of a body, the inevitability of a body slowly swaying, tipping, falling forward without this applied resistance, this reverberative force of another person. The repeated instruction to stop, stay still, remain here. Prolong the moment, keep this going, just a little longer. Just this, only this. The forefinger against him; the arm over him; the legs wrapped at his waist.

They watched the sun from inside. The glare continued through the three days, warping the front part of the house, reflecting on the windows and the mirrors and appearing to build new space. So much room, so many things to do. No-one had known him, no-one had seen so much of him as she had in those three days. Running her hands along the pale pink scars where his wounds had healed over, pressing them as if the new, risen lips could speak, could tell her what had happened. He had changed, and there were alien parts. Licking the mark on his neck, making a soothing noise, drying him with her breath. Her eyes over him in the bed, matted hair tied up, lower body circling over him. New scratches, blotches, lumps and bites on her. Ankles stripped bright red against the sheets. The blood of opened bites, the blood she drew from biting his ear, the contraction of her abdomen, the jerk and spasm of her hips as she came. Her sweat, the new colour on her face, her neck, her hands, her lower arms. The ease with which moisture came from her, the humidity she apparently still retained, the scent, even, that she brought with her from the park. Her ripped nails, the dirt deep inside her ears. The black and green that came out from her nose. Waking up and prodding him in the night, a distant expression, unable to speak. Requiring only the evidence he is there, awake, he is with her, he is conscious. Shaking her head when he goes to speak, putting her forefinger to his mouth. Waking again in the morning, locked. The reflex of a smile in the light, the space around them, the time ahead. The reprieve, the unbelievable reprieve of the continued present, the sustained world.

Feeling her warmth, the change in her breath, the slight stirring of her body, he waited for her arm to lift over him. He pictured this in space, surrounded on all sides by darkness, untraversable distances, immensities beyond understanding, beyond purpose.

————————

He crept out of bed, stopping to watch Doll in her cot, and turned on the kitchen light. He sat at the table and opened his laptop. Shel came in, bouncing Doll on her chest. 'What are you doing?' she said. He read the time; he had been working hours.

'What are you doing?' she repeated. 'Do you have to do that? Do you have to work on that thing, now?'

'I'll come back to bed soon, I promise.'

She turned to go, and then paused, nodding to the window sill. 'Will you throw these out tomorrow, too?'

The garlic had withered. He hadn't fed it and it died.

He laid everything on the floor: the two base towels; the waterproof mat; the soap solution; the cloth; the change of clothes; two nappies; the basin. He peered inside the basin and decided he should disinfect it first.

The water had cooled to lukewarm. He removed the babygrow and took Doll from the cradle. Her puffy arms and legs were red, the rolls of excess skin bunched up. He took the small hand-towel, dipped it in the lathered water, rinsed it. He wrapped her lower half first and dabbed at her skin with the hand-towel. She flinched occasionally but didn't cry as he'd expected. He used one hand to support her, tipping her gently to the side so he could wash her back. A reminder of the almost nothing weight of her, the mildest resistance to his arm as it moved through the air. He washed her lower half and changed her nappy, and lastly washed her hair, putting the basin behind her head, scooping up water in the hand-towel with his free arm. He padded her dry with a fourth towel, shook and rubbed a little hydrating powder over her. He reached for the fresh babygrow and cursed as he saw, underneath it, the large white hooded towel he was supposed to have wrapped her in.

He put the babygrow around her and then the hooded towel over her as well, feeling a sudden chill through the room, an arrow of sharp colder air. Looking back at her while he walked, he checked the heater controls in the corridor. Behind the heater, spreading over the wall, beneath the window on the far side of the house, were the beginnings of a new black-green growth.

He apologised, lifting her – she had been about to sleep – and took her with him through the perimeter of the house, checking the lock and seal on each of the windows and on the exterior doors. He went back, testing them again. Then as he returned to the living room he closed each of the inner doors he passed. He felt her, in her cradle – she looked a little red, although her temperature was fine. He laid her on the second mat on the floor, stretched his arms and dug the heels of his hands into his eyes. He had taken so long to accomplish such a simple task. He'd washed her many times before. He looked at her and realised he'd forgotten to feed her. The alarm hadn't sounded or he'd blocked it out. He paced to the kitchen – he counted, now, three times in one afternoon he'd broken the vision line – and took the bottle to her, disturbing her and drawing protests as he lifted her up, sat on the floor by the mat, with his back against the wall, the top of his head just reaching the wood base of the sill, wet by a trickling condensation line. He set her in front of him, falling back into him, and fed her.

Later, he heard something. Her crying stopped; she spluttered, coughed. She made a slight moaning sound that momentarily paralysed him. Putting his face to her, he thought her breath seemed slightly shallow. The sound – the light, fragile moaning – repeated in his ears.

Shel texted. She would be home in thirty minutes and was there anything he needed. He was surprised; she rarely got away early. He looked at the time stamp on the message – 5.30. He hadn't noticed, hadn't even seen the dark. He quickly dried the floor and put the wet towels and used clothes in the laundry. He cleaned out the basin and left it to dry. He phoned her quickly, apologising, asking if she could pick up some takeaway, he'd got sidetracked. She said she would go to the Korean, their favourite, an unusual treat.

On the fourth day he heard Shel retching in the bathroom. She'd thought it was finished, that whatever had begun in the park was over. She had undergone a battery of tests at the clinic and then immediately after in the capital. But nothing had come up. It was something else. Something had eluded them. Something from the park, she said, remained inside her.

They drove to the doctor's in silence. The sunlight mocked them, showing the scenes outside as thin and insubstantial, revealing the dirt and flaws and the incipient decay of the buildings. A feeling of torpor, of redundancy, of pointless repetition. They stared ahead in the waiting room, convinced something grave was about to be pronounced. Her name was called. He waited twenty, thirty minutes, watching the closed door to the examining room, his anxiety increasing. When finally the door opened he was surprised to see a broad grin across the nurse's face. She placed a hand, additionally, lightly, against Shel's elbow. Shel was white; she appeared to be in shock.

He was to visit the offices the next day, his first meeting with colleagues in almost four weeks. A car arrived to pick him up. He was energised, exhilarated. He couldn't keep the smile from his face. Shel told him not to, it's too early, he shouldn't say anything, not yet, it's bad luck. Just in case. As the car drove past security, over the created lake, pulling in to the business park, the long network of block buildings carved out of black glass set elegantly into the landscaped green hills, his excitement grew. Ideas, future projects, tumbled out, rushing forward with every roll of the tyres. He opened the door, stepped onto the cushioned tarmac and approached the reception building. No, he would say. I feel well. I feel better than I have in a long time. I'm ready to resume work immediately.

Recent investors had made money available for new initiatives and speculative projects, work that would be done independently of Network Engineering Solutions, over and above the day-to-day running of the company. What these investors – the venture-capitalist arm, he learned, of an enormous multinational – were doing was supplying lavish amounts of money to NES to effectively pre-empt the peripheral creativity of its employees, on the condition that everything they wrote would be offered first to themselves. At the same time, NES was one of several companies bidding for contracts on the new high-speed Perpetua Wi-Fi that was soon to be installed throughout the country. Available everywhere, at all times, free of charge, impervious to outside systems, Perpetua was explicitly a response to the productivity losses entailed in several recent episodes of aberrant weather. Never again, the promise went, would citizens be stranded from online life.

———————

Shel soothed her and laid her on the mat in the bedroom, asking him to turn on the ceiling light so they could make clearer contact with her eyes. She raised Doll's legs gently, one at a time, and pushed them slowly towards her body, making a cycling motion. Then she took both legs together and moved them by increments forward, bending them in again. 'She's fine,' she said, wiping the hair out of her eyes, 'just a bit of gas, bit of air. Nothing to worry about.'

He began the following day brushing, vacuuming, spraying, wiping. Looking over the room, he thought he could do better.

He wanted to banish any traces of dry rot from the walls. He wanted to order their things so that everything they had would be visible, easy to get to, easy to quantify.

He scrolled past the photographs he'd taken of the mould. It was nothing, minor, barely noticeable, but as a precaution he'd arranged for someone to come out and look at it, test the walls, the windows, the doors. Across the days he saw its movement, the illusion of the fungus travelling in real time. As if directed towards something. Hunting nutrients, Shel said. That's what it does. And he was reminded of something she had said about her father, towards the end of Ivan's life. She said his cancer was distinct, that it had its own character, a wholly other order, with its own imperatives, customs, values. It had its own sense of time, its daylight rhythm. The idea stuck with him, disturbed him. And as he zoomed in on the individual lines that composed what he had earlier seen as an indistinct greyish-green cloud, he looked at the way they turned, the angles and rhythms they expressed, the suggestion of a spiral inside, and he remembered, with a shudder, the mania that had overcome him in the cottage.

Shel's note on the fridge, her writing a blur, her distinctive letters tall, jagged, narrow like EKG displays or mountain silhouettes. He had to hold it away for a few seconds for the meaning to come through. Her writing looked laterally compressed, more so as the years went by; he wondered how it would appear if you eased it, stretched the letters out. Both of them wrote through the house, index cards and printed sheets overscored in pen. She said his pages of formatted data – his robot words – ended up in the strangest of places, in the fridge, in the back of a kitchen cupboard, behind the cushions on the sofa; sometimes she thought he was trying to code for the everyday objects in the house, firming up their identities through a back-up script.

He still occasionally wore the wrist brace – the physiotherapist recommended it for prolonged spells at the keyboard, his hands locking down in the familiar animal grip. Shel was against it, said it was an enabler, the whole point was that he was to take time away from work. His joints had strained from overwork the past year, ever since she'd come back from Westenra. 'We're building a house, we're expecting a child, of course I'm going to do long hours,' he said. With the new investors and the Perpetua bid there were opportunities, and he didn't want to be left behind. If you didn't come up with something now, at the start – if you didn't have something for them – then you were effectively dismissing yourself. It wouldn't always be like this, he promised her, it was a temporary thing. So for the seven months leading to Doll's birth he'd worked longer and harder than before. At first it was about ideas. He generated various proposals but then settled on one and began developing it. He took his laptop everywhere. Some nights he'd stayed over in the office. It wasn't quite superstition, but he had a rule of not telling Shel the details of a project until it was finished. The bulk of it he'd been able to do on his own, with minimal help from the team. Within those seven months the invisible part of the app was essentially finished; he now had to decide on the front-end design. He was making it drag on, slowly pushing around features and playing with different graphic options. He went back to it at weekends, or occasionally during evenings if something was nagging at him and Doll was sleeping particularly well.

———————

Are you sure? Are you sure it's okay? Are you sure it will be okay? That nothing's wrong? I was sick for a long time in the park. I was exposed to lots of different things there. I had lots of tests afterwards and I don't know exactly what they were. I have bites all over me. You need to ensure I am fit enough to carry this, that nothing is critically wrong. You need to tell me that nothing I may have contracted can be transmitted to my child; do you understand? I can't do this otherwise. I know the first weeks are crucial and this can't have been an optimal environment. You can't imagine what it was like. You just can't imagine – all the things that happened there. Are you sure the child is not in danger? Are you sure this is going to be all right? Can you tell me this? There's just no point going on otherwise. I won't, I can't.

———————

Her voice had changed. She spoke lower, quieter, slower. She was sure it would wear off – it was just a delayed effect of their habituation to the park; they had adapted the way they talked to minimise their disturbance. They had found, inside, that slower, slightly lower vocal expressions were less liable to produce alarm in the troop and without really thinking about it, certainly without discussing it, had adjusted accordingly. Loose, fluent, higher speech seemed to disturb, to disorient the animals, who looked around in a panicked fashion, then upwards to the higher trees, the canopy, searching for where the sound was coming from. They must have thought that birds were making this, that this long trilling was the product of things in flight. Still, it surprised her how noticeable the difference was, right from Arrivals there was some concern, some suspicion, she thought, in the way he looked at her, the way he listened to her, and he must have expected that the difference would quickly fade because he had waited a full three days before addressing it.

Obviously, as well, the three of them were isolated throughout the bulk of their time inside, isolated from each other, from any kind of company with whom they could communicate. They'd grown used to speaking less. He would have to be patient. She was sure he'd understand.

Her cracked lips as well, how it appeared, he thought, to hurt her to say certain words, which meant she then avoided those words, used them less, which made her sound different in all sorts of ways. She never complained about the pain. She kissed hard, and he only later realised the cut, realised he tasted his own blood too. You could see her consider the labour of speaking, scanning the anticipated lines and the arrangement of the tongue, teeth and lips, and deciding against it, deciding it wasn't worth it, abandoning the words and all thought of the words and saying something else.

Later, in the first days at home with Doll, he noticed Shel speaking in this hushed, concentrated way again, slower, focused, less fluent. He watched the way she closed doors, the way she walked, how she opened out the windows. Slowly, carefully, surely. Don't alarm Dorothy, don't frighten her. Shel was curious about the differences he saw in her after the park, saying drily this was conditioned, learned behaviour, that under the extreme example of WEBG she was obsessed with watching herself, monitoring her reflection, observing her tiniest actions too.

————————

Bathing Dorothy in the evening while Shel worked in the next room, he watched the water slipping over the edge of the basin. He padded her with the sponge, going around her, lathering the soap over her dark hair, her forehead, her crown, the base of her head. Water dripped directly from the sponge onto the carpet; water fell from his hands and from her head and splashed onto the basin surface and slipped over the edge. The amount of time it had taken him to pad every part of her head was visible as water; it implied her, a volume commensurate with her head. He was tired; he was unclear. The scene appeared as fluid, blurry. He set the sponge carefully down, lifted the towel. He dried her slowly, methodically, remembering this time, after he had changed her, to slip her into the thick white hooded towel, wrapping her like a cloud. He looked from Doll to the basin to the water-stained carpet. A displaced surface. He put his arms out helplessly. For a moment he had lost her, for a moment she was loosened, her edges came away, her form spilled across the room. He had to gather her up quickly, put her back together, before it was too late.

There she was, dried, warm in the white hooded towel. The panic passed as suddenly as it had arrived. He was just tired. Lack of sleep and the perfectly routine amount of strain he was under.

He heard something. A knock. He waited, listened for Shel. Nothing. He left it. No-one knocked. No appointments were scheduled. A call would come first, a message. Hearing nothing further, he released his breath.

He kept looking at the hooded towel later, after he had dressed her and put her back in the cot. He watched the dip, the hoop, the lip around the rim, the bunched-up hollow hung along the back of the chair. The shape that would be pushed out, formed, with Doll inside. Her shape was implied through the house, in the safety seat in the car, in the cot, the fabric cradle, in the sling they wrapped her up in when they carried her. The premature plastic safety fittings on the table corners, simple blue clasps, instructed her to grow, to age, to stand up, to not be hurt. Later, these would be discarded, still carrying her marks, stencilled lines from where her body hit it. Tens of thousands of years in oceans. Marine life nesting in the plastic folds where her head had nudged. Dorothy sluicing away in the displaced water, her volume an overspill on the carpet. The first baby hairs already falling from her head. The simple fact she aged and grew, ungraspable. The impression of her changing shape in the towels and mats, the basins and carpets, the sinks, the fabrics they put her in, the cradle and the cot, the little indentations the cradle made by virtue of her weight on the wooden table in the kitchen. The tiniest scuff on the oak wood panel where the rolling corner of the rocking cradle swung. The gentle way she turned and stretched, tensing her little arms, pressing the base corners against the wood, creating the faintest line upon it. This line, this little scuff on the table, turned him over. His breath quickened; his vision blurred.

He went to the kitchen, put on the light, put his hands on the table. He couldn't see the mark. Couldn't find the line. He examined it. He was sure there was a mark. A surface mark – so they had washed it, cleaned it away. He got up, and he veered, in impossible tension. All but weightless, she was the whole of the world.

———

Construction resumed quickly, and by the second time they visited the site the whole of the foundation was laid. The progress from here on was astonishing. He stopped en route to work, leaving earlier, going out of his way just so he could get a glimpse of what they'd done. He pressed the agent on the cause of the previous suspension to the work. Bureaucracy, she told him, nothing important, a piece in the planning process they'd had to smooth out. And then, of course, the weather hadn't helped, that fog. Everything had since been settled and resolved, and they were now more than making up for the lost time. Didn't he agree? Of course, if he was anything less than happy she could speak to the developers, but this only risked upsetting momentum, and she really didn't think it was justified.

———

In the first days she was red with a purple edge, raw, internal, like they hadn't finished making her, would go on making her for years. Her back was marked with grooves and wrinkles from the sheet in the small cot in the hospital. Their fingers, as they held her, made impressions in her, appearing to push through her. He was talking quietly about taking the sheets home, washing and sterilising them then ironing them so the surface was entirely smooth, with no blemishes or creases, nothing that could mark her next time, a perfect flat surface that would hold her without breaking through her. Each time either he or Shel or one of the nurses went to lift her he was afraid she would slip through their fingers, a burst of water, the inclination in water always to descend, to reach a lower level. They examined her from a new light's glare and he thought he saw her shadowed organs, and through them the white, the other side. He couldn't believe they were taking her home, that they said that she was ready. She didn't have a name. They had prepared a name, the name was ready, but now that she was there they couldn't present it. It wasn't right, it didn't feel right. He had to document her later, externally, at the Renfield Building, the Registrar's House.

Peeling the curtains they saw the blue midnight sky. It stretched up and up and up, deep blue banks dusted with glimmering white lights. Further still, vast distances, faint streaks of colour, star clusters he'd never seen before. Unusual conditions, brief light intensities telescoping further reaches of space. They looked up, beyond the thin, damaged upper atmosphere, the protective film around them weakening all the time, straining out their window, both inside and outside the world.

———

Shel's debriefing continued, interviewed alone and with Alice, interviewed by the department and the faculty at the university, interviewed by foreign office officials and police representatives, interviewed by members of the legal team hired by Jane's family and by a roster of experts attached to WEBG. Each time she came back drained, ever paler. She just wanted it over. She knew it was necessary, knew these talks were important, but she'd given the same answers again and again, repeating an identical story. She'd told them everything she knew. She couldn't account for what had happened; no amount of repetition was going to change that.

Still he saw her, late at night or in the very early morning, quietly stepping out of bed, thinking he was sleeping, taking out her laptop and writing. He heard her fingers on the keys, recognised the posture of her shoulders. He tried to intuit her words from the bob of her head and the way her fingers descended. The counsellor said it wasn't unusual, that she remained in a state of prolonged shock; she would tell him more when she was ready. The inquest went on, reports were drafted, conclusions still to be made public. It was the park, she said, WEBG exerting its influence. Anything unfavourable would be quashed. Money was paid out to Jane's immediate family, legal agreements signed discreetly in remote office suites. Alice had heard they were going to destroy the animal. Forensics teams, recovering what they could from the scene and from Jane's body, had built up a profile. WEBG insisted it was acting in good conscience, doing the only thing conceivable in the circumstances. In addition to the tragedy, they had the well-being of the troop to consider. Shel and Alice both stressed this was a mistake. There was no indication the animal represented a threat to the troop. The hunt was clearly misdirection. The animal was not the issue at hand. Again and again, they repeated throughout the interviews, to the glazed eyes of the legal reps, the fault lay with the park, with WEBG. The decimated ecosystem created an imbalance; the animal was acting under unnatural pressures. 'You know,' Shel said in one interview, and as she told him late at night, a bitter laugh emerging through her tears, 'if you want to find an individual to blame, then blame me. It was my fault. I insisted on staying, when already we should have left. And I'm guilty of more. I should never have been there, from the start. Don't you see,' she spoke into the one-way glass in the interview room, and past his shoulder in the darkness of their bed, 'none of us should have been there, that's the point. If you want the report to be accurate, then focus on that. We should not have been there. I should never have let her come. I should never have taken us into the park.'

'The bonobo, with its greater anthropomorphic potential over the common chimpanzee, will be carefully rebranded as a new domesticated species, infantilised, bred in captivity in stable numbers, sold as pets and exhibits, becoming increasingly human-like as certain qualities are artificially selected, either through careful breeding or cut directly with CRISPR tech. Year by year, domestic bonobos will spend a greater proportion of their time walking on two legs. Their capacity for expressive emotion will be harnessed and exaggerated. They will be heralded as the most human of all animals, supported by anecdotes, speculations and historical evidence, such as that they are disturbed by loud noises and sudden movements, that they are afraid of other animals, that they are particularly fraught during the night, that their sleep is fractured and they experience especially savage nightmares; that, unlike those animals who can predict certain natural disasters including earthquakes, an uncanny attribute making those animals separate and strange, bonobos suffer like humans do, experiencing the event as it happens; that during the bombing of Munich eleven captive bonobos bellowed from their enclosure dozens of miles from the edge of the devastation, and when their keeper went to inspect them the following morning she found all eleven had suffered sudden massive cardiac arrests and died; that no other animal in the zoo was affected; that their acknowledgement of war made them already all but honorary humans, with a perceived nobility in the face, an observation similar to the one children often make on seeing coastal hamadryas baboons cleaning and picking themselves first thing in the morning, the animals bending and arcing one arm and pointing their head in the same direction, and which it is almost impossible to describe, at least the first time you see it, as anything other than the animal acknowledging the sun, the breaking day, the persistence of the world; that what had destroyed the bonobos outside Munich, rather than being the direct physical effect of sound and tremor, was something else; that the bonobos, in reality, were so terrified not even by the bombs themselves but by the possibility of the development and increasing sophistication of weaponry and warfare, that, in the instant the bombs fell, the imaginative capacity of bonobo chimpanzees compelled them to understand there was no place for them, that they couldn't live here, that the world was going to become stranger and more inhospitable; that their fear of flowing water is instructive and might also be described as reverential; that somehow, across still unknown means of genetic storage, bonobos are aware that water created them; that the fact, long ago, that certain members of an ancestor species decided in fear to avoid a body of water, decided not to cross it, had the effect of isolating them from the rest of the troop, who moved through the stream and became divided; that the physical, behavioural limitation of this new fearful group, who were limited to staying in the same relatively small areas of forest bound by water, was compensated in other ways; that a greater imaginative demand was placed on them, now having to anticipate, react to and consciously deceive other animals; that they had to learn to devise new, elaborate, unusual paths across the land, which affected their idea of time, desire and reward; that over many generations the descendants of this small group became genetically distinct, developing parallel to but separate from the common chimpanzee, being more imaginative, displaying greater anxiety and continuing to avoid, and to fear, flowing water; that it was easier to ascribe to the bonobo than to any other animal the existence of an innate origin story, a story their behaviour continued to pay tribute to; that their fear of water was an unconscious reverence for the means of their creation; that flowing water represented not only the original topographical feature which isolated, separated and adapted them, but was identical in some way to the slippery, mutable, unreliable manner they experienced the world; that the bonobo was made, largely, of water, even, and particularly outlandishly, the claim that this fear of and reverence for water marked the bonobo as a species so sensitive and remarkable that its behaviour continued to acknowledge the water-based origin of all life, even beyond and prior to animals.'

———————

They bought old newsprint from a warehouse, stacks of it, placed sheets over the mat by each of the outside doors and lined a path through the house. However careful they were, shaking off snow on the steps, removing boots immediately inside, taking coats off and hanging them in the porch, water persisted and scattered through the house, trailing their movements in overlapping lines. Spilled onto the floor, it attracted and fed the mould. Roads were closed after heavy snowfall overnight and the company wouldn't be able to come out and look at the walls until later. They gathered up the newsprint three, four times a day, one of the little tasks he enjoyed, taking in the old print and laying down fresh sheets. Early morning, still in darkness, the snow piled up from the night's fall, fresh and untouched and with the illusion of a glow inside it, a wider silence around it, absorbing the birdcalls and the sounds of any traffic. He went silently along the corridor whispering to Doll in his arms, the snow beginning to fall again, thick and heavy and oddly slow, still gathering, flickering as he saw it through the opened curtains in the rooms they passed, the snow all around the house, the whiteness absorbing not just the vegetation and the roads and the fences and the parked vehicles but the houses too, the walls as well as the roofs, the white stone and wood panels, similar enough in tone that the snow all around the houses seemed to absorb them, to be consistent with them, to make them depthless and appear only as a series of isolated, unsupported, floating and gravity-defying windows and doors.

Attaching her in the sling, he went to the kitchen, the white glow of the covered garden casting an odd effect over the darker space inside. Carefully, he opened the cupboard, checked the heating and picked out the fresh bag of print. He told Doll what he was doing, describing the two of them walking in lines through the house, laying out the paper they would step on, predicting all the places they'd go to through the day. 'I think we need to change you,' he said, conscious of the odd turn in the pronoun, as if it was somehow more reasonable to suggest the baby's assistance. 'After that,' he said, vision line held close, 'why don't we go outside? The snow will stop soon, and we won't have the light left for long. Why don't we go outside?'

———

Forensic preservation was priority, above all else. This was made clear to them in the hours immediately after. Read the animal from the shape of it remaining. Find out what did this, what it was. They had guided them in messages relayed from the gates. Over the tent and around it Shel helped hang the remaining blue tarp to block immediate rainfall, and past the last of the evidence they dug a makeshift barrier from stones to at least offer some resistance to flooding. They used torch lights under the tarp and in the tent, illuminating the premature darkness while they recorded every aspect of the scene. They observed the arrangement of the body and its relation to the emptied blood. The way it had been dragged out of the tent. They spent what couldn't have been really but which felt like hours on the prints, recording them from every perspective.

One of the stories she heard later but was unable to verify was that WEBG had wanted them to sever and partition Jane's body, carry it with them on a single journey out of the park. Put it in boxes. Overcome the inconvenience of a distinct body, which is heavy, and long, and difficult to carry, by separating it out, folding it up into separate containers, then lifting it away as discontinuous pieces. A drastic response to the urgency of the moment, the necessity of getting all of them, including Jane, in whatever form, out of the park as quickly as possible. And a cost-saving exercise. Even after all that had happened, all that she had learned about WEBG, she still found it impossible to believe that such an option had actually been considered.

———————

The paper was warmed from the boiler in the cupboard so, as he handled it and despite its age, it seemed freshly printed; Catherine said it was relatively pure, germ free, that her mother told her midwives would sometimes bring sheets on home visits so that, if there was nothing else in the house, they could use it to wrap the child. It became a charm, putting the child in newsprint, where its wet body came through on the page. An impression of the child – edgeless from the twisting and turning – appearing as a gap, an absence, a shining transparency on the page. This was the document. The family kept this damaged paper, holding its impression of the first moments of life. They folded the sheet and put it in a safe and hidden place, somewhere a stranger wouldn't think to look. Under a floorboard, into a roof panel, in a sealed bag inserted in a cut in the mattress. They put it into the fabric of the house, she said – blending it.

For some time the smell would remain. Periodically the family, usually the mother, would take out and unfold the page. They would check that it was okay, that it remained together. The paper, after several months, became hard and brittle, with a sort of ribbed effect. Holding it up, rather than seeing anything inside, anything that came back at you, anything meaningful or instructive, you looked through it at whatever was the other side.

———————

It wasn't just the interviews themselves – it wasn't as if those periods were limited to the ninety to one hundred and twenty minutes that were recorded in each session – she was preoccupied for days before and after. They were always delayed. She would drive in to the sub-level car park and take the lift up to the conference suite and there would be tea, coffee, light food; she would be encouraged into small-talk with the several cheery personnel, different individuals each time, and she knew all this was being recorded too and that, as well as waiting for her to say something that might be leveraged against her, WEBG was also making a display, offering a glimpse of its reach and power, a warning. It had started to make her a little paranoid. Though it was probably nothing – she regretted telling John immediately – she thought she had observed the same individual several times, in an unlikely series of settings. A café; walking past faculty reception; through the window of a passing car. Even if it was the same man then it could be explained as an unusual though hardly impossible set of coincidences. The clearer point, which he agreed was a concern, was that WEBG was getting to her. Each time she only thought she saw the same pale elderly male face, hairless, eyes glowering, long thin arms reaching out below, she became more convinced that she knew him from somewhere, that he was familiar and that this cluster of near meetings pointed back to something else. She strained her memory, thinking back to the airport, the hotel in the capital, the gates before and after they entered the park. Where had she seen him originally? If she could place him definitively with the firm she would be vindicated and she could stop questioning herself like this.

When they had got out of the park scores of vehicles blocked the road, officials swarming amid the tents and trailers and other makeshift buildings. Alice was taken to one room and she was put in another and they were told this was a response to the trauma, that the people interviewing them were professional medics, grief counsellors, and even in the shock of those first days she knew this was bullshit, knew this was the beginning of WEBG's stage-managing of events. The interviewer, a thin woman in her twenties, walked up and down the small room while insisting Shel remain seated. When she stopped, she made and held direct eye contact for several seconds before resuming her long stream of words. She introduced several phrases which would come up again and again over the following months. Shel found herself nodding, soon using some of those phrases herself. They were being coached, she told him, to speak about what had happened in a way that didn't mean anything, using a banal, neutral set of terms, preparing them for the later periods when they would be officially interviewed, sessions that were recorded as part of the formal inquest. WEBG had made a concerted effort, from as soon as the news had reached them, to get around all responsibility and potential liability. The more she thought about it, the surer she was that every single action they took was calibrated towards this end. But again, she questioned herself; she asked him, at the cottage, later, when she felt up to talking about it, after those first few days back when they'd done all they could to push the events away, to be only with each other, as if nothing else mattered and might as well have been a dream, whether this was further evidence of paranoia, or did he really think the firm could be quite so brutally efficient?

Through the immediate debriefing at the gates, the interviews and battery of physical and psychological evaluations, she and Alice were made to sign several documents which they were told at the time were simple, routine medical consents but which she later understood to include various non-disclosures limiting what they might say to an outside organisation. The firm's efforts towards not only containing but in a sense adapting, rewriting what had happened, were extraordinary. Of course they should have read the full text of anything they signed, of course they should have said they wanted to defer it, but then he didn't, he couldn't understand the pressure they were under, he couldn't have any idea how it felt those first days after the killing, sipping mint tea to the sound of the industrial generators, looking blankly ahead, trying not to think and then becoming incidentally aware of something in the room, something that reminded you of Jane, a pen, a stack of papers, a mug, and then standing and gripping the papers and realising that the heft of them shared some basic, banal relation to the resistance she'd felt holding the blue tarp as she and the rangers briefly carried the body.

The thing with writing code, the thing that was so addictive about it, was that it actually built the product in real time. It was all making. It wasn't just description: it was the thing itself. (Sometimes he added, embedded within the script, English language notes – reminders, clarifications, things that would jump out on a later reading. These were the only parts that weren't directly influential, the only lines that didn't build. In Shel's terms, this would be the junk part.)

When you wrote something, it happened. Two of his colleagues in particular were very earnest about this; he knew they were religious, and the appeal was obvious enough. He was surprised coding hadn't drawn more of a religious following – perhaps it was considered idolatrous. He told himself he wasn't interested in this, but he couldn't deny the feeling of power was attractive. He had tried to tell Shel what it was like, but as usual he'd stumbled, backtracked, undermined and contradicted himself. It's a thing, tactile, and it's also a form of speech. There is nothing else like that, he said. There's nothing provisional about it. You state the idea, in the defined terms, and then suddenly, if you've done it right, it exists. You jump directly there. It's made. It's incredible.

Doll's latest appointment with the doctor was scheduled for the coming weekend, Saturday morning, time that he could use, Shel told him, to work; there was no reason for him to come along too – these check-ups, as he knew, were routine and, besides, she'd note everything and repeat it all to him later. 'John,' she said, her shoes tapping on the floor, her coat pulled on, the collar raised, protecting her neck from the cold, 'are you listening? Look, I've got to go, I'll be late for work, I'll see you in the evening.'

It was still dark in the mornings when Shel left so they had the lights on in the front room and the kitchen and sometimes the corridor, the house like a little laboratory, harsh forensics exposing them as they rushed and prepared for the day ahead, bread lightly toasted, cups of filter coffee multiplying, laptops on the table, Doll needing changed and fed, Post-its stuck to the worktop and the fridge with incomplete lists, things that he was to remember to get from the supermarket and prompts for emails she was supposed to send and administrative deadlines she had to meet. She was sure 90 per cent of her time was occupied by admin.

He didn't notice at first the time that passed because the lights were set to read the changing glow and to dim in sympathy, a process that happened slowly, and often he only realised the lights were already off – that it was no longer dark; that the day had come out – when by reflex he had gone to press the switch, overriding the controls. He emptied out and rinsed the mugs, wiped the table, the counters, put everything away in what felt like an unnatural quiet after the bustle of the morning and now that Doll, for however short a period, was sleeping. He looked round the kitchen, peered out above the back garden covered in a thick layer of white. Reaching for the basin dishes he caught a colour on the edge of the garden, a brief movement he barely registered. He leaned forward, pressing his face almost up to the glass pane, but whatever he'd seen was now gone. A blackbird; a crow; a smudge of colour against the snow, fluttering and flying away.

He packed their things, dressed Doll in her layers and strapped her onto his front, then closed and locked the door, standing on the top step with his back to the garden. It was cold. He felt his breath catch sharply in his throat; his fingers slipped and dropped the keys. He turned on the step, checking for ice, and then reached back and tried the handle again. Rather than going directly to the gate and the driveway he waited, looking out on Shel's boot prints on the path. He could hear her again, he saw her striding out, sensed her perfume static in the freezing air. Looking across the garden, it was clear something had got in from the field. This was what he'd seen from the window. He heard the quiet creak as he trod past the powder to the harder snow, stopping when he reached the prints. Hesitantly, trying not to disturb Doll, he crouched down. The prints were large and deep and spaced closely together. They were hooved. Unlikely though it seemed, it must have been a deer, stalking and lunging at a bird. A single line led through the garden, ending at the house. He looked around for any feathers or for the light impression of the bird's feet on the snow. He looked for further deer tracks but there weren't any. Eventually, seeing Doll's pursed lips and the darker red of her nose, he got up, left the prints behind, opened and locked the gate, strapped her into the safety seat in the back of the car and started the engine.

———————

She was convinced, at the funeral, the second burial, that that wasn't the real body, that Jane remained in the park. Bryan ignored each of the many messages she sent and neither he nor Selina attended the ceremony. Her feeling was that they had left her there, that Bryan hadn't stood guard at all but had either followed them after a short delay or exited by another route. The body by that stage was surely beyond recovery, and the story about waiting by the tent, with the gun, was ridiculous, a ruse prepared for her and for Alice, who might otherwise have refused to leave.

Before the ceremony began a small woman walked towards Shel and in her grief-struck face she saw a sunken replica of Jane. She told Shel her daughter had never been as excited about anything in her life. She said Jane had been fully briefed beforehand, she knew the risks and they weren't to blame themselves. Shel watched as they lowered the coffin, noting the strain on the bearers' arms, trying to measure this against her own experience of the weight. Was it life-like, this weight? How much would the body have lost since? In addition to Jane's remains there would have been the preserving fluid put inside her and the corrective work done to the face, which she was told had been reconstituted, a cosmetic team building up, based on photographs, a likeness over the soft tissue. It took Jane's brother, Edward – a tall, thin man who walked with his sister's stoop and who had flown out immediately news of the mauling reached the family – sixty days before permission was granted to see the body, and then only briefly. It may still have been a substitution. Jane, Shel believed, was not inside.

Jane had been taken apart in the park and she was put into the ground there and she remained there. Anything inside this box was simulation.

———

She remembered what Shel wore in the morning – wide raincoat or mauve winter coat extending as she put her down, boots rapping on the floor walking away, faint scent of sea-salt perfume floating – and linked them to her leaving. She was irritated at first when Shel came home again, arrivals and departures carried by the same means. Just the sound of the boots rapping on the wood floor made her cry. He and Shel discussed this, even talked about concealing her leaving, keeping her things by the door so the exception of her clothing didn't mark it. But the problem, once they started, was that the project would consume them. As Doll aged, she would become aware of objects further from her and start picking up subtler clues. They wouldn't be able to display keys or bags. They'd have to avoid certain conversations, various keywords.

She stirred, coughed, and he snapped towards her, watching her eyes peel open and a yawn split her face. He rocked her back and forth, holding her gaze and singing to her quietly. Her breathing still sounded different, he thought, shallower. He tried to soothe her with sounds, patterns. Catherine called and told him she was visiting the next day. The garlic; he was still to come up with something. He spoke quietly, almost whispering. Catherine, on the other end, whispered too. She was talking at him. She told him Doll was already picking up on what he said; he should speak to her as often as he could. She said it comes up on you so quickly, you don't even realise when it's happened, already they're talking, then they're walking, as if one carries the other up, and then they're gone.

In a very simple way Doll was what the world had given her, and it was obvious, but it could surprise him too. Her little body implied everything; you could start from her, only her, and from the power of what made her construct the whole of the universe again. He could only do so much, adapting the house for her, turning her head. Watching her, recording her. If it helped her – if there was even the slightest chance that it helped her – to feed her first from his right arm then his left, and to come towards her, gathering her from a new angle every time, so that she always looked towards him differently, then he would. He would do every little thing he could, of course he would.

It was unbearable, sometimes, and impossible to predict, these moments of collapse from somewhere inside the overriding exhaustion, sparked by something as innocuous as an unexpected glance at a bottle she fed from, or from the appearance out of place of one of her tiny socks, dropped from the laundry onto the floor. He would turn away, try to be reasonable, tell himself it goes on, it all goes on, she will grow, she will probably, in some broad sense, be okay. And then the little opening inside the single sock, the shadow, the intimation of its depth, would be enough to bring him down again, back into hopelessness and impossibility, into the certainty that whatever happened she would be hurt, she would finally be hurt, and he just wouldn't be able to accept that. Feeling like this, in one of these spells, necessarily brief, he would look around him at the immediate space with a kind of bald and naked wonder. Over the carpet was the footprint then the whole form of every person who had stood there. Figures stretched from the prints and marks over the reflective finish on the countertops. Every word spoken billowed out as waves. He stared at it for as long, perhaps, as a single second, before a new piece of information – the brush of his knee against a chair leg, an itch on his back, a mild stirring of hunger – re-established balance and brought him back to his habitual self, a perspective from which the previous thoughts – one, two moments ago – appeared completely ludicrous.

———————

Of course I think back to what happened; I think about it all the time. The first days afterwards were some of the strangest of my life. Almost the first thing Dr Andrews did, at the gates, when we finally made it out of Westenra, was put a needle in my arm. We hadn't even washed. Joseph must have called ahead because they were waiting for us. A team actually entered the park and escorted us from a couple of kilometres in. They had vitamin capsules and saline solution; they were immediately solicitous, the questions quickly sliding from what did we need to what did we know. People were clustered and jostling and staring at us. I didn't know what they'd been told. I was exhausted, severely dehydrated and probably, in retrospect, would judge that my recall wasn't unimpeachable, that my defensiveness might have coloured what I saw.

One group was around me and another around Alice and very carefully, very effectively, like it was practised and they knew exactly what they were doing, they led us in different directions, increasingly further from each other. This was the last I saw of Alice directly for three weeks. Four days at the park gates tested and interviewed, kept in different rooms, monitored round the clock. Unable to sleep through the night, I became hysterical, demanding to see her, demanding to know what was happening, what this was all for. I thought something terrible had happened to her too. Later, when I glimpsed her through the window, walking over the track now quickly drying out in the blazing sun, the fading puddles on the red ground glimmering, flanked by staff on both sides, I felt a thrilling, anxious, unbearable expectation that Jane would appear immediately behind her.

They told us only that everything we saw was done to protect us and that it would all be explained later. We had to submit our phones and laptops, and when I got mine back I saw the engineers had adapted the settings, that in order to make a call I had to go *through an authorisation process, and when I sent a message it was delayed, everything checked over before being released. Alice and I had our respective numbers blocked so we couldn't talk to each other. They asked me the same stupid, irrelevant questions again and again. I just wanted to be out, to be home, to have this nightmare over, and as I knew it wasn't going to happen for at least another few days I tried to sleep as much as I could, long, disturbed drifts in the afternoon, waking with a bitter taste in the back of my throat, the feeling of a fever developing, the air-con always turned up just a little too high. Why were we being kept apart? What did they think we knew? I almost laughed when I considered, much later than I should have done, that they might actually have suspected us, not necessarily of doing something awful to Jane but maybe of being guilty of gross negligence, and that in keeping us apart they were stopping us from coordinating our stories. Maybe they had something, I thought. Maybe they were right; maybe we really were guilty. Jane, in the last week, had been increasingly withdrawn, and it was tempting to posit some kind of foreknowledge on her part, which is ridiculous. I told them it was my fault and they barely flinched, told them the only reason we stayed so long was because of me.*

I considered what kind of story they might have imagined, whether it might have passed their minds that Alice and I did it, that we tore Jane open by ourselves, with our hands. I watched them and tried to conceive of them thinking this, tried to see it in the way their eyes held us. The first reports they would have had came directly from the rangers who met us inside. How had we reacted? How had it looked to them? How had we seemed? I remembered very little, only that none of my answers were satisfactory, that the rangers were insistent there was something else, something we still weren't telling them. It seemed extraordinary to me to really imagine this, to think that when they first came upon us in the park, guarding the body, they considered the possibility that Alice and I were not only responsible for this scene but that we had instantly generated a story to cover it up. It seemed almost as unlikely that we could have invented a story as that we could have murdered her. Two scientists traumatised in a micro-park, acting outside our minds, then collaborating, speaking quietly close together, compiling a long story to try to fool the authorities and cover up what we'd done.

What exactly had we heard? What did we see? What did we think it was, coming towards us, that last week in the park? All our data was copied; all of it was taken from us. All records of the prints and the animals' shrieking was removed, forensics, I imagined, cross-referencing everything, putting the data against the evidence taken from what wasn't a crime scene, because there was no explicit human error, no culpability other than what I'd attributed to myself in my myopia, but was still a sealed site marking where someone had died. I kept expecting the air transport to arrive. Whenever I heard a particularly heavy engine I'd look out, relieved but also confused. Where were they? What had they done with Jane's body? They waved my questions away, told me not to worry, told me it was all being taken care of, that an expert team was going through everything. Did that mean she was already out? I said. Then where is her body? Where is Bryan? They changed topic; there was another test that couldn't wait; something else had come up.

———

The rule was that he would try not to work from home; it was the only way they'd manage. He was irascible, defensive, shut off when he worked, and she wouldn't tolerate this stranger around her. Sometimes he had this glow deep in his sunken eyes, a glimmer of a rich happiness, but this was rare. Most of the time she saw frustration, anxiety, occasionally something approaching a total loss of confidence. It wouldn't work and he didn't know why. It should work; why isn't it working?

Describing what he did every day, trying to be open, to be less insufferable, he said it's this constant doubt, this incessant checking. If you could concentrate entirely on only one level it might be okay, it might be manageable; the problem, the impossibility, was working on both levels simultaneously, re-reading each letter in every command to make sure nothing was out of place and at the same time maintaining a constant visualisation of the entire structure. You had no option but to be vigilant at both scales at all times. You have to exert absolute control, he said, because if you don't, if you make a single mistake and you don't immediately find it, it won't work, it will collapse. Not just this one module, but the whole program, everything. From one error, a single mistyped character. The program tries to run only it reads the error and it can't go forward, it starts stuttering, it focuses all its energy driving round and round this error and it produces something that's decayed, that's rotten, that's full of this redundant, infuriating energy. It's broken, it's gone, you've lost it.

———————

Dr Andrews performed the majority of my tests, a small, wiry man with an earnest, serious demeanour, always concentrating on something close at hand, peering in through his horn-rimmed glasses, fascinated by some minor detail that apparently meant the world to him, and almost pathologically unable to stand up straight, to look out, to make firm and direct eye contact with anyone. He seemed on the cusp of being overwhelmed and hence his efforts to keep the wider picture at bay. I watched him and he almost always avoided the windows. He kept his head down but it was even more obvious when he was outside; he seemed afraid of looking, afraid of what he might see and the obligations and responsibilities that might be forced on him. For some reason I was sympathetic to him. I didn't quite trust him but the edge, the tension and compression, the lack of ease in his manner seemed more appealing and certainly more relatable than the general blanket neutrality of the other staff.

In retrospect, it was obvious; he knew I was pregnant and for some reason had been told under no circumstances could he tell me. It must have been clear if not from the first moment he saw me exiting the park, or from as soon as I began listing symptoms, then directly the first results came back. Neither he nor anyone else from WEBG ever acknowledged my pregnancy. Instead, tests and medical questionnaires appeared listing every other conceivable explanation for my vomiting, my nausea, my loss of blood, the feeling of difference and change throughout my body. When later, back at home, I saw Alice again, she told me she was given exactly the same questions, indeed that many of the same symptoms presented now in her as well. It was not beyond the realm of possibility that even had I not been pregnant I would still have been vomiting, would still have been presenting myself as in some pain. There was some talk about the contributing effect of 'psychological factors', triggered by what we'd experienced in the park and which, if they weren't actively causing our symptoms, at least exacerbated them. At my most generous I tried to conceive a scenario in which Dr Andrews genuinely had my best interests in mind and where in testing me he considered the vulnerabilities of my unborn child, that the tests were conducted in a genuine, earnest attempt to rule out the presence of an illness, an infection, an invasive agent that might threaten it. He may actually have convinced himself, justifying his enforced silence, that the pregnancy was dangerous precisely in the way some of its early effects could be mistaken for illness, and that using the word 'pregnancy' to account for and to explain everything could in fact be the worst possible thing to do, diagnostically speaking, given that it might distract from, might hide entirely, the stealth presence of something else, something other, inside me.

It was entirely possible they were still searching for pathogens and wanted to have a full measure of my health before giving me the news. Because the first thing I was going to think when I did get the news was 'Is it okay? Is the fetus stable? Is its development within the normal range?' And if they couldn't give me those answers because they were still not sure what else I might be carrying, what other agents I might have picked up, then I might become – they might think I might be liable to become – hysterical, creating all sorts of other problems for them.

Alice, when I finally found her, after they'd split us up, after they'd put us in different hotels and on different flights, and after I'd already been home several weeks, said with WEBG your first thought regarding motive should always be money, i.e. potential claims to liability. Some obscure contract clause stating that so long as pregnancy is not acknowledged under the period in which the individual is working for the firm, said firm cannot be held responsible in any way for later difficulties or abnormalities that might come up in the development of the fetus. And WEBG – through the employees conducting the interviews back at home – told me with a straight face they had no knowledge of the pregnancy and that it was entirely a personal matter. Though I didn't want to be dramatic – and I was lightly aware that in dwelling on this I was distracting myself, or trying to, from Jane's death – I let myself imagine a certain look on the green-grey faces of the legal staff and the administrators in the conference suite, a look between fear and a kind of remote concern, suggesting there was something I still didn't know, some other piece of information they were privy to, something that had come up in the tests and with clear implications for the development of my child. I would lie awake and think that when they tested me, when they looked inside me, they had found something else, something impossible, unnameable, and that even if they had wanted to tell me they wouldn't have had the words.

He heard the engine start and then the car pull out of the driveway. He looked around the kitchen, sure there was something he was supposed to have seen to, something he had overlooked. He collected her babygrow from the table and a thread came away in his hand. Resisting the impulse to pull on it, the material tightening as it unravelled, he took the scissors, cut it off, folded the thread and put it in his pocket. All her clothes were kept in a small white box, or rather three boxes of ascending size nested inside each other, a present from Catherine anticipating Doll's growth for the next several months. It was supposed to be about perspective, about declaring how quickly the child was growing, making it obvious. 'What will go round a baby isn't much,' Catherine said, awkwardly he thought, handing the boxes over.

He lifted the top off the largest box, wet his finger, took the thread from his pocket, pushed it into the saliva and placed it against the white inner wall, where it stuck. *What will go round*, she said, round and round, the way he had rocked Doll minutes ago, away to sleep, before Shel lifted the cradle and took her away to the doctor's. Turning her round, always, as he had been told to, as he must, adjusting her position, lifting and rocking her from different sides, coming towards her variously, rotating the pictures along the sides of the cot.

Catherine was only half-right, he thought, taking out the clothes from the middle box. As Doll turned, in little revolutions in the house – in her cot, in the cradle, in the mat and in their arms – she turned against everything, and that friction aged her. Had Catherine meant something like that by the phrase, not gravity necessarily, but something commensurate with it, the impersonal, everything around her?

The paediatrician loaded them with information on their first visit, and despite all the practical advice and instruction which he had forgotten, strange, unlikely fragments remained, such as that inside Doll, already composing her, was a fine filament which, if you were to untangle it and spool it out, would measure the full circumference of the world. That already, in a direct, material sense, she encompassed the world. The white thread in the box, pulling on it, a magic trick, pulling on it again and again as it came spooling out, a guide, a map used to mark a great journey, tracking every single movement across a life. Shel had rolled her eyes, had told him on the way home it wasn't even true, that it might hold for an adult – in fact it was probably longer, a greater distance – but not for a newborn. He was always being amazed, she told him; he was such an easy audience. The doctor, not much older than them, had seen him coming, someone who could flatter her, and so she had pulled out an arbitrary fact, something from an in-flight magazine.

He stirred, groggy, opened his eyes. For a moment he was unsure where he was. Colder, the day darkening. He had meant to work. Fallen asleep in the chair by the window. He reached for his phone on the table, looked at the time again. Where were they? he thought. They should have been home already. He clicked through to the messaging app and saw she wasn't active. He sent a text, *Everything okay?* Waited, stretched his arms, got up, collected his laptop, still time to do something.

The counsellors stressed how important it was we experience what we thought was private communication with our loved ones, that it was a crucial, integral part of our recovery. Of course what they didn't tell us until later was that all these calls were recorded too. The passing, predictable smirk as the staff went through all this, showing where I'd signed consent, careful not to too obviously express relish over the full access they'd had to the video calls between John and me.

However many times I said I didn't know anything, that there was no value in what I said, they didn't listen. 'You might not know what you know,' was the latest contorted justification for their intrusions. 'It might be something that seems insignificant, a small detail, something you'd never think of mentioning to us. But, put next to something else, some other piece of information we already have, it could prove revelatory. We just don't know; we have to gather as wide a net as possible – I'm sure you understand.'

For those four days at the gates they were obsessed with us. They kept saying if there was anything I needed they would do their best to see to it; they wanted me to be as comfortable as possible. With all the activity and personnel the place was barely recognisable. There was a chef, dressed in whites, ridiculous and immaculate with the humidity and the insects and the wet earth everywhere. Something common to the staff was their pristine attire, incongruous in the setting but somehow functional, reaffirming their separateness and aloof neutrality, this idea they were above things and their experience was virtual, not contingent on anything outside. He quietly consulted with me and asked me to think hard, recall the finest meal I'd ever had; if I could describe it in sufficient detail he would render it again. He asked me to write it down and then go to the sealed office and wait. An odd, instantly effective indulgence, taking me away from there, recreating the past, closing my eyes and with every mouthful *lingering on the taste, not just of the food but of everything around it, the smells and the sounds and colours, I was right there, inside the original experience, and when I opened my eyes I saw a broad tinted-glass window overlooking the park, a slightly faded wooden interior, felt an immediate, awful sterility, a blankness.*

Given the remoteness of the place I had no idea where all this food was sourced from; it seemed uncanny, as if this quiet, obsequious figure had performed alchemy, had really transformed the limited material around us into something other. My mind was still a fog, I wasn't thinking, but even then I remember feeling this isn't right, this isn't straightforward, something else is going on here. And there were lots of things, I suppose: distraction from the tests, shifting and managing our perception of the firm, trying to establish a kind of loyalty in us which might prove instrumental further down the line, in the inquest.

Our own questions failed, bounced back at us. The staff had been trained to respond like this, to give nothing away and press us on our own interpretation of the motives and assumptions behind what we said. 'So what was this?' I said once. 'Your best guess – a boar?' The young woman shot me this startled look from behind her tablet, standing above me, unnerved and suddenly flustered, not expecting this at all; she visibly composed herself, breathed and took half a step back. 'Why do you think that? What makes you say that?' And on.

Whatever had happened in Westenra – whatever sickness had afflicted the original animals; the real reason behind their decision to invite us and accommodate us in the park; the encroaching into our camp by a predator; the ongoing terror experienced by the troop; ultimately Jane's mauling from inside her tent, impossible, remarkable in so many ways, not least because it is such anomalous behaviour in almost every animal I can think of, they simply wouldn't do that, stalking a human, as if determined, coming after them, seeking them out at night, knowing they were inside and slicing up the tent – it remained out of reach. Much later I confided in Alice my suspicion that throughout it WEBG had been in control, that the whole three weeks comprised some kind of test, that the officials watched us, that they were on the periphery, that the whirring, clicking sounds I sometimes heard and that we picked up more than once in the audio were indications of drones floating above us, recording us, filtering through the trees. That they had put us in that situation as an experiment, just to see what would happen. It was no secret that WEBG knew more than they were saying, but the idea that our invitation was a charade was startling. Was it possible, I thought – again this was indulgence, grief distraction, fantastical speculation – that WEBG had known that something terrible was in the park and by putting us in there they were hoping to goad it, provoke it, tease it out? To see it better? To capture it, harvest it? Something like a weapon? And that though they had been watching all that time they had recorded no direct footage of the predator, and so, rather than the relentless interviews that followed being rhetorical, or some kind of attempt to establish their innocence, they genuinely were at a loss in the end?

The interface still wasn't right. He had tried everything, he had thought it would take care of itself, it would come naturally, but whichever style of graphics he chose it was wrong, it was underwhelming. He needed to find a way of visualising the data that was both simple and comprehensive, that worked at different scales, a style that would communicate information in a single glance but would also reward sustained analysis. He set his laptop down and began walking, stepping over the lines of newsprint laid out earlier that morning.

He saw columns of text on the pages and columns made by the linked pages and columns in the individual letters composing the words. A self-reiterating shape; a pattern repeated at different scales; a basic fractal design. Adhering to the principles Shel noted in cell biology, the fact that every cell in an organism contains a nucleus inside which is a description of the whole organism. It was a perfect, breath-taking illustration of data compression.

DNA, then, he thought, as a naturally occurring storytelling graphic, expressing fractal movements in the cells, organisms and eco-systems it created. In one sense, nature itself was an unsurpassable surveillance machine. Everything that hap-pened, however trivial, contributed to the ongoing shaping of the environment, which formed the individuals, who in turn affected the environment. Every single creature, everything that lived, every animal and every blade of grass, every spore and seed, every hint of a virus trailing in a breeze, told not just the story of itself, where it had come from and where it might be going, but told the story of every other thing, animate and inanimate – mountains, sedimentary layers, varying ocean levels. Everything that happened, irrespective of how distant or how far back in the past, was there in the fullness of every living cell, in the adaptations of a lineage that could still be traced. He brushed a fine powder from the sill and felt molluscs descending and calcifying and forming new sea beds and appearing aeons later as a white cliff wall, as the unstable, mobile surface of a desert. He was losing the thread, the significance, the practical application. Concentrate, he told himself, closing his eyes: data compression in fractals; multi-level information capture; aesthetically pleasing, self-reiterating patterns.

He pictured Shel's face tilting, a patient smile appearing as she gently told him the comparison of DNA to a language is as old as the hills, that even Darwin, confounded, noted that the number of languages arising in a given area broadly matched the area's biodiversity, as if words too bred from the soil.

Shel's mouth when she returned, when she stepped out at Arrivals, her lips peeled from the sun, the slight sense that it hurt to speak, or at least to say certain words, that she wasn't ready to speak yet and talk about it, everything that had happened, it was too close, there was too much of it, and she was traumatised and in shock and more than anything else, she said, slowly, as they walked towards the exit doors, she was exhausted. He thought of her lips again, of the first slow, gentle kiss by the doors, the rough, hard flakes of skin, hint of blood. He remembered Shel, years before, when they would talk all night, when they were young, when they were still unfamiliar, asking about his work, asking whether synthetic languages, machine languages, the languages that he worked with day in and day out, and which in volume now occupied, he supposed, the greater part of his communicative experience, given the little he was able to read outside of work, given, now, how tired they both were and how little, relatively speaking, they saw of one another, and how little he saw of other people, and given that the words he used in Doll's presence tended to be limited and repetitive, she asked if these artificial languages adhered to the same principles as natural languages, like the one, she said, we're speaking now. What do you mean, he said, by principles? Do you mean grammar, because—? No, she cut him off, extending her legs over him on the sofa – he noticed she'd pulled a single sock halfway down her foot so it covered only the toes, he felt the rub of her heels on his thighs – I mean things like word frequency, you know, how the frequency of the most used word is supposed to be twice as great as the next one, which is used twice as much as the third, and so on. Does this happen, I mean, she asked him on the sofa, with the languages you write in, too?

Something had happened – a phone call; water boiling over in the pan – and he couldn't remember getting back to the conversation. But they must have, he thought – they must have done. So why couldn't he remember it? And why was this particular conversation, this incomplete memory, coming back to him now?

At work, a language profile built up for every employee, holding every report they wrote, every search they entered, every email they sent, every email they drafted and ultimately didn't send, everything they coded too. This data trove was examined by software initially built by the same employees – so that it was a kind of self-analysis, the software examining its own origins and generating *prints* for the staff, an identifying unconscious mark that came through in everything they wrote, the employees expressing more of their own tics and flaws in attempting to understand them. The objective was ostensibly to give 'transparency' to the workplace, to make it clear in every system they designed which individual was responsible for which part.

The same software studied language and behaviour in video and audio, watching lips move, noting the changes in facial muscles, pupil dilation, body temperature, the vocal stress coincident with certain words. The software made original observations which it then used to rebuild itself and improve its own performance and its understanding. It did this autonomously. The staff watched this but didn't understand it.

Self-created languages built more efficient systems, which led to even more advanced understanding, new languages, further systems, exponential increases in productivity. In answer to her question, he thought, and which he must remember to mention to her whenever they get back from the doctor's – what, he thought again, was taking them so long – part of a conversation that had happened so long ago that she would probably look at him blankly, saying, John, what are you talking about, saying for the life of her she had no recall whatsoever of ever having had any such conversation, saying that, in fact, it just didn't sound like her, is he sure, she would say, that he was remembering it correctly, and he hadn't in reality simply invented it? In answer to her question he would say something like, I don't know.

Shel, again, her lips, her voice – there was a further significance, something he just wasn't realising, a breakthrough waiting for him just out of his reach. Graphics and data, anatomy and a life's work. Shel, language, everything that she said, everything that he remembered. Her arm unconsciously rising over him last thing at night and pushing the dial so that the music stopped, deceptively at first, and then darkness, dreaming, blank sleep, morning again. He remembered his rehabilitation under the doctor's supervision, the feeling, prolonged over the days and nights that followed, of a whole world fanning out from a single concrete detail, one movement, one line – a beginning – Shel, his partner, lifting her arm over him. He had remembered

– he thought, now, he had remembered – every movement he had ever seen her make, every one of which he treasured and wanted to hold onto, hold close to him, to feel the warmth of it and never lose it again. The fact of their lives had overwhelmed him, lying in the quiet, dark room upstairs in the cottage all those months ago, because for the preceding days he had lost it, lost an unbelievable, unrealisable data-stream.

Now, he thought, concentrate, focus, realise the implications. Every movement of a life, beginning from the smallest thing, a newborn child, Doll, her first breath, her tiny body—

A sound, a vibration, the phone in his pocket. *Shel.* 'Yes?' he said, putting the phone closer to his ear. 'Shel?' he said. 'What is it? Shel? What's wrong?'

Acknowledgements

I wish to thank everyone at Atlantic Books and Georgina Capel Associates, especially James Roxburgh and Rachel Conway.

I am indebted to Andrew, Kirsten and family for their generosity in Castlebay in winter 17/18.

Matt, Diana – my brother and my sister-in-law, in Mexico City, in Panama City – for giving me the space, for making me feel at home, for enabling me to write this book: thank you. I won't forget it.